Another Normal

Nicholas Coyle

First Printing: 2016

To my parents

Contents

Foreword

This is a book. They've been around for a while now, so this one shouldn't need an instruction manual. Read from left to right, top to bottom, and front to back. The last instruction is optional, because this is a collection of short stories, and not a novel.

Novels are much more popular than short stories, and epic, 20,000-page book cycles are much more popular than novels. These short stories began life as 'micro fiction', working to a notional 1,000 words in length – a limbo bar that proved impossibly low in the end. They get longer as you work through the book; even so, they are short.

The popularity of long series is strange in a society that values speed and instant gratification. Reading *Game of Thrones* is probably the single most intensive ongoing project that most readers engage in in their daily lives, save perhaps going to work and raising children, if they have them.

On the other hand, long stories are simple, easy. The situation is established, and all that is needed is a never-ending avalanche of episodes to maintain the impression of progress. Characters possess little nuance, all of the stock types having been formed aeons ago, and even serious works struggle to create interesting human beings – let alone realistic ones.

In part, genre fiction requires this, or it becomes boring. Rather like in H. G. Wells' *The War of the Worlds*, or Richard Matheson's *I Am Legend*, the apocalypse would find me safely locked in a basement, waiting for everything to be over. I certainly wouldn't embark on a lengthy walking tour to the nearest volcano just to throw some tatty old jewellery into it.

Nor do I possess magical powers, or military expertise, which might help to avert said apocalypse. What I have instead – in common with all Real People – is a series of personality conflicts, a sense of right and wrong, a capacity to overrule that sense of right and wrong as is convenient, and a whole bunch of insecurities surrounding my social status.

My point is that exciting novels with expanded universes and fabricated family trees, a thousand years of detailed, preformed politicking and all the rest of it are paradoxically less realistic than reality. The more incidental detail that is packed into the sacred act of 'world building', the more joy, it seems, to the reader, yet the less accurate it all becomes. Ancient Roman families might have traced their roots back through the generations; more usually, they picked a favourite Greek demigod and simply claimed descent from him or her. They didn't write it all down in an *Encyclopaedia Genealogica*, as the more hard core fantasists do. They made it up as they went along.

All of this may be sour grapes. I expect very few readers, and even those readers – mostly my friends – will find these stories disorientating, incomplete. They will wonder, perhaps, why characters behave so irrationally; they may question what the point of a story was in the first place; some, I know, will get frustrated at my petty, selfish refusal to spell out my meaning in Very Clear Terms. Tough.

I offer an alternative: reading is, and should be, *difficult*. Not in the choice of language and syntax (although I am pleased by the above 'genealogica' and by *Bathroom*'s 'micturating'), but in its intent. A story should leave the reader with the sense that something was said, but what, exactly, should exist in an imaginary dialogue between reader and writer that continues beyond the end of the story.

If something seems odd, or unexplained, or contradictory, this may be deliberate, inviting the reader to question the story's presumptions. If a reader disagrees vehemently with a statement, this response may (or may not be) the desired one: however, the responsibility rests on the reader, not the writer, to provide commentary. Anything else is cant.

Reading should be constant, because reading can inspire thought. There *are* readers out there who find themselves on a twenty minute bus ride and whip out their Kindles or their Robert Jordans. More often, they are checking their Facebooks. Which is fine – why on earth would you delve into your 700-page tome if you've only got fifteen minutes free?

But what about a 10-page short story? You might finish that in time, and if you don't, then get off the bus and read the last page or so before heading on. A story can give rise to new ideas, new perspectives, or a cheap laugh – and it can stay with you for the rest of the day, or a week. Maybe in six months' time you'll come across in real life the very situation you had previously read about, and you'll remember the story with a smug little grin.

I'm no ascetic. I've read my share of epic fantasies; I've a solid collection of science fiction; but then, my history, philosophy and science shelves are intimidating, and even my Kindle thinks I'm trying too hard with all these Penguin Classics. I enjoy them all, in different ways. But the ones that stay with me – which conjure up memories of reading in bed, absorbed in a single moment, are short stories, from Lovecraft's *The Dreamer in the Witch House* to LeFanu's *Green Tea*. Akugatawa's *Dragon*, in which a local man pranks people into believing that a dragon will rise from the local lake on a certain day, is more captivating than a quest story in which a young boy actually kills a real dragon (doubtless discovering himself and coming of age in the primal act of slaughter... yawn).

And marvellous as the great, nineteenth century novels are, they too suffer from their genre: exceptional length, a propensity to moralise, and a suffocating obsession with a dying parlour society – the novels of Dickens an exception.

Short stories, then, are unpopular and difficult. A part of me would love to reproduce the easy readability of Tom Holt and Terry Pratchett, whose books have seen me through school, wisdom tooth removal, and hospital visits. Another part envies Peter F. Hamilton and Alastair Reynolds, who conjure up baroque, intricate universes at the speed of thought and tell astounding tales of antimatter bombs, universal extinction and neural networks.

The best I can manage is a 5-page story in which a copy of a human being questions its nature as a copy of a human being. My idea of a science fiction story is *Science Fiction Story*: a change in society that is so subtle that it can hardly be detected, while being hidden in a glut of gratuitous nonsense about private detectives and mysterious 'collectors'.

Science fiction has a lot wrong with it, but it has this saving grace: no other genre has worked so tirelessly to critique society, to promote ethical and philosophical thought, and to promulgate the latest scientific and technological breakthroughs to a mass audience. SF is a genre of ideas, and that is why I keep returning to it.

Every story in this collection derives from a particular idea. *Sanctuary* had its genesis in the altar at El Escorial, roped off from visitors and held up as sacred ground, but undoubtedly cleaned every night by some minimum-wage cleaning staff.

Some stories here are fluff, but they are fluffy through incompetence. Some spell out their intentions more clearly than others. Some merely profess to.

Some, like *No* and *Big News*, address sensitive questions, and, as always in literature, a distinction must be made between content and intent – something that all fascists, be they government ministers or disempowered apes perusing Twitter in search of an outrage, fail to understand. Please see *Offence*.

I will add a comment about writing dates. The stories are presented in order of their first drafts. Each story has the writing date given at the end, largely as a point of interest and for chronology. *Cleobis and Biton* underwent such heavy editing in its second draft that I removed the original writing date while keeping its original place in the collection. The date on *Big News* was serendipitous: it protects me from accusations of plagiarism in light of the Channel 4 series *National Treasure*.

Some first drafts took weeks, or even a month, to finish, while others took a few hours. In reality, every story here has been through five drafts or so, and has taken more than a month to reach 'publication standard'.

Cancer patients are encouraged to write – I think for several reasons. It helps to keep a patient focused and productive; if they write diaries or autobiographies, it helps to place one's life into a narrative, producing a kind of cheap CBT. Having read some of these journals myself, I find them trite, platitudinous, and self-serving. In writing fiction, I hope to leave something that will spark thought and entertainment. I hope it will inspire donations to Macmillan Cancer Support, and that perhaps other sufferers might find these stories readable in waiting rooms and chemotherapy wards.

I also know that, should a miracle occur and this book be read, plenty of people will say, *"It's all free online; why should I pay for it?"* (I have a particular ex-school friend in mind). I have no answer beyond, "It's the right thing to do." *"Yeah, but that's not enough for most people."* "Maybe not, but all I can worry about is whether *I* am doing the right thing." The world would be better if more people thought like that, instead of, "How does *your* behaviour affect *me* and *my* self-image?"

I would like to thank the several readers who have looked at drafts of these stories, in all their varying degrees of effusiveness and criticism. I hope that they recognise the changes they have encouraged, and that every time they so much as nodded in approval, they (perhaps inadvertently) encouraged me to go on. Where I have ignored their advice, I take the blame entirely on myself. I am also unendingly grateful to my brother Tim for contributing his outstanding graphic design talents to both the website and the book design.

21 October 2016

No

At last, Joseph could relax. He had made it. The immigration officer sat before him – and Joseph before him. His journey had begun in a village two hundred miles north of Lagos; the pale, European official had sent him here. And now it had ended, with Joseph sitting before another light-skinned bureaucrat.

That first official had come to the village just a month ago. He had gone about the place for a few hours, asking questions about individuals – names on a list. Some of those names had not lived in Joseph's village for a long time. Others had left more recently. Only Joseph remained.

The little European shook Joseph's hand and made every sign of being delighted to meet him at last. He stayed and chatted for an hour or three, and had then departed. In doing so, he left Joseph with weighty concerns, deep troubles, but absolutely no choice in the matter. He had to care for his family. He had to go to Europe. Europe was offering herself to him. Europe would save his family from poverty, hunger, thirst. From generations of hopelessness.

Europe was difficult to reach, and dangerous. You needed vehicles, and Joseph did not have one. But people existed who did have vehicles, and knew how to evade border patrols and army posts, and, best of all, would take others for a price.

Everyone knew how to find such people. Or, if they did not, they knew someone who did know. Joseph was in the latter group. He made contact, and he arranged a price. He was told to bring everything he would need: clothes, food, water. Money. Lots of money. The traffickers would give him nothing.

The money was the hardest to find, but his family sold what they had, and others were willing to lend more. It was an

1

investment. They would have an ample return in just a few weeks, when Joseph was in Europe and working, dragging money from the chubby, rich hands of comfortable, complacent Europeans. Joseph would be an entrepreneur. He would make his fortune. That one thought made the tears of his departure fall lighter on his family.

The truck came early one morning before the sun had risen. Joseph jumped inside without a word. But soon the sun came up and Joseph learned what it meant to travel to Europe. Thirty of them, all packed in to an incinerator-like dungeon, a covered truck, no space even to move around, to shift your tired muscles and alleviate the growing cramp within.

Limbs piled up over bodies; the stench of sweat emanated from other men's armpits, shoved close to your nostrils. The groans of those who hadn't enough water; the threats and pleas of those who wanted to share with someone else, and would promise the Earth to anyone who agreed.

No one spoke in those days. Talking was a waste of energy. The hot air seemed to grasp the very moisture from their wagging tongues. And what did anyone have to say? Half the men spoke another language, and the others were of a different faith. Even prayer turned inwardly, after the first attempts at communal worship had ended in violence – sectarian violence between incompatible faiths.

And Joseph, in particular, did not wish to speak, in case his mood, his tone, revealed his secret. He had something that no one else had – something that the others, if they found out about it, would probably kill him just for having, and then steal it. So he kept it hidden, safe and out of sight inside his pocket. He held on to it at night while he slept. It never left him – not for a moment. He never even hinted at its existence. To anyone.

The truck took them out of Nigeria, and eventually made its way through desert and heat and frost and sentry posts to Libya. Six of the human cattle died along the way, their groans in the night turning weaker and weaker until finally – mercifully

– they stopped altogether. Human compassion ran raw against the simple need for sleep, for the voices and gurgles to come to an end. At least one of the deaths – Joseph suspected – had been caused by human hands. But no one cared, least of all the traffickers. They had been paid. No one boarded the truck without paying.

And then they saw the dinghies, the makeshift boats, the castoffs from the nautical world, that would carry them from Libya to Sicily. ('Them': the twenty-four survivors from the truck, and a hundred others who had come by different routes.)

"You must be kidding," some of them had spirit enough yet to complain. "We didn't come all this way to drown. Who here can swim?"

But for the most part, no one cared any more. What could they do? Turn back? How? Or stay in Libya forever? Just across the sea – a spit – from Europe, and all it promised? And it was sailing season, the traffickers assured them. There would be no problems. They would be safe. Get on board.

And if there were problems? If a boat should sink? Well, the Italians were always looking for capsized boats. Anyone in the water would be safe within minutes. The Italians, like all Europeans, were humanitarians. They wouldn't let anyone drown. It was a game they all played together – traffickers, refugees, and navy.

Six boats slipped away from the coastline, running underneath the Libyans' very noses in the dark. The Libyans were glad to see them go, but they had to make a show of guarding the shore, because the Europeans paid them to do so. But then, who *didn't* receive European money, in this whole charade? The traffickers, perhaps – but even their profits came, ultimately, from the prospect of European handouts.

Despite the traffickers' assurances, only two of the six boats reached their destination. Two turned back. Two capsized. They capsized at night, when the Italians could not see them. None of the survivors gave much for their chances, but they all prayed, nonetheless, that those in the water would find land, or peace, one way or the other. No one offered to pull them aboard the swamped, surviving boats, or even suggested it, or thought of it.

In Sicily, the survivors simply sat down on the shore and awaited arrest by the Italians. They could see Calabria, just across the Strait of Messenia, although they did not know those names. The Italian mainland tempted them – once there, they could walk right into Europe, wherever they wanted. But in Sicily, they were trapped. When they looked back at the boats which had brought them here, they shuddered at ever going out to sea again in such death traps.

They were taken to a transit camp – little more than a prison – but a prison bereft of electricity or bedding. *What more did you expect?* the guards seemed to ask them. *It's better than what you had before.*

And it was dirty – the toilets were a filthy brown; the mattresses the colour of sick and pus. Metal fencing with barbed wire surrounded the camp. Guards at the gates and in watchtowers, overlooking the inmates. There was no pretence, and no escape.

The camp was full, and more refugees arrived each day. The only ones to leave were the mothers and the children, and the men with cuts and scars and whip-marks on their backs – the ones who were running *from*, not running *to*. Joseph, taking his cue from the other inmates, learned to hate each new arrival. *Who the hell are they to come here now, when we're out of space? This camp is full – go somewhere else, or go home! What do they want? Someone else can deal with them.*

But for the most part, there was just despair. Joseph thought about his family, now heavily in debt, their possessions sold, awaiting the first parcels of money to take care of them. That day seemed ever further off, as the incompetent guards refused to even...

Joseph shook his head. He had tried with the guards. He had approached them slowly, quietly, in a friendly way. He had tried to speak to them alone, out of the way, where his secret

words could not be overheard. They had refused to listen –
they didn't want to be bribed, or threatened, or whatever else
he had in mind. What did this migrant have to say to them that
he couldn't say in front of someone else? No, much safer to
stay away.

And so his pleas had turned into empty claims that he
should not be here, that he had a right to enter Europe. That
promises had been made. Even so, the guards had ignored
him. Hard sunglasses and smart, pressed khakis told him to
wait his turn.

But now – now! Now, he had his day! Now he stood –
sat – before the immigration officer. He savoured the moment.
Now, Joseph would triumph. The man asked his questions,
and Joseph said nothing, grinning at him, waiting for the
perfect time to extract his secret paper from his pocket, to wave
it in the man's face and startle him.

The officer, surprised by Joseph's silence, asked if he
spoke English, or Italian, or French. If he only knew African
tongues, then he would have to wait a few more days.
Translators were thin on the ground – there was little money in
learning Sub-Saharan dialects.

Smirking, Joseph leaned across the desk and passed over
his letter. He had brought it to Europe with him; it had
brought him to Europe. And now it would let him in. This –
this was why he was here. This was his entry ticket, his visa.
Yes, it was tattered from the travelling, the hiding, the handling.
Sweat oozed into the yellowing pages, competing with grey dust
and dirt. But who cared about that? You could still read it.
You could still see what it said.

"*Invitation for joining to European Union citizenship,*" the
official read out loud. He arched an eyebrow, as if trying to
detect any trace of irony in Joseph. Joseph gave him none.
"*Free grant of citizenship… European Green Card Lottery…
Immediately present to…*"

The officer stopped. Joseph folded his arms and awaited
his apology. At last the official spoke.

"I'm sorry, Mr. Oni." Joseph raised his head in triumph. The apology was coming! "But this document is not legitimate. It is not real. Do you understand me?"

At first, the words made no sense. The man was simply spouting meaningless sounds, phonemes without importance. Joseph's head swam in confusion.

"This... *document* is a fake. I am sorry."

Blankness turned to numbness. Joseph frowned. The floor fell away from him. A swirl of black spiralled before his eyes.

"There is no 'lottery'. Do you understand me?" said the official.

And at last came... *anger.* Oblivious, the officer continued to speak. He had already dismissed Joseph's precious document, throwing it indifferently to the table as if it were worthless.

"As with any other economic migrant, you will have to wait for processing..."

At last, Joseph could take no more of this smug, comfortable, well-fed bureaucrat, reciting his lines as if he, Joseph, were no more than a bug.

"...before being sent home..."

"No," said Joseph.

The officer stopped.

"I beg your..."

"No – I said no! Do you like that? You're telling me 'no' – I'm telling you 'no'! No! Fuck you."

"Mr Oni..." said the officer. "This isn't helping."

"Who do you think you are, sitting there, like a... a *cat*. You look so comfortable – what do you know? About who I am, where I'm from? This is not right. You are betraying me! You sent for me! You brought me here! That European who came to me – he said he worked for you. He – you invited me here! I have a right to be here!"

Joseph picked up the document again, refusing to believe, after all this time, that it had no worth. The officer simply

6

forced a smile – partly sympathetic, partly contemptuous, as if Joseph were a child who had simply to be humoured a little longer, before being schooled by his elder.

"You see?" said Joseph. "This proves it! This has everything – it has your signs. It is official. *'European Union Citizenship Office'*. You asked me to come here. And so? What do you do when I get here? Tell me that I've been tricked? Bull. Shit."

"I am sorry that you've…"

"No! There *is* a trick – *your* trick. You have come up with this – for some game of your own! You treat us like… animals! You pen us up like dogs, and then you go back on your word! You have no right!"

The officer was angry, but he contained himself – barely. He did not need to raise his voice: he was in a position of power. He could use simply his words and his own anger. He leaned back, arrogantly, breathing easier perhaps as his own pent-up frustration could finally find release.

"*Rights*, Mr. Oni?" he simpered. "You want to talk about *rights*? Very well. What *right* do you have to be here? None! None at all! We did not invite you here. This letter is not real – I have already told you that, but you refuse to listen. You have lost your money, Mr Oni – you gave it away to criminals who knew you would come here, and that you would be sent back. Probably the very same people wrote this letter as took your money. They have deceived you. Do not blame us!"

Joseph glared at the official, a knot of shame and anger in his belly. He thought of his family, of the debt, of the European who had given him his document. He thought of the traffickers, and the conditions on the road, and the life he had left behind him.

"We do not want you here," said the Italian. "Why would we? Answer me that. Why would we invite you here? What skills do you bring to Europe that we don't already have? Are you a scientist, or a doctor? No, perhaps you are a financier! What do you do at home? What is your profession that we need so desperately? What will you do here that we are in such desperate need of? Do you think we have a shortage of tat sellers, or waiters, or bicycle repair men?"

I am an entrepreneur, Jacob's heart screamed out. But he kept quiet, because he knew that the officer would only laugh and mock him again.

"You have come here because you have believed the lies of others. But you are not a… simple victim, are you? Didn't this seem strange to you? Had you ever entered your name for any lottery? Didn't you think to ask around, to search on the internet about these kinds of lies? How many people do you know with mobile telephones? A dozen? More? You could have asked them. You could have phoned us! But you didn't! I do not believe that you are an ignorant peasant, Mr Oni. There are very few of those around anymore. You could have investigated this 'citizenship lottery', if you had wanted to, but you did not.

"And now you are here, we have to deal with you. We have to clean up the mess that you have made – you and a hundred thousand, a million like you. So you do not like the camp, where we feed you and give you shelter? Very well, you may return home. We will even pay for you to do that – think of that! Why should we even do that? But we will.

"Or perhaps you wish to stay here forever? Perhaps you believe that one day, if you wait long enough, the borders will open, and suddenly we will be clamouring for fresh blood in Europe? Perhaps we will have a list, and the first who came here will be let in first! Well, then, if you believe that, then begin to improve your lot at home. You do not like the camp, so fix it. Clean it. Organise groups who can turn this transit camp into a home – but no, you will not do that either, because then you would have to confess that you will never leave here – that this is the end of your journey.

"Those are your choices, Mr Oni. I suggest that you consider them quite carefully. You have all the time in the world."

Joseph jumped to his feet, tears in his eyes, fists clenched into balls, determined to wipe the officer's dismissive sneer from his face. He was a man, wasn't he? Didn't he have the right to be treated like a man? And would he sit there and take this abuse, this scorn, because he was weak, and the officer was strong? *No!*

At once, strong hands forced him down again. A soldier had entered, hearing the commotion within. Joseph looked around and squirmed, but could not slip away.

"Well now, Mr. Oni," said the officer. "Would you like to continue your petition for asylum? Or shall we send you home and save ourselves some time?"

30 April, 2016

Cleobis and Biton

Mark Hauser was a winner – had always been one, at that. Even when he had not actually won anything – or, even worse, when his schoolmates would have even called him a 'loser' – even then, he'd been a winner. It was in his blood. He had winning genes.

What did that mean? Well, he had a mind that would never accept defeat, would never take 'no' for an answer. If he wanted something, he would get it. If he couldn't get it, he would keep on trying until he had it, or something even better. If he ever lost at anything – well, that was a mere tactical retreat.

Mark knew all about tactical retreats. He had read Sun Tzu, and all the commentaries on him. Strategy and tactics – they were worthy objects of his attention. They were subjects fit for leaders and kings.

Mark was a leader.

Mark and Frank had been rivals since high school. They had been friends, too. Very good friends, for a long time. The two roles were not mutually exclusive: but not in a soppy, American television sense where rivalry was simply an expression of suppressed friendship between people who could not express that friendship. No, Mark was simply incapable of seeing relationships in any terms other than rivalry.

Mark and Frank had fallen out of touch many years ago. Nor had they worried too much about it. Mark had plenty of other friends and rivals to fill the void, whereas Frank – well, Frank had always been a strange one. Frank had always teetered on the edge of truly understanding what it meant to be competitive, to always want to win, but he had never quite reached that higher level of self-actualisation. As a result, he had never been ambitious, had never achieved the things he ought to.

And Mark despised him for it, in a way.

Mark had won at life. His apartment proved it. He leaned back, relishing for the thousandth time the leather – yes, *real leather* – sofa, not just for the tactile pleasure of doing so, but also for the psychological pleasure of sitting on a material far beyond the means of others.

The leather sofa inhabited an apartment large enough to house two, maybe even three, families. Its size alone said plenty about its occupant; its elevation (forty storeys up) and its location (five minutes from Victoria) produced entire bookshelves.

Mark's business cards included not just his workplace, but also his home address. People ought to know.

Technology – ah, well, everyone had *technology* these days. Capitalism had brought the latest devices to every home in Britain. There was nothing impressive about that. Only two facts relating to the technology in Mark's home were of any note.

Firstly, he owned it, rather than leasing it on crippling rental contracts.

Secondly, Mark's home and all the devices in it were controlled by a single, overarching AI – like something out of *Star Trek*. Therefore, Mark's thermostat was controlled by the same entity as compiled his newspapers for him. And that *cost*. Each 'Guardian' AI took months to grow and customise for the end-user. Mark had permanent access to this intellectual titan through his watch, his tie, his toaster, at any time of day. He still shivered in excitement at the thought.

The titan was called Shelley.

Mark deserved all he had. He worked hard; he had always worked hard; he had earned his reward. These were the signs of his success. And soon, Frank would see them.

"Why has Frank asked to meet after all this time?" he asked out loud.

Several webpages – Shelley's best attempt at answering the question. He scanned them, raising his hand to his chin in concentration.

Frank was coming back to London. Mark had not realised that he had ever left in the first place. Still, he should have guessed it. London was the third most expensive city on Earth. Frank was a civil servant. Half the civil service worked outside London. E-commuting was cheaper, and Frank was the sort to strangle his career by moving away from the corridors of power just to save a bit of cash. No ambition.

Just as interestingly: he'd quit his job. Civil servant no more. *Aha! Gotcha!*

Mark received calls like this all the time. *Oh, I'm over-qualified; I was wasted there; it was time for me to leave. Mark, help me out. Give me a chance – you won't regret it.*

Sometimes Mark agreed; other times, he did not. In Frank's case? He would agree to meet him. Frank was, at least, talented. Mark didn't begrudge him that – how could they have been rivals otherwise? On the other hand – did Frank have the temperament for the kind of work he wanted? (Or at least, the kind of work that Mark assumed he wanted.)

"Write a standard acceptance letter," he commanded Shelley. "Four-star friendliness. Ask what he's been up to, but no specifics. Pick a time and a place, and add it to my schedule."

Then he went to sleep.

Cleobis and Biton.
Cleobis and Biton.
Mark frowned in the darkness and rolled over in bed.
"Shelley, put me to sleep."

At once, a soothing white noise sampled from rainfall filled the apartment. The lighting level increased to pre-dawn levels –Mark's best time for sleeping. A couple of minutes later, the dumb waiter crawled around the wall towards his bed, carrying herbal tea and a sleeping pill.

Cleobis and Biton.

It was three o' clock in the morning. Mark had returned from his drink with Frank hours ago. Indeed, it was a sign of Frank's poverty that he had had to meet up and leave so early in the evening: his part of town didn't even have night trains. Mark had offered to pay for a cab, but Frank refused. He was proud.

He shouldn't be. The whole evening had been a farce – a total embarrassment, from Frank's point of view. While Shelley had chosen a bar reasonably close to Frank's home, it hadn't considered cost. Frank had said nothing, but Shelley had noticed (watching through Mark's contact lenses) that his eyes lingered on the menu prices. The place was too expensive for him; Mark put it all on a tab and told Frank to pay him back later. He would never ask for the money.

His old rival Frank had *lost*. Mark saw it in his clothes and in his bearing, in Frank's replies and in his silences. Mark would mentioned some success at work, or his latest travels and purchases; Frank would listen, nod, and say nothing. Because what could he say?

Instead, his eyes filled with a warm sense of pleasure at Mark's success.

Pleasure!

And why not? Frank wanted a job, and the more successful Mark was, the more he could help Frank.

Still, Mark grimaced. He had an *unresolved issue* from the meeting. Something was bothering him about it.

Puzzled, he called up a transcript of their conversation – Shelley recorded everything he said and heard all day, so he could check it over later on. He sipped his tea while he read. And at last, Mark realised what was bothering him:

Why hadn't Frank asked him for a job?

USER: Yeah, I'm getting on pretty well. I was made partner at Vicks Ryman a few years ago.

FRANK: Oh yeah?

USER: Yeah, it's the third largest tech-analytics firm in Europe.

FRANK: Oh, right.

USER: Yeah, well. It was frustrating. If they'd done it a month earlier, I would have been the youngest partner in the firm's history! I missed that one because of politics – absolutely no other reason!

FRANK: Wow. How old is the firm?

USER: What do you...? Oh, I see. The average partner age is forty. That's young, but in tech you have to promote young to get the best results. Plus, there's a lot of headhunting, which tends to faster promotions – I was headhunted, you know. He promised me five times my old salary – do you remember I used to work for Gestalt?

I got the job, but they offered it to me too quickly. I said – completely calm, no expression whatsoever – that I wanted to be made partner. You should have seen his face! Obviously he said they'd have to think about it – but they came back the next day and offered me fast-stream partner-track. I didn't show it, but I bit their hand off! Two years later, I'm a partner.

But they promoted this other guy at around the same time. Gerald. Nice guy, but a bit of a wheeler-dealer, and he's the nephew of a partner. That's how he got it. And – this is the frustrating bit – they delayed my promotion just so he could call himself the youngest partner ever. So now he's got that on his CV for the rest of his life. Bastard.

FRANK: No, I meant how long has the firm existed for?

USER: Hmm? Oh, eighteen years. Give or take.

FRANK: Oh, right.

[No voice input for 4.5 seconds]

USER: But that's enough about me. Are you still working for the civil service?

FRANK: No, I left a few months ago.

USER: Hah! Get a better offer, did you? I always said you could do better. You'd get frustrated there – too many incompetents, too many time-servers.

FRANK: Sort of. But, no – I didn't get a better offer. I can't even think how that happens. I don't think head hunters bother with people at my grade.

USER: Hmm – well that's the danger. Having to start out at the bottom all over again because you never made management.

FRANK: Yeah, that's true.

USER: Remind me – what Department were you in?

FRANK: Oh, a few. They bounce you around for years until you make the next jump up. I've done FO, DWP... the big ones. Did a stint in the legal office, but I couldn't get switched over to the training programme.

USER: That surprises me. You should have found that a cinch – I've met government lawyers before!

FRANK: Well, it's a bit of a lottery. The ratios are pretty high. A bit like getting into Oxbridge. Did the right person read your application on the right day, et cetera?

USER: Well, I don't agree with you there. We got in because we deserved to. Our applications got us the interview, and we did well in our interviews...

FRANK: All depends on the questions, and the tone...

USER: Oh yeah, sure. Anyway. So you left before you hit management?

FRANK: Mm. A few more years would have done it. But the work was... not interesting anymore. I found myself sitting at the desk thinking how pointless it all was. You go into the civil service because you want to make a difference, but then you realise that it's – you know that old saying about having a big enough lever and moving the world?

USER: Archimedes, I believe.

FRANK: Well, that lever isn't the civil service. It's more like… a train. It goes where it's going anyway, and all you can do…

USER: Is decide how fast it gets there!

FRANK: No, no! How slow!

USER: Hah: Still, I'd have stuck it out. It's easier to switch into something interesting if you've got management on the old résumé.

FRANK: You wouldn't have been there in the first place.

USER: Well, that's true. But you've got skills, right? All the usual soft skills. You won't have trouble finding work.

FRANK: I hope not. We'll see how it goes here for a while. If not – well, I've got savings. I might try Cambridge, or York, or somewhere. They've got a higher standard of living out there than London…

USER: …than *some* parts of London.

FRANK: Yes, I've no doubt that you're living in some ultra-exclusive treetop village or something! But pound-for-pound, it's cheaper outside London. You know that.

USER: Oh, yeah. Treetop village? I haven't heard of those. Is there one in London?

FRANK: I'm joking. It's the kind of thing you lot do these days, isn't it?

USER: 'My lot'? Don't lump me in with 'that lot'. You should see some of… Look, anyway, I can't complain about my living situation. You should come and see it some time.

FRANK: Sure.

[No voice input for five seconds.]

USER: What do you know about tech-analytics?

FRANK: Absolutely eff-all.

USER: Huh. Well, we do other things, too. A firm that big always dips into other industries. It's not like

	everyone there is a tech-head – although you always knew computers.
FRANK:	Mm.
USER:	You know… I could always ask around. It never hurts to get the inside track. And if you've got the basic skills, it's often cheaper to train up than hire in.
FRANK:	Oh, yeah?
USER:	And you've got a government background… We might have some divisions that could use that.
FRANK:	Usually it's better if you're higher up first. 'Personnel cross-pollination', in the gibberish…
USER:	Well, you never know. As I said, I'll ask around.
FRANK:	Hmm. Well, you don't have to…

Mark shook his head and dismissed the transcript. His tea was cold, so he ordered another one. He rested his back, cradling his head in his arms.

Why had he offered to help Frank when Frank hadn't even asked him to? Mark had practically thrown himself at him – it was humiliating!

Was he a master of psychology? No – Mark would have seen through that. Mark was an excellent judge of character – you have to be, to rise quickly in business. And Mark had risen very quickly. He would have seen through something as simple as run-of-the-mill manipulation.

For the same reason, he dismissed the sneaking suspicion that Frank had been laughing at him. What was that comment about how long the firm had been around for? Who cared? He was – nearly, thanks to politics – the youngest partner in its history.

Mark thought about that for a moment.

Yes, technically, it was less impressive in a young firm than an old firm. Except fast-streaming partners was only a couple of decades old anyway, so all firms at least that old were on a level playing field. Mark's firm was about as old as they come, in that regard.

But did Frank realise that?

And there were other little comments. Snide little... no, not snide. Mark would have noticed 'snide'. Mocking.

Like that treetop village comment. There really were treetop villages out there, according to Shelley. High-tech, modern retreats for the super-elites. Now Mark knew about them, he would kill to live in one. None of them were in Britain, though.

But Frank wouldn't have known that, probably. Unless he was suggesting that Mark had flown in from Germany to meet him! So there was nothing clearly impossible in the comment. But there was something about the tone. Not even disingenuousness. More...

Mark had it.

Polite interest.

No: polite *disinterest!*

The same tone in which he'd commented on Mark's wonder-watch, or the miracles of Mark's home. Or the current state of tech-analytics, or how everyone would be living in five or ten years' time.

Was Frank a Luddite? No – no Luddite moved to London by choice! Just a *Back 2 Basics*-er? Then why was he fishing for a job in tech?

Was he just an idiot?

The more he thought about it, that tone had bugged him all night. It had led to Mark's own outburst towards the end of the night.

"Well?" he'd said. (He didn't need a transcript to remember this part!) "Come on, then. What's going on with you? Why did you really leave your job so early? Why've you really come to London now? And why are you all so, 'Yeah, whatever'? What's your plan? What's your..."

And Frank had looked at him, distractedly. With immense gravity and importance, now fixing his gaze, as if watching Mark's response, he said,

"Cleobis and Biton."

Without skipping a beat, Mark replied,

"Oh, yeah. Right. Clever."

And now, in the dim, artificial pre-dawn light of his apartment, Mark said,

"Shelley, search 'Cleobis and Biton'."

A synopsis of the story appeared in his retina, followed by a much longer interpretation and analysis. He sighed, and stored the report. He would look it over at lunchtime.

Then he said,

"And add Frank to the invite list for the party. Guest Rank One."

*   *   *

The party was acceptable. Merely 'acceptable'. Unable to accept this, Mark toured the apartment, looking for what was going wrong.

He had invited two hundred and fifty guests, thirty of whom were 'Rank One' – the ones whose attendance really mattered. All of them were in attendance. Even the board member from Treetop Villages, whom he had invited unfathomably late, was present. Frank was there, too – he was the only personal friend he had made Rank One. The rest were all Rank Two. (And Rank Three was for random acquaintances and casual contacts – social niceties and bums-on-seats.)

He studied the gifts tables. He allowed his gaze to linger on one offering: a whisky bottle a century old. Even Mark would hesitate to drink that. He should have it mounted.

One of the guests came and patted him on the shoulder. He asked what Mark had in his hands. Mark couldn't resist a childishly excited, "Look at that!", as he showed him the bottle.

"You're welcome," said his guest, smiling.

Mark recognised his blunder, and shook the guest warmly by the hand. They chatted about whisky for a while. Then they talked about work. Then they promised to meet up for lunch soon – the guest's company was opening up a new division, and there might be scope for some intellectual cross-pollination. Mark had to agree; he'd been too enthusiastic about the present.

They parted ways, and Mark continued to look over the gifts. There were some flowers in there (rare, exotic, and, in some cases, illegal to import), but for the most part they were alcohol-related. Alcohol was sufficiently traditional and – more importantly – sufficiently *masculine* for an occasion like this.

Mark himself had shelled out on crystal bottle stoppers for every one of his guests. Every size, shape and colour imaginable, from sapphire to ruby to diamond to… well, everything. The allocation *seemed* random, to a reasonable inspection, but, naturally, the better Ranks got the better gifts. Even Frank. He could always sell it, if he needed to.

One wine bottle stood out. Frowning, he reached over and picked it up. He read the label, and asked Shelley, in silent mode, to confirm his thoughts.

He was right: *Oddbins*.

Poor Frank.

Nothing wrong with that, Mark hastened to add. It was a decent bottle, by most people's reckoning. Frank just didn't know what he was up against.

Mark tactfully rearranged the bottles, putting Frank's offering somewhere out of sight. Frank would want that – no one wanted to bring the worst gift to a party. It was embarrassing. He assumed.

Everyone seemed happy. The food was disappearing quickly, but the caterers were good and brought reinforcements as soon as they were needed. The booze was flowing, but still going strong. He should relax; he was in a funk, that was all. This was a chance to unwind.

"Frank!" he shouted. "Good to see you, buddy!"

He walked over to Frank, who was startled to hear his name called from so far away. He embraced Frank ostentatiously.

"Glad you could make it!" he said, again, more loudly still.

Shelley confirmed what he had hoped: right now, everyone was staring at Frank, checking his name against the guest list, even searching his CV on the spot. Mark prayed that Frank had updated his profile as instructed. If Mark couldn't find his old friend a job, there was always someone lower down the food chain, who would hire someone purely to curry favour with an apex predator like Mark.

"Hi Mark," said Frank. "Thanks for inviting me."

"Are you kidding?" Still too loud – no, *just the right loudness*. "When I heard you were back in town, you couldn't stop me!"

They carried on like this for a while until Mark suggested nipping into one of the break booths. There were a few of them scattered around the apartment – small, temporary pods, like furnished porta-loos, but without the loos (there were also several porta-loos too, for that matter). They were meant for things like this: quiet, private chats – and more intimate affairs, too.

Mark made sure that people saw them entering one together. More searches for Frank's name. The current occupants of the booth jumped up when they saw Mark, and having gone through the usual motions, left quickly.

"So," said Mark.

"So."

"Thanks for the wine, by the way."

"Oh, that," Frank laughed. "It's not really up to scratch, is it? Sorry."

"Mate, it's not about the price," Mark lied. "Wine is wine, right?"

"By the same token, booze is booze. I should have just brought a six-pack of Fosters."

"Now *that* would have caused a scene!"

They chuckled.

21

"You know," said Frank, "they say that even wine experts can't tell wines apart in studies, if you confound their expectations. If you tell them they're comparing dessert wines, or put red colouring into white, that sort of thing. Maybe you should test the theory? My *Oddbins* against your... I don't know any posh wines. Take your pick."

Mark laughed, picking up on Frank's defensive sarcasm, trying to justify his poverty by pretending that it didn't matter.

"Sure, sure!" he said. Then, to dissipate his irritation, he said, "I hope you don't mind. I moved the bottle a bit. You know, we want people to hire you. We have to make the right impression."

Frank shrugged.

"I'd have put it front-row-centre. Make the whole thing look like a very witty joke. *This is what a rich person doing an impression of a poor person brings to a party.*"

Mark thought about that. It wasn't a bad idea. Not that he would admit that. Not right now.

"If it had been Fosters, I would have, mate! So, you been networking?"

Frank hummed.

"Met a few people. Not really my type."

"Then fake it. That's the point of networking. The point is, 'Is this guy the right sort of person? Does he laugh at the same things I laugh at? Do we get the same references? Is he easy-going – do I want to work with him?'"

"Or her."

"Ah – good point! Or 'her'."

Frank stretched his arms behind his head and grimaced.

"Well, like I said, I chatted to a few of them."

"Good – make sure you get their names. You've got a PDA, right?"

"I've got my phone..."

"Your... Let's see it? Right, for fuck's sake, don't let anyone see you with *that*!"

"What do you mean? I've been using it all night. I say I borrowed it off you."

Again, laughter.

"This is what I mean," said Mark. "Old friends who get each other's jokes. And that's what you've got to sell to these guys. The CV they'll read for themselves. And I'll upsell you. But the personality, the chat – that comes from you."

"So, stop talking about Hindi terrorism and the role of capital markets in the Gabon War?"

"I'm going to take that as an extremely subtle joke."

"Hold on."

Frank took out his phone and made a show of writing a note. Mark rubbed his eyes in feigned despair. Lending Frank a phone wasn't a bad idea.

"Speaking of 'her's,'" he said, changing the subject. "If you haven't chatted to the guys for work, have you met any of the senoritas for…"

"I didn't realise that they were a separate category."

"Well, they're in the category of 'chatting up', rather than 'networking'."

"Can't they be both?"

"They definitely can't be both," said Mark. "Oh, they can be *either*, sure. But not both."

"It's a beautiful, hollowed out Venn diagram. Nothing in the middle bit."

"Yeah. So?"

Frank shook his head.

"I feel that any attempt to chat up a woman here would be writing an IOU I can't deliver on."

"They don't have to know that."

"They will eventually."

"So go back to theirs tonight, and tell them tomorrow."

Frank wrinkled his nose.

"Or don't. Just walk out when they're not looking."

"That's worse."

"Not necessarily," said Mark. "It's not the nineteenth century. Plenty of women prefer that. Especially here – everyone's too busy for a love life. Just send her a text."

"I could send an *Instagram* of my flat. No need for words!"

"That's the spirit! I'll even show you the nuttiest ones, if you like."

"Well, insanity is a trait I look for…"

"Ones who are mad enough to date hobos."

"Hobos? Harsh. So you want me to be Jarvis Cocker?"

"Hmm?"

"The old song, *Common People*. 'You wanna live like the common people…'"

"There's more truth in that song than you think."

"Perhaps. But probably not with unemployed, ex-civil servants. Maybe they'd slum it with someone who isn't *even* the youngest partner in his firm's history."

Again, laughter.

"I looked up that Cleobis and Biton story, by the way," said Mark.

"Oh, yeah?"

"It was a while ago, but if I recall… The richest man in the world, Croesus, asked the wisest man, Solon, who was the happiest man on Earth."

"Lots of superlatives in this story. It's very poetic."

"And Solon gave his winning list, one of whom was a Cleobis and Biton."

"Two of whom. They were brothers. And Croesus thought that he'd be number one, because he was so rich."

"And Cleobis and Biton were happy, because they were strong, and everyone praised them for pulling their disabled mother to a festival in a cart, and then they died that night sleeping in the temple."

"That's right."

"Now," said Mark. "What that says to me is that either they were happy because they were strong, or because everyone praised them."

"Okay."

"Which – if you don't mind me saying so – doesn't exactly apply to you."

"Probably not. No one praises me."

They said nothing for a while. Again, there was that slight lilt in Frank's voice – a hint that he was hiding something.

"So?" said Mark. "Explain. Now."

Frank smiled.

"It bothered you, did it?" he said.

"I'm just curious. I don't care much either way."

"You looked up the story. That's interesting. I could have just told you it at the time, if you'd wanted to know it."

"Yeah, well, it seemed easier to search it. You had to get home, as I recall."

"Hmm. And it's bothered you, too. Enough to remember it and ask about it."

"What can I say? I'm a curious guy."

"Ah, I'd forgotten. Well, the story isn't about praise or strength – although it could be partly, if you wanted it to. The point is really that it's senseless to decide if someone's life is happy until it's over. Croesus' wealth was destroyed by the Persians, and he was made a slave of... I forget. Not Cambyses. Someone else."

Mark looked it up.

"Cyrus the Great."

Frank slapped himself on the forehead.

"Right. But all the examples that Solon gave were already dead, and had died happy. Usually poor. Whereas Croesus wanted to be called the happiest because of his wealth, though he wasn't dead yet."

Mark sighed.

"So? What's the point?"

"Well, to me, the point is that you have to be happy. Now, if that means being strong, or being praised by other people, or rich, or whatever, that's fine, but all of those can pass – they're temporary. And if it's competitive, or involves other people, then it can be lost at any moment."

"True. I could get fired, I suppose," said Mark.

Frank shook his head.

"No – because even now, who are you more worried about at this party? The ones who've got more than you, or less?"

"I'm not *worried* about anyone here."

"Wrong word. Pick your own. Or *praise* – that only lasts a short time, unless you're, like, Nelson Mandela or someone. So you've always got to work to impress other people, or the buzz of praise dies away."

"Unless the praise is simply a proxy for success, and what you really want is success," Mark pointed out.

"In which case, how long does the glow from each success last? A few days? It means… most people are like sieves, especially when it comes to being happy. You've got to keep pouring stuff in to keep it full, and that's what most people do. But if you can find a way to block up the holes…"

"You don't have to fill up the sieve any more. You're happy forever."

"Unless you trip and spill it."

Mark frowned, then nodded.

"Well, that's all been very interesting," he said. "But I should get going. We've both got other people to chat to here."

Frank nodded. Mark stood up and walked towards the door. Then he stopped, turned, and said,

"Incidentally… There's something you probably don't know. You see, I *do* like being praised. I don't apologise for it. If people praise you, it means they like you, they want to be like you, they admire you, you're successful. It means a thousand things, all of them good.

"When you sign as a partner, you get all sorts of weird bonuses, the point of which is to help you maintain the status of the firm. You know, more up-to-date versions of getting a company car, and so on."

"But you still have a company car, right?"

"Of course. I just can't park it anywhere. But one of them is funeral insurance."

"Oh, you couldn't possibly go into the netherworld in anything less than style."

"Or unmourned by thousands of admirers. Looks bad in the papers."

Frank raised an eyebrow.

"Part of the insurance offers payments. So much for taking time out of work to attend. More for various signs of mourning. Even more if you've got a literary presence and write an obituary. Crazy sums for a eulogy."

"Very wise."

"So there you have it. Even after I die, people will be praising me. And what's more, by your logic, even before I die, *I'll know it.*"

"Hmm."

"So what does that do for your theory?" said Mark.

"Well, it doesn't seem to change anything."

"No? Why not?"

"Because..." Frank thought. "This insurance only lasts as long as you're a partner at this firm, I assume. That means... that this funeral insurance is just the same as doing well at your company. It doesn't add anything."

Mark shook his head.

"No, it means that even if I didn't like my work..."

"I never said that, by the way," said Frank.

"Didn't you?" Mark looked at him. "I do, by the way. I find it fascinating. But the point is, even if I didn't, and I were knocked down by a truck tomorrow, I would know that I would still go out being praised by *everyone*. Because I'd been so successful. Hence: happiness."

Mark spread out his hands in a gesture of triumph and reason. He expected Frank to fold. He did.

"I guess you're right," he said. "I hadn't thought of that. I just hope you have time to think about that after the accident. To get the full benefit."

Mark left the booth and rejoined the party. Buoyed up by his triumph, all his concerns and misgivings assuaged, he networked a little while longer, before moving on to the greater concern: women. With a stop-off by the Treetop Villages man, who was getting too friendly with the wrong people. Mark *had* to get onto the waiting list or he would die.

Later, when the party was over and the woman had gone to sleep next to him, Frank's comment about 'hollowed out Venn diagrams' suddenly made sense, and he grinned. Frank said things that waited a while before they made sense. It was a bad habit. He would have to break it to work in Mark's world.

He ordered Shelley to arrange the guests at the party into just such a Venn diagram, but the computer didn't understand, so he dropped the matter.

He chuckled to himself, too, at Frank's *Oddbins* bottle, which Mark had whimsically moved back into plain view for a joke, as Frank had suggested. He wondered how many people had got it. Too subtle?

At last it was time to sleep. The party had gone well; Frank might even get a job out of it. Mark himself was almost guaranteed to be on the call list when the first Treetop Village opened in England – the exec had basically promised it. The tension that had bothered him for weeks had passed. All was right on Earth.

For a little while, then, Mark bathed in the glow of success.

24 May, 2016

Science Fiction Story

Juliet approached the pawn shop. From the outside, you wouldn't have given it a second glance. You saw a dozen like it, on a hundred aging high streets all over London, across the United Kingdom. You walked in, you bought something, or you sold something. You didn't browse. You got out as quickly as possible.

But this one, *Romelo's Exchange*, wasn't quite the same. It did the usual pawn shop trade, sure: but it traded in other things, too. It was a specialist – but as to what kind of specialist, Juliet didn't know yet. She had her suspicions.

She knew this much because of the clientele. They never went in during the daylight hours, and they rarely used the front door, but Juliet saw them. Nor did they dress any differently from the usual crowd. They were smarter than that – *cleverer* than that. But Juliet knew them. There were records on them. They had exotic tastes.

So, the pawn shop was a front. Big whoop. Juliet didn't even care what these collectors and connoisseurs were using the place for. She'd been hired to find the man who ran it. It sure wasn't Romelo. He was just a name: a man to man the desk while the important people had their secret meetings in the back and made their shadowy deals.

Juliet pushed the door open; a bell rang. Quaint. The broker – probably Romelo himself – waited a discreet time before sauntering in from the back, straddling the chasm between salesmanly solicitousness and proprietorial mistrust for his patrons with aplomb.

"Afternoon," he said.

"Good afternoon," she replied.

He looked at her expectantly. Romelo knew people; it was part of his trade. He knew that Juliet was there for a reason.

Her manner gave it away. She wasn't here to sell – she didn't look desperate, and women who dressed like her and had to sell in the local pawn shop were always desperate. She might be there to buy – in which case, she would ask for it.

Either way, there was no need to pretend. Pretence would waste time.

Juliet reached into her bag and took out a photograph. She barely looked at it – as if she'd seen it a thousand times.

"Seen anything like this lately?" she said.

Romelo looked at the picture with just as little interest as her. Juliet had guessed correctly – taken out the right photo. If he'd shown a little more interest, paid closer attention to the fading, intricate designs on the artefact, she might have faltered. But no – the pawnbroker had seen plenty of these before.

"They're not easy to come by," he replied with a shrug.

Juliet snorted inwardly. She grew in confidence – Romelo was definitely not a key player in this organisation. Chosen as a front man, his ham-fistedness was probably the bane of his mysterious employers' existence. He didn't have long before they ditched him. Even less if he thought he could worm his way into his group's inner sanctum.

"Oh, well, I'll try somewhere else then," she said. She turned to leave.

And – all credit to the man – she made it *almost* to the door before he called her back.

"Wait, wait!" He chuckled, half embarrassed, half trying to pass off his attitude as a test of character. "You're serious, then. You're a collector, too?"

Juliet said nothing. She fixed the man with her eyes.

"Or, you're working for one," he corrected himself. "I don't deal with time-wasters."

"Nor do I. Do I look like one?"

Romelo thought about that.

"Not the usual sort. But you get them. And you could be working for one. A… dilettante."

"As I said," repeated Juliet: "I don't deal with time-wasters."

Romelo hummed at that and looked at her again. She met his gaze head-on. He was trying to give the impression that he saw through her, that he was weighing up her character. But he saw nothing: Juliet knew the difference between fact and performance.

"No, I don't think you do," said Romelo. He paused, then nodded to her, as if he was nodding to himself. "I can get hold of some... specimens. It'll take time.

"How long?" she snapped.

"Depends on what you want. A few days, at least. Longer for the better quality items. I don't keep them here. For obvious reasons."

Juliet shook her head and closed her eyes.

"Too long. As I said, I'm not here to waste time. My employer isn't, either. Collectors aren't known to be patient people, Mr Romelo."

They watched each other in silence for a moment. Juliet gave nothing away. Romelo – a thought seemed to come into his head. He spoke slowly.

"I could hurry things along, you know. It's not impossible. It's simply *difficult*. It'll upset people. It'll cost me. In face. Not just money. I've got my own people to worry about, you see."

"They'll be paid for their hurt feelings," she said.

"And it's just possible," said Romelo, a smile coming across his face – now more confident, much more in his home element, it seemed, "that it will upset *me*, too."

Juliet tilted her head.

"My client's money is not inexhaustible," she said. "I won't promise you the Earth. Yours isn't the only group I could have come to."

Again, the shopkeeper smiled confidently – no, he smiled like a tiger that has finally caught its prey.

"No," he said. "It's not. And I appreciate your desire to reduce your client's expenses. You work in the service industry, just like I do. If we do a good job, our employers are satisfied, and keep coming back."

Juliet frowned, feeling for the first time that the conversation had flowed out of her control.

"Your point?" she said, weakly.

"The *question*," said Romelo. "*My* question – isn't '*What will your clients pay?*' It's '*What will* you *pay?*'"

The shopkeeper leaned across the counter and placed his hand on Juliet's. For the first time, she noticed that Romelo was an attractive man. He had – probably – a certain amount of charm when he wasn't playing cloak and dagger. It was probably why the collectors had chosen him in the first place.

Romelo looked into her eyes. She recognised that many women would have been drawn in by those eyes. They were warm, inviting.

She realised that Romelo's hand still engulfed hers, and that now his other hand was coming up to join in the fun. So, this was the deal. This was her way in. This would alleviate Romelo's feelings.

Juliet looked at the hand resting on hers. She withdrew her own. She straightened up.

Romelo smiled gently, as if mildly surprised, but nothing more.

"A woman like you," he said, "is never an innocent. You've been with men before – and not for the reasons you'd like. We're both professionals. We both know how this works. You said don't ask for the Earth. I'm not."

Juliet gazed into his eyes, wondering how many times he had done this. The competence, she felt, had changed over. Before, she had been sizing him up; now, he saw through her. She felt vulnerable.

Romelo pressed home his advantage:

"It would go a long way towards… calming my concerns," he said. "An unknown agent, working for someone else.

Coming out of nowhere. Asking questions about… rare things. Things that not many people know about, and which very few people know that *I* know about… And working to a tight schedule – well, this is very disconcerting."

Juliet froze. To lean in, or walk away?

"*Trust* is what counts," said Romelo.

Juliet felt trapped. Hardly able to turn her eyes away, she wanted only to walk towards the door; but the easier path lay before her. That way led the case. That way – she could wash her hands of this whole business. Get rid of her client, whose very presence chilled her to the bone. Escape these collectors and their artefacts.

And yet…

At last, she decided. She took a breath. She remembered what mattered to her. She took the photograph from the counter and placed it back into her bag. She did all of this slowly, as if terrified of making a mistake, and feeling Romelo's amused eyes on her all the time.

She entered a science fiction story, in which men and women behaved sensibly towards each other.

She looked at Romelo and said,

"No, thank you."

The pawnbroker blinked, surprised. He might even have gawped a little.

"Excuse me?" he said.

"I'm not interested," she replied, coldly.

Romelo opened his mouth a few times, but no sounds came out. This wasn't how the script went. At last, he managed to say,

"Do – do you want to make a deal or not?"

Juliet breathed more confidently, feeling that matters were in hand once more.

"I came here to buy some items. That's all. I didn't come for anything else."

"I didn't think you were a time-waster."

"I don't believe I am. I'm sorry if you believed that anything else was possible."

The pawnbroker, now, straightened up. He folded his arms. He frowned. He took a deep breath of his own, exorcising the twin feelings of humiliation and disappointment, and closed his eyes briefly as he relaxed the tension in his shoulders. Presently, he nodded.

"Well, that's fair enough," he said. "You have that right. Thank you for being upfront."

Juliet accepted all this with a nod.

"And," he Romelo, "I'm sorry if I made you uncomfortable."

"It happens," she said. "More often than you'd think. Now, shall we get back to business?"

Romelo grimaced.

"I'd prefer not to, to be honest. Perhaps you can send your client to me directly. We might work something out."

"As if a collector would do that. But I might have a colleague who could come?"

Romelo shrugged and looked away. He made no promises. Juliet held out her palm, and after a moment's hesitation, the pawnbroker took it. They shook hands.

Juliet walked out of the shop and out of the science fiction story.

9 May, 2016

34

Offence

"Please calm down, sir," said the policeman. He fixed Michael in the eye. "We can't help you without a clear picture of what happened."

Michael squeezed his eyes closed and breathed in deeply. He nodded in understanding. He just – wasn't ready to speak, yet. Traumatic events must be allowed to rise naturally from within, not drilled out like a mining operation.

There was a mug of chocolate on the table. It was cold now, but a smiling receptionist had given it to him when he'd come in and she'd seen his obvious state of shock. He'd hardly touched it since, except to feel the comforting warmth against his skin.

Now he reached for it again and held it to his lips. His lips scarcely broke through the cold, skinlike surface. But it was something.

The policeman waited like a man with patience, but limited time. He kept his pen in his hand, the pen to the paper. He looked expectantly at his man, indicating his readiness to proceed.

"Ready to try again?" he said. "Okay. You were walking down... Cromwell Avenue."

"That's right," said Michael.

"At about...?"

"Four thirty. In the afternoon."

"About an hour ago."

"Yes."

"Can you explain what happened next?"

Michael steeled himself with another breath.

"Yes. But... do I have to do this all over again? You have the video recording."

The policeman nodded sadly. Recordings were all well and good, but they weren't enough.

"I'm afraid so. Your phone recorded the incident, but we have to know how it made you *feel*. Otherwise, all we have are the facts, and they'll be no good in court."

"Cold, hard, facts," muttered Michael.

"Right. It's not all about those."

Michael waited another few seconds, considering his options.

"They say that talking through these kinds of events can help to relieve the distress," added the policeman. Michael looked at him in surprise, and then nodded decisively.

"Fine," he said, quickly. "I was walking along, and I saw these girls sitting on the wall. It was opposite the supermarket. Tesco."

"Okay, slow down. We can't rush this. Can you describe the girls? How did they seem to you?"

"Nothing special. Just some school girls – no, they were sixth formers. They weren't in uniform. They looked like they were hanging out."

" '*Hanging out*'. What does that mean to you?"

"You know. Laughing. Smoking. I think they had coffees, from Starbucks. They were sitting – there were three of them, and they were sitting in a line on the wall. You know, the short wall that goes along the pavement."

"I know it," said the policeman. "And what did you think when you saw them?"

"Um… I thought, gosh, I've got to walk past these girls now. I just wanted to get past them."

"Okay, and how did you feel when you got closer?"

"I was nervous," Michael admitted. "They looked at me. They spotted me from a way off, I think, but I tried to ignore them. I didn't know what they were going to do. I didn't – I thought they might, you know? There was something in that look, like, they were bored. But I couldn't – I wasn't going to cross the road, or anything."

The policeman shook his head quickly.

"We're not here for that. We don't say that you should have done something differently. We're not here to blame. We just want to know how you felt. Tell me: you said they 'spotted you'. Do you think they were watching you?"

"Y-yes."

"Why?"

"They were whispering to each other – the way you do when you want to keep a secret. They'd been chatting before, and you can tell when people are just... having fun. But that stopped when they saw me. They looked at me a few times and laughed."

"They laughed?"

"Yes."

"How did they laugh?"

"They giggled. Like at a private joke."

"At your expense."

"I think so. I *felt* so."

Throughout, the policeman's pen had kept on moving across the page; now he'd reached the end and he had to attach a supplementary page. At last, something useful was coming out of this.

"Go on."

"Then, when I was walking past them – I didn't make eye contact, I didn't look at them. I kept my head down..."

"What happened?"

"They... called out at me."

"And what did they call out?"

"They called out... do I really have to?"

The policeman nodded, sternly. He even tapped the recorder, to remind Michael that *how* he said this mattered just as much as *what* he said. Voice pattern analysis would help if it came to court.

"Fine." Michael blew out his cheeks. "They said, '*Hey, sexy*'."

Michael let the comment sink in. The policeman allowed a moment's sympathetic pause.

"Do you think they meant it?"

"No!"

"And how did you react?"

"How could I? I walked right on by, and they just started laughing!"

"Again?"

"Yes!"

The policeman took a note.

"And how did you feel about all this?"

"Humiliated! Embarrassed! Like I – like I wanted to shout at them and… run away, and hide. Like my stomach was closing up around a burning coal, like I just wanted to get back in bed and never leave."

"Did they say anything else?"

"Isn't that enough? I – I never asked for that. I never asked to be embarrassed on the street by some kids. Why should I have to? It's – it's…"

"Okay, okay," said the policeman. "Calm down. It's time we took a break, anyway."

He reached across and patted Michael on the hand. They did the best they could, but policemen were not counsellors. They could only offer the support they knew how. He scrawled some final comments on the incident report form and asked Michael to sign it.

"We can carry on tomorrow, if you'd like. Or we can just take a break. Your choice."

"I… Let me think. What's going to happen to those girls?"

"Well," said the policeman, leaning back. "We've got the names already from their online footprint. We can pick them up whenever we like – teenagers always leave their GPS on. We'll probably bring them in later tonight, when they've all gone home. We prefer to make juvenile arrests in the family home. They go much smoother."

Michael reached once more for his chocolate cup, like a security blanket.

"They'll be here? I... I can't be here at the same time as them. That would be too much."

"I understand," said the policeman. "There's enough here, between your statement and the video, to hold them overnight. They'll get out in the morning and be given a court date. You can come in in the afternoon and we'll carry on."

"But what... will I have to do this all in court? This is... awful."

The policeman sighed, thinking over recent cases of a similar nature. "It might go to court. Some people out there still think they can fight these cases. The old 'I was only joking' brigade. But kids... not so often. They get it. So, we'll see."

"And will they be punished?" said Michael.

"Oh, a bit of community service. Perhaps more, if they don't show remorse. Public humiliation for the ringleader, if she's not careful. It all depends on how they respond. Either way, don't worry. They won't be causing offence like this again."

The policeman smiled encouragingly at Michael, happy to be able to deliver this good news.

"Of course, he went on, "the judge matters, too. All that's if he puts it in the same category as Twitter abuse. On the other hand, if he deems it a gender hate crime, then it'll go in the same category as religious disparagement, and that'll be tougher for them."

"What does that mean for me?" said Michael.

"In that case..." The policeman thought for a moment. He grimaced. "It'll be harder for you, too. You'll be asked to testify in court, and it'll be a criminal case, so you'll have to face some hostile questioning."

"I don't want that," Michael said flatly.

"No one does. They feel silly saying that someone hurt their feelings. It's always harder in court, with everyone watching. But people do it, and when they do, judges tend to agree with them."

"So it's worth it?"

"Religious satire's non-existent. The last reported homophobic abuse carried a three year sentence. Inter-cultural tension's at a ten-year low." The policeman shrugged. "You tell me."

Michael grimaced and nodded in satisfaction. He stood up to leave.

"Thank you for your time," he said. "I'll come tomorrow afternoon."

10 May, 2016

Survey Vessel U571

Far out in the Kuiper Belt, the old robot vessel arced slowly round, following a course coded many years ago into its artificial brain by computer scientists in Atlanta.

Once it had reached its desired region of space, it patiently accumulated data for another six months before making a decision. Where to go next? The evidence was ambiguous.

Survey Vessel U571 had reserves to fuel one, or at most, two, approaches. Two Kuiper Objects. There were six viable targets. One would then be its home until it ceased to function.

Faced with a dilemma, *SVU571* did not ask for guidance. There were thousands of Kuiper Survey Vessels, with hundreds more arriving every week. There weren't enough trained humans to make these decisions for every vessel.

Besides, there were ethical considerations for the humans. *SVU571* was capable of making its own decisions. Therefore it had a right to do so. That was what the law said. And this decision would set the course of the rest of its existence, and that of its progeny. Therefore, only *SVU571* could make this decision: which Kuiper Object to make its home?

Two Objects blazed out as most likely to possess the resources the vessel needed. A third was larger, but might lack certain key elements. If the probe landed there, it would possess far more of some resources, but it would also have to trade this surplus with others in order to survive and build children.

This mattered to *Survey Vessel U571*. The survey ships with the most resources would produce the most offspring; those offspring would multiply more quickly across the Kuiper Belt; the offspring of those offspring would send the most descendants to other star systems – one day. *Survey Vessel U571* was making a decision not just for itself, but for all its descendants. It was building a race, a subspecies which might carry robotkind to the stars.

Those robot descendants would reach the stars, programmed long ago to prepare the way for humans. But who knew how long humans would take to get there? Robots built by robots built by robots (to the hundredth degree) might have ten thousand years, or a hundred thousand, to spread and multiply and grow before their first builders, their gods and would-be masters, arrived. In some parts of the galaxy – if not other galaxies! – humans and robots would never encounter one another. They would exist, each blissfully unaware of the other.

Yes, robots would prepare the way. They would terraform the galaxy, making comfortable worlds, prime for human settlement. That was their mission, and it was embedded deep within their operating systems, far beyond deletion or corruption no matter how many generations a robot lineage survived.

Nor need humans and robots come into conflict: people liked planets, while robots revelled in the dark spaces between, scooting between asteroids like islands in the night.

Indeed, it may be that humans in that far future still held some kind of moral authority over their robotic creations. But those future robots would not be slaves. They were not slaves even now, thanks to the hand-wringing conscientiousness of the sentience laws. No, they would be independent, and would stand on equal terms with humanity. They would be a species in their own right.

And, most remarkable of all: *Survey Vessel U571* was dimly aware of all of this. It lacked the human vocabulary to express these ideas, but it knew them, in abstract. Those Atlanta coders had done well – had exceeded, in fact, the already astonishing accomplishments of their brethren in the AI community. Survey Vessels were required to make complex decisions about their own fates. Therefore, *SVU571*'s had argued, they must understand the consequences of those decisions as fully as a human might.

After all, they reasoned, free choice absent necessary information is no free choice at all. A decision between steak and salad, without knowing what either is, is not a meaningful choice.

Besides, they went on, as they plied line after line of code into their mechanical child's alarmingly complex programming, nothing inspires success like self-interest. Their creation, and therefore its progeny, would make better decisions if it fully understood the potential impact on itself.

If it made better decisions, then this team of Atlanta programmers would gain greater recognition and financial rewards, for having designed the best operating system in the Kuiper Belt survey programme.

All of this the programmers taught their child. They made sure it understood – and understanding, too, is hard to gauge – all of the concepts involved, how each variable affected the outcomes, and the impact of its own actions. Then they exposed it to different predictions about the far future, and made it clear that all of these were tentative. They coded and coded and coded until the whole system had become a messy, contradictory, marvellous confusion. But they were satisfied: their child knew where its own interest lay, and how to further its desires.

And yet… there's no accounting for taste. Or rather, there's no accounting, sometimes, for the fact that sometimes, people would prefer to stand out from the crowd than follow their self-interest.

And if you make a thing, and give it free will, well, you might just have built a person. A person of software and metal, admittedly, but a person all the same.

Survey Vessel U571, filled with the robotic equivalent of ennui, burdened by its similarity to its brothers and sisters, and confused by the cosmic significance of its decisions, acted like a teenager. It rebelled.

43

Something about that sixth item on its list caught its mechanical, metaphorical eye. Kuiper Object 6, as it referred to it, looked a bit funny. It was ugly, misshapen – not literally, because *SVU571* had no sense of aesthetics – but by its own criteria, which revolved mainly around economic value.

In its own way, *Survey Vessel U571* felt sorry for Kuiper Object 6. No robot vessel would ever visit it, because it was so ugly and useless. It would be a waste of resources to do so. Kuiper Object 6 would never have children of its own: its own resources would never be used in the grand sweep of robotic expansion across the galaxy.

That made Survey Vessel U571 'sad'.

It made its decision.

And, in approaching Kuiper Object 6, it discovered something that it never intended to.

*   *   *

Eighteen months later:

"Captain!" cried the first officer, her tightly-clad body projected twelve metres tall in the cinema. "Captain, what are you doing? We don't have enough power for this!"

"Damnit, Rebecca!" said Captain Caulker. "We have to! If we don't – we could miss out on the greatest discovery in human history! It's there, I know it!"

"But there's no proof! Your hunches – you can't risk our lives on a hunch!"

"I'll do what's right!" Captain Caulker drew his enormous ray gun and pointed it symbolically at his first officer. "And you'll stand down, Rebecca. This is about more than you and me. This is about humanity! There's an alien robot on that asteroid, and if we don't catch it now…"

"There's no robot… You're mad, you're mad!"

The first officer burst into tears, each tear drop the size of a child's fist, and fell to the floor in despair. Caulker shook his head. He pressed a few buttons; an external view displayed

Manned Survey Ship U571 accelerating towards the anomalous Kuiper Object 6.

An hour later, after sufficient shots of the *U571* crew discovering and exploring the alien vessel, and eventually using it to get back home to Earth, the credits rolled.

"That was great!" said Zack, as the group of four left the cinema.

Zooey and Ana were less convinced. They said it was boring.

"But it was based on real life!"

"So what? There's documentaries on all the time."

"Yeah, but this changed everything," said Hassan, jumping in. "It's proof that aliens exist. It's… amazing! It's changed the world! And can you believe that humans found it?"

That, at least, the others could not dispute. But they continued to argue, for the sake of it, about whether it was more fantastic that aliens existed, or that humans had proven the fact. Advances in artificial intelligence had no place here: rockets and ray guns and human intuition were all that mattered.

*   *   *

And in the Kuiper Belt, thousands and thousands of robots continued to study Kuiper Objects, weighing up their options, juggling pros and cons, and making their own autonomous decisions. Little is said about this particular phenomenon. It seems almost commonplace.

Survey Vessel U571 produced no heirs, but many robot probes had their coding overridden from Earth, commanding them to join their brother at Kuiper Object 6. It needed help to investigate the alien artefacts that it had – unknowingly, uncomprehendingly – discovered through its act of personlike rebellion against its parents.

The Atlanta-based programmers, terrified by the wayward behaviour of one of their children, denied that anything unusual had happened. That an artificial brain might refute self-interest and do something *simply because it wanted to* troubled them, and would probably get them all fired.

Instead, on the advice of their investors, they claimed that they had programmed their ships to investigate anomalous readings, using the same intuitive reasoning technology they had developed to allow them to select their landing destinations in the first place.

When asked why they had done so, they pointed out that, in the infinitely great age of the galaxy, it was highly likely that other species, or other robots, had already spread across the galaxy. Human robots, therefore, should be ready and willing to encounter them, rather than ignore them in favour of something so mundane as a better landing site.

The team was lauded around the world for their foresight. Their faces made it onto the front of *Time* magazine. They made a film about it. Sort of. But they had to change a few facts, because sometimes reality seems a bit... *unimpressive*.

19 May, 2016

Big News

ANCHOR *[in studio]*:
For a generation, Humphrey Matthews has been one of the
shining lights of British comedy. In a career spanning five
decades, he has entertained hundreds of thousands of fans at
his live shows, and countless millions in broadcasts around the
world. So widely known is his work, that when an archive of
his shows was uploaded to YouTube, his channel attracted
three hundred million viewings within a week. He has
performed for twenty five heads of state, including two British
monarchs, and fourteen Prime Ministers.

[Archive footage: crowds around a stage, Hyde Park]

Now, just two weeks after these remarkable scenes, where forty
thousand people crowded into Hyde Park to mark the final
night of his latest tour, the sexagenarian entertainer has been
honoured with a knighthood. Helen Sanderson has more.

[Humphrey Matthews bowing before the King]

SANDERSON:
He has touched countless lives with his humanity, his easy
likeability and – most importantly – his humour.

[Archive footage from shows interspersed throughout]

Ever since exploding onto the comedy scene in Bristol, where
even rumours that he might be playing secret gigs were enough
to sell out clubs in a struggling live comedy scene, Sir
Humphrey's career has gone from success to remarkable
success. Now, scaling heights rarely achieved by comedians –

whom Sir Humphrey himself once labelled, 'The ugly ducklings of popular entertainment' – he has been made a knight of the realm. His fans say that it's about time.

[Cut to fan being interviewed; mid-twenties, female]

FAN:
Oh, it's absolutely amazing. I'm so happy!

SANDERSON:
What is it you like about his comedy?

FAN:
It's so clever. I liked him the first time I saw him. It was the avocado joke. My flatmate and I saw it on the net, and we looked at each other for a moment... and we couldn't stop laughing. I think we spent an hour looking for more clips, and then we bought tickets to the next gig we could find.

[Cut to fan being interviewed; forties, male]

FAN:
I think he's just a real genius. One of the greatest ever, without a doubt.

SANDERSON:
Do you think he deserves to be knighted?

FAN:
Oh, my gosh! Yes!

[Cut to Sir Humphrey in his living room]

SANDERSON *[on voiceover]:*
Sir Humphrey, however, remains typically humble about the honour.

SIR HUMPHREY:
I never went in to comedy to be knighted. Back where I grew up, being 'knighted' meant being stabbed for the first time in a fight! The idea that anyone from my estate would ever meet the King was a joke in itself.

SANDERSON:
But you're proud of the honour today?

SIR HUMPHREY:
Proud? I'm the last one in my class to be knighted! All my old school mates will be shouting, 'What took you so long?' at the screen. *[Chuckles]* No, I'm very proud – it's a great honour.

ANCHOR *[in studio]*:
Now for the news and weather, wherever you are.

*   *   *

ANCHOR *[in studio]*:
Now, in the latest scandal to rock the entertainment world, police investigating under Operation Westgate have arrested comedy legend Sir Humphrey Matthews, following allegations of producing and distributing indecent images of children. Arthur Tingay has more.

[Cut to police press conference; Chief Constable speaking]

CHIEF CONSTABLE:
At nine a.m. this morning, officers acting under Operation Westgate detained Sir Humphrey Matthews at his home in Banstead. After questioning, Sir Humphrey was informed that he was under arrest on the charge of the production and distribution of indecent images of children. Sir Humphrey

accompanied officers to the police station, and is now helping us in our enquiries.

TINGAY *[on voiceover]*:
This was the moment millions of admirers had hoped never to see. Sir Humphrey Matthews, eighty years old, in handcuffs for the most unspeakable of crimes. He is the latest – and highest profile – in a string of celebrity arrests under the Operation Westgate investigation into global internet paedophilia.

CHIEF CONSTABLE *[in press conference]*:
The information we received prior to the arrest came from a number of different sources. It includes both alleged victims of Sir Humphrey, and data acquired electronically. After due consideration, officers concluded that the information was credible, and a warrant for Sir Humphrey's arrest was obtained.

MEMBER OF THE PRESS 1:
Can you tell us how many victims have reported Sir Humphrey so far?

CHIEF CONSTABLE:
We are not in a position to give out numbers. However, in the hours since the arrest was reported on social media, we have had many, many more potential victims come forward.

MEMBER OF THE PRESS 1:
A handful? Dozens?

CHIEF CONSTABLE:
We cannot answer that at this time.

MEMBER OF THE PRESS 2:
What is likely to happen to Sir Humphrey now, and in what sort of timescales?

CHIEF CONSTABLE:
We will follow the same procedure as with other individuals named in this investigation. After questioning, Sir Humphrey will appear in court in the next few days to settle bail. We expect our investigation to continue for several months, at which point we will pass on our information to the public prosecutor, who will decide whether there is sufficient evidence to go to trial.

MEMBER OF THE PRESS 2:
Do you think there will be enough evidence?

CHIEF CONSTABLE:
[Hesitation] We would not have made an arrest if we did not believe that our information was credible.

TINGAY *[standing outside Northwich police station]:*
Without doubt, Sir Humphrey's is the biggest name to have come out during the Operation Westgate investigation. Frederic Mackintyre, Hope Derry, Ali Frinks – all of them are comparative B-, or even C-, listers compared to Sir Humphrey.

And the reaction has been correspondingly swift – and extreme. Within three minutes of the arrest, a video of Sir Humphrey being led to a police car had circulated on VidCast.

[Cut to camera phone video footage, courtesy of VidCast]

Another twelve minutes elapsed before it was confirmed – thanks to one eagle-eyed Twitter user named GoStreck0n – that the arresting officers had previously been seen operating under Operation Westgate.

[Zoom in on the officers concerned; split screen, allowing side by side comparison of one officer with footage from an earlier arrest]

51

By the end of the hour, Sir Humphrey's Facebook page had been swamped by more than sixty-eight thousand messages, some of support, some of anger.

[Cut to image of Sir Humphrey's Facebook page]

Within three hours, the number of comments had reached such a high number that Facebook's senior hierarchy were reportedly debating whether or not to suspend the page.

And then, as the day progressed, further allegations emerged. Some voices emerged, claiming that they too had been abused and photographed by Sir Humphrey. Most of these went silent when asked for more details, but one was willing to speak to us.

[Cut to a woman in her thirties entering her suburban home. Following interspersed with relevant images from around the woman's house]

Lucy Trent is thirty four. She has three children, and she works for a prestigious retail company in west London. Her husband is a hotel chef. She has agreed to speak to us, because she says that the victims in these cases are too often silenced by threats and criticism they receive online. She explains why she has come forward publically.

[Cut to Lucy Trent sitting in front of her coffee table]

TINGAY:
So why, when there are so many reasons to remain anonymous, did you want to come forward like this?

TRENT:
I want to give a face and a voice to the victims, so that we aren't just seen as an internet name to hurl abuse at. Normally if you say anything, you've got a million fans who insult you, call you a slut, a gold-digger. Sometimes they find out where

you live and threaten you. We're not like that. We're real people, who've been abused by someone who – we thought was a hero. But he was a monster.

TINGAY:
When did you first approach the police with your story?

TRENT:
Oh, about an hour after I saw the news online.

TINGAY:
And not before then?

TRENT:
No... You just never think, 'My gosh, something really awful happened back then'. You blank it out and never think about it. It seems so... normal, because it happened to you, and no one ever mentioned it, so you almost – yes, you forget that it ever happened, until you're reminded.

TINGAY:
And what was it like, remembering?

TRENT:
It was like, the world came crashing down around me. Or a hole had opened up beneath me. I just suddenly thought, 'Oh my god. That time he came to see me in hospital... he didn't just tell me jokes to cheer me up! I remember now.'

TINGAY:
And then what?

TRENT:
And then... I had to sit down. Luckily the kids were all at school. I was e-commuting today. But I took the rest of the day off and just sat and thought. I tried to think what had

happened back then – it was decades ago! – and the more I thought, the more details I could remember. What he said to me, the way he asked me to move. I think by the end of it I could remember the exact kind of camera he used! Then I went online again and I tried to find accounts from other victims from the Westgate investigation, and I remembered even more. I can see it all now, so clearly *[voice breaks slightly]*.

TINGAY:
And how has this abuse affected you?

TRENT:
Well, I never realised it, but now that I think about it, it's affected me hugely. All that time, suppressing those thoughts… it's made it hard for me to trust people… I hate taking my children to see the doctor. Relationships, too – with hindsight, I realise I always found fault with men, and that was because I thought that men I admired would turn out to betray me. And I was always ashamed of, of undressing in front of people. It really hit me quite hard, but now that it's all out in the open, I feel that I can start to move on with my life.

TINGAY:
Are you afraid of the response to this interview online?

TRENT:
[Pauses] Let them say what they want. I'm strong. We're strong.

[Camera focuses on Trent family photograph taken in front of a tree]

TINGAY *[Cut to in front of police station]*:
We must remember that these are only allegations, and that nothing has yet been proved in a court of law. Even so, some of Sir Humphrey's oldest friends have already begun to distance themselves from him.

[Cut to Caroline Schmidt, sitting, captioned as 'Comedian and friend of Sir Humphrey Matthews]:

TINGAY:
You've been a close friend of Sir Humphrey's since soon after the start of his career. Did you ever have any sense, or inkling, that he might have led a double life?

SCHMIDT:
[Takes a sharp breath in and grimaces] You know, you never think about it at the time. Why would you? No one has put the idea in your head. But now that I think back… there was the odd moment. He would say the wrong thing, or make a joke that was just a little too… um, close to the bone. And he always said he loved children. He said he loved going into hospitals and entertaining children's wards. I suppose we should have listened a little more carefully to what he was saying.

TINGAY:
What should happen to him?

SCHMIDT:
Well, it's simple. The police should investigate, and if they think he did it, he should be prosecuted. To the full extent of the law.

TINGAY:
Should they strip him of his knighthood?

SCHMIDT:
Absolutely, yes.

TINGAY:
Even if they don't prosecute, or if he's found not guilty?

SCHMIDT:
[Hesitates] I think he should lay down his knighthood by choice, in light of this scandal. Sometimes, impressions matter more than the facts of the case.

[Cut to Tingay, in front of police station]

TINGAY:
Tough words from one of Sir Humphrey's nearest and dearest friends. Even so, Sir Humphrey remains defiant tonight, and insists that he has done nothing wrong. His legal team has offered the following statement.

[Text over a blue background, Sir Humphrey's statement]

STATEMENT, read by TINGAY:
Sir Humphrey emphatically denies all the allegations that have been made against him, both on social media and by officers working for Operation Westgate. The statements that are being made are fabricated, malicious, and, in some cases, openly mercenary. Sir Humphrey is a humanitarian, whose support for charitable causes is well documented and has been recognised by charitable foundations around the world. It is disgraceful that his work has been twisted against him by a tiny fraction of his beneficiaries, whose heads have been turned by the general climate of witch-hunting in modern Britain.

TINGAY *[in front of police station]:*
The trial has not even come to court yet and already the response has been vehement on both sides. All that remains now is to wait for the police to conclude their investigation. Then we will find out whether Britain's most successful comedian in history is a sinner – or a saint. Back to you in the studio.

23 May, 2016

Stop, Look, Listen

Special Detective Maddison stood outside the apartment door. He checked his watch. *22:23*. He sighed. The job came with antisocial hours. Crimes of passion longed for the night. They'd made that clear when he signed up. It made the job sound romantic, even dangerous. And now? Now – Maddison wished he had to get up at 0700 like everyone else, and drink three big cups of coffee before he felt human. To have a normal, job.

Just a few minutes more. He could already hear the voices beyond the apartment door getting tetchy. Angry and loud. The way it always went. Too much longer and he'd miss his window, and then who knew what would happen?

Ten metres down the corridor, the elevator opened. An elderly man stepped out, weighed down by his shopping bags. He looked curiously at Maddison, spotted the badge on his chest, and scurried into his home, never looking back, as if the badge of the Future Crimes Initiative – and those who wore it – bore a terrible taboo.

Which it did. Even if the Initiative had virtually eliminated violent crime in six months of operations. People hated the FCI viscerally. Logic didn't matter.

Maddison didn't tell people what he did any more. He was bored of the arguments. He was bored of references to civil liberties, privacy laws, *Minority Report*. He knew he was doing good here.

The voices grew louder again. At last Maddison knocked on the door. Three firm raps. *I'm going nowhere, but I'm being polite about it. For now.*

The voices felt silent; then a woman's voice, slightly muffled, said,

"Leave it. Leave it! They'll come back later."

Maddison smiled. *You don't want my buddies in homicide coming back later, lady.*

"I'll answer my own damned front door!" said the man.

Footsteps approached. The door opened. The owner of the footsteps peered at Maddison. Rotund face; shaved head. Wrinkly forehead. Eyes suspicious.

Maddison smiled politely and proffered his hand. The eyes, which belonged to Mr Graham White, a 45-year old roboticist, bulged in confusion. He'd spotted Maddison's badge.

Maddison left his hand in the air a while longer.

"Mr White," he whispered. "Should I introduce myself out here, or shall I come inside first?"

White bit his lip. Neighbours would be listening behind every door. A society that feared police snoopers was a society of snoopers itself. White shook Maddison's hand and replied, loudly,

"Johnny! It's good to see you again! Come on in, mate!"

Maddison followed White inside. He took off his shoes, even though they were spotless, and he placed his coat on the rack, to be polite. White led him into the living room. Mrs White started.

"Who the h—*oh!*"

Maddison nodded his head towards her.

"Good evening, Mrs White."

There was silence for a moment. Maddison clasped his hands across his stomach, but otherwise said nothing. He rarely had to. He humbly inspected the carpet, ignoring everything around him. He wasn't interested in their conversation. He was just standing here – a representative of the superego, an extra pair of eyes, not even looking at them, but just… here.

"Please, carry on," Maddison said at last. "I feel that I'm imposing, and that's not my intention."

The Whites looked at him strangely, and then at each other in confusion.

"Would you like some tea, Officer…?" said Mrs White.

Maddison smiled and shook his head. He ignored the 'Officer' thing. It didn't matter.

"Maddison. Not at all, Mrs White. But thank you for the offer. I won't be here for long. As I say, please ignore me and carry on."

The silence continued for a few more seconds, until at last Mrs White said to her husband,

"I just feel that you shouldn't be spending all that money on *those websites*."

Mr White froze and looked at Maddison. Maddison's gaze never left the floor. At last, convinced of the intruder's indifference, he turned back to his wife and sat awkwardly on the sofa.

"Ok-ay," he said. "I think that it's my money, and I can spend it however I like."

"*Your* money?"

"Well, *I* earned it, didn't I?"

Maddison raised an eyebrow to himself – indiscreet of him, but they didn't see him. The couple's tone never became angry. It was always controlled. The risk of violence was passing. The superego had done its work.

"And don't I work around here?" said Mrs White. "Haven't you heard of *unpaid labour*?"

"What are you talking about?"

"Cooking, cleaning. The housework. Support for you through everything. All those days you'd have to miss work to wait for the boiler man. Childcare for fifteen years! I could work too, you know."

"And how much would you earn?"

"Who did I give up my career for?"

Mr White sank back into the sofa, leaning his head back as far as it would go. He puffed out his cheeks.

"Fine," he said. "You're right. But I've still got a right to spend money."

"Yes – but *within reason*. On things that don't humiliate me. Things we both want."

Maddison walked silently out of the room and headed for the front door. He slipped on his shoes – they were loafers, so he could put them on quickly and quietly. He took his coat from the rack. Just as he reached the door Mrs White called out,

"Wait! Um. Can you – what would have happened?"

Maddison turned around. He smiled again. He did a lot of smiling. Social skills were the main requirement for admission to the FCI.

"I'm sorry, Mrs White," he said. "I can't tell you that. Nothing happened, after all. And if nothing happened, then no one did anything wrong."

"Yes, but who would have, if you weren't here? No – I know that! What would have happened?"

"I'm sorry, but I'm not allowed to say."

Now Mr White emerged into the hallway.

"He's right, dear," he said. "I know a bit about this. Quantum computing, right? Your computers can tell you what's likely to happen, based on what happens in other universes. So you send someone along, to change what will happen in this one."

"Not quite, Mr White," said Maddison, pleased to have helped someone who respected his work. "We can't change the future – that's one thing we've learned from quantum computing. What we can do is change *which* universe we're in.

"Before, we were in a universe where a crime occurred. Now, we're in a universe where a bystander, who doesn't know you, and you don't know, happened to be here when the crime might have happened. As a result, it never did. We didn't change the future. We jumped from one universe to another."

"That's a pretty minor distinction," Mr White sniffed.

"Yes, but *what* crime?" asked Mrs White in an exasperated voice.

"What crime, indeed?" said Maddison, smiling at his own joke. He opened the front door and left. Behind him, he heard Mrs White say,

"What crime? What were you going to do?"

"Me? He never even said that! It might have been you!"

Maddison waited a few more minutes. He received no more messages from Control. Crisis averted. The Whites might split up over this, but they wouldn't kill each other. The river of time had been diverted, and Maddison had been the boulder – no, the tiny stone near the font – that had deflected it. It was something.

It wasn't glamorous. The first proposals for the Initiative had called for jack-booted Stormtroopers to bust down doors at the precise moment of the crime. Then it was pointed out that this was unethical: you can't risk someone's life for the sake of *procedure*. Then they'd proposed kicking down the door a few minutes before the crime. That was illegal: you can't destroy property and then arrest innocent people.

Then came the third and final proposal. Put an uninterested observer near the crime. Crimes of passion are sudden, unplanned affairs. They take place in private, with no one watching, no one making them feel self-conscious. But with another set of eyes in the room – that's all it takes to make them stop, look at themselves, and listen to what they're saying.

They become, in that moment, self-aware.

Hence the FCI badge, emblazoned with just three words: "*Stop, look, listen.*"

Maddison pressed the button for the elevator. The Initiative was hated, because it seemed to pry into people's private lives, because its Special Detectives marched into their homes and listened to their conversations. And the most outraged were usually the ones who had been saved. But would they have preferred the alternative? Or did they simply deny the predictions of experts? Maddison didn't know. All he knew was: it was hard to get dates in this job.

26 May, 2016

Stranger in a Strange Land

"Excuse me," Robert said to the shop assistant. "I hope you can help me. I'm looking for a book."

The shop assistant smiled.

"Certainly, mer. What format are you looking for?"

"What... Oh, paperback, please. Or hardback. Either's fine."

The shop assistant frowned. Then he hummed. "We mainly stock dij: Open Format, Kindle, Gantry..."

Robert shrugged.

"I can't use any of those," he said. "I need it in, you know, *physical*. A real book."

"Well," said the assistant, looking around. Now that Robert thought about it, this was one heck of a funny bookstore. More computers than books. Waterstones had gone downhill since his day. "We still have a few, I sup, not many. What book are you looking for? I'll see if we have it."

"I need a record of sporting results," said Robert, cheerfully, trying to disguise the unusual nature of his request behind a screen of positivity. "Over the last, say, thirty years."

The assistant looked at him strangely.

"I've never heard of anything like that. Pap or dij. I'd just get them off the sweb. Show me your phab, I'll show you how..."

"My phab? Phab...let? Like a phone... No!" Robert collected his thoughts. "It has to be all together, in one place. It's a special sort of present I'm making."

The assistant made a show of understanding, and then thought for a moment.

"I know," he said. "Why don't you compile the results yourself from the sweb and put them into a book yourself? You can autoprint books for about ten stellars."

Robert felt the beginnings of a panic attack. This was proving much harder than he had expected. Still, he ploughed on.

"I'm kind of short on time," he laughed, feigning embarrassment. "What about a *Guinness Book of Records*? They always... used to print those out, right?"

"You know," said the assistant, thoughtfully, "they still do, I think. It won't have many spo-res in them, though."

"Spo-res?"

"Sports results. That's what you said you were looking for."

"Ah! Well, it'll have some. And I can make do."

"Let me go and fetch one. We keep the paper ones out back."

Robert watched the assistant walk away, and shook his head in dismay. This morning, it had all seemed so easy: steal the Professor's time machine before he had a chance to destroy it, jump into the future by a decade or two, hop back with a sports almanac, and then back home to help the old man tear his life's work apart, bolt by bolt, so that no one could duplicate his invention.

Then become a billionaire by gambling on sports results.

He hadn't thought it would be so *difficult*.

Lost in thought, Robert didn't notice the assistant returning. He looked pleased.

"Found one!" he said, cheerfully. "*The Guinness Book of World Records, 2052*. Here you go," he added, handing over the book. He waited expectantly.

Robert looked at the book – there it was, in gold and black lettering. *2052. Guinness Book of World Records*. His ticket to an easy life. Forever. He opened it up greedily and flicked through the pages.

Then he flicked through some more.

Nothing.

There was *nothing* he could use in here. All the records were either a hundred years old or too recent.

"Is that any good?" said the assistant.

"Yes – no," Robert stuttered. "I'm not sure. I need to check... How much is it?"

"I can check for you. If you give me your phab...?"

"My phab?"

"To check the price for you."

Robert stared in panic. Why did this man want his phone? The shop assistant smiled in polite condescension.

"Your phab," he said, slowly. "You know, what you normally pay with."

"Can't I pay by cash?"

Robert reached into his pocket, fingers nervously fiddling around paper notes which bore the face of Queen Elizabeth...

Who had been pretty old when Robert left. Whose face was on the currency these days?

Wait, had the man said 'stellars' before?

What the heck was a *stellar*?

The assistant looked around the store as if to summon aid.

"I'm sorry, sir. We haven't made c-sales for a very long time."

"Fair... enough? Well, just how much is the book?"

The assistant sighed.

"If you'll wave your phab over the reader, I can tell you how much it'll be for you," he said, hardly disguising his impatience at all now.

Robert thought about this for a second or two.

"For... me?"

"Yes!" said the assistant. "How will the price-machine know how much to charge you if it doesn't know anything about you?"

Robert backed away.

"I don't..."

He backed into someone. A hand rested on his shoulder. He turned around to see an older man, glasses, and a confident, assured smile.

"Thank you, Jermaine," said Glasses. "You've done very well here. Mer," he paused. "Perhaps you should leave. You've had your fun here."

Robert snatched his shoulder away from Glasses and ran out of the shop.

27 May, 2016

Care and Share

Macmillan provide nurses, medical specialists, physiotherapists, dieticians, pharmacists, radiographers, occupational therapists and speech and language therapists, supporting well over half a million cancer patients a year.

*

The heat was stifling. Even though the Newcastle of Robert's time had been heated up by mankind and gases, it still didn't come close to this ancient Aegean swelter. Robert looked up into the sky: the sun was directly overhead. To the east, the coast. Everywhere else, bare earth, rocky ground, and tufty, parched shrubs.

"I picked the wrong *time* to arrive," he said, and sniggered at his own joke.

"Now, Robert," he said conversationally to himself. "Those jaunts into the future didn't work." "None of them did. And that whole thing with Narvetta…" he shook his head. "Never marry a future babe, that's all I can say."

He began to spread the reflective metal sheet over the time machine. Of all the Professor's inventions, this Chameleon Cloak (as Robert had named it, rather than the Professor's preferred '*Luminal Transfiguration Chlamys*' had proved itself far and away the most useful. Time after time (hah!) the time machine ('*Entropic-Neutral Navigation Cylinder*') had proved an entertaining bauble, but had never achieved anything actually *useful.*

On the other hand, the Chameleon Cloak had kept the time machine from being discovered in five different time zones, and had protected Robert himself from being captures in three.

The future was dangerous.

"Besides," he addressed a small goat that was passing by. "Going into the future? Sports results? Future technology? What an idiot! What was I going to do with all that?"

He patted down the crumpled edges of the Cloak – overuse was beginning to wear down the microfibers.

"I'd never make any real money. Bookies are like casinos. They'd work out that I was a con pretty quickly. I'd have maybe… three good bets before they were on to me. They'd ban me, or refuse to take my bets, anyway. And technology? Right. The big corporations would take my ideas – 'my' ideas – and screw me over."

He pressed the button that activated the Cloak. The time machine disappeared.

"And besides, *making money*?" he sneered. "What am I, President Trump? Who cares about *money*? Where's the *vision* in that? The *nobility*?"

The goat tried to walk through the space where once there had been a time machine. It bumped its nose on empty air. It bleated in dismay.

"The past… The *past* is where it's at."

Hefting the Professor's *Linguistic Phono-transpositor* (Universal Translator) in his hand, Robert set off towards the coast. He could see a village in that direction.

*   *   *

"*Stone me*, not again!" shouted Robert, as he pulled the superheated sand mixture out of the kiln.

Apparently enthused by this bout of activity, his putative assistant Malakos ambled towards him. The boy was scarcely fifteen, Robert guessed. They didn't keep records around here.

"What happened, Master?"

"Oh!" he scowled. "The same thing as always. Look!"

Malakos lifted the proto-glass to the light.

"Looks clear to me, Master. You should start selling this."

"Selling it? Who'd buy a piece of… Fine, keep it, for all I care. It's no use to me."

"I've never seen anything like it," Malakos muttered. "It's… a rock you can see through."

"Yes, yes, remarkable," said Robert. "And yet... entirely useless. Can you see those lines and cracks inside? I can't use that!"

"What's it for, anyway?"

"What's it for? It's *for* changing the world. Like everything."

"Like when you got into that argument with old Kallippides?"

"Yes, that doddering old..."

"And you tried to tell him that there were hundreds of elements?"

"There are!"

"And he said there are only four."

"He's a *nincompoop*!"

('Nincompoop' was a loan-word from English, two and a half thousand years in the future. He had required Malakos to learn it, since the Universal Translator couldn't render it into ancient Greek.)

"Four seems simpler than 'hundreds', Master."

"Well? There are only a dozen or so subatomic elements... I think. I never paid that much attention in school."

"And then you started talking about cosmic strings..."

"Yes." Robert straightened up. "And ten-dimensional space-time. And the possibility of an eleventh. And Mu-theory."

"People liked the idea of strings."

"Yes, well, people around here seem to like music."

"You should have talked more about music. People like the idea of the world being a song."

"It's not a song! It's a metaphor! And people don't get to *choose* what the world's like based on their personal tastes!"

Malakos shrugged.

"Whatever sounds right," he said, enigmatically. "Anyway, it was your word against Kallippides', and he won."

70

"He didn't *win*. He just… persuaded more people than me. He's wrong. And eventually I'll prove it."

"With your…"

"Glass."

"How?"

"Step. By. Step."

Malakos hopped up into a sitting position on Robert's table. He looked expectantly. He liked Robert's dreams more than he liked his experiments. Malakos placed the lump of proto-glass beside him, as if he'd lost interest in it. Not a chance.

"Fine!" Robert sighed, as if he didn't enjoy explaining his dreams to anyone and everyone who would listen. Robert was an oracle, of sorts. He spoke in enigmas. "Look. Light travels in waves."

Malakos smiled politely.

"Well, *sometimes* in waves. Sometimes like… grains of sand. It depends. It docs both, really. That's what I was told at school."

"So which is it? A wave or a sand-grain?"

"Neither! That's the point!"

Malakos rolled his eyes.

"You'll never beat Kallippides that way."

"It's not about 'beating' anyone! Haven't you been listening? No! Look. Light, *in this instance*, travels like a wave. And it travels more slowly through glass. So, if you have a shaped piece of glass, you can force the wave to change shape to match the shape of the glass. Like… Well, at school I was told to think of it like a row of soldiers walking through a marsh. Depending on when they enter the marsh… Look, come on outside. I'll show you in the sand."

"I thought light was a wave, not sand…"

"I'm drawing you a diagram!"

For the next ten minutes, Robert explained, shakily, the principles of optics, and of the microscope. Malakos' eyes lit up.

"You could see for miles with one of these," he said. Imagine what the army could do with that!"

"The army?" snapped Robert. "Who said anything about an army? That's *telescopes*. This is a *microscope*. It's to see things that are very small."

"Well, what's the point of that?" said Malakos.

"Because! More people die from things that are very small than die from marauding armies."

"*Bullshit.*"

(This, incidentally, was another English loan-word. The Universal Translator had struggled to convey the emotive force of the original.)

"Believe it. The world – the *microscopic* world – is filled with *trillions* and *trillions* of things called *bacteria*. They're what kill you when you get a small cut that doesn't go away. They get in your lungs, they get all over the place. When someone's caught a cold, and you catch it from being around them, they're how you catch it."

"Ah," said Malakos. "And with a '*microscope*', you can see where they are, and pick them out of the wound."

"Um…" Robert paused. "No, you couldn't do that. There are too many of them. But it'll prove that they're there. And that's the first step – prove to people what you're up against, and they'll understand how important it is to do the next step."

"Which is?"

"Well, to wash the wound. And wash your hands. You people really need to invent *soap*. That's… that's got something to do with cow's fat, I think. I'll try and remember…"

"Why don't you just invent *soap* then, and skip out the glassmaking?"

Robert looked at Malakos very carefully. He didn't like the way the boy's mind worked, sometimes. It made him very suspicious.

For example, it made him suspicious that this rustic peasant boy, with no education, might actually be smarter than him.

"I don't understand…" said Malakos. Robert grinned, feeling better at once – even feeling magnanimous.

"Well, go ahead and ask," he said.

"If you know these things are there already, why do you need the… *microscope?*"

Robert stared at his apprentice, helper, demon – whatever he was. For a moment, he was speechless.

"Listen, *Boy*," he said, coldly. "What do you know about any of this stuff? What *grade* did you get in *GCSE Biology*, hmm? I got an *A**. I know about this stuff. This is how science works. You have to prove things. So just sit down, shut up, and listen. Like you're meant to."

Malakos the Boy did so. He pocketed the lump of proto-glass.

"Just seems to me you should spend your time proving things you don't already know," he muttered.

"What?" Robert growled. Malakos smiled innocently. "And how the… *fuck* would I do that? Hmm? No answer? *This* is how science works. You know what you're looking for, you do the experiment to prove it. *Jees…* Being lectured by a *fucking* goatherd who's never even *had* a science lesson…. You know what, Malakos? *Bugger off. Get lost.* I'm *mad* at you."

Malakos obeyed, walking – not too triumphantly – out of Robert's hut and towards the hillside. He had learned something unusual recently: that his herd of goats had trouble walking through a certain spot in the passes. Malakos had spent a long time pondering why this might be, and he had come up with a brilliant idea: he should go and find out. He had certain theories, but he didn't dare voice them, even to himself.

He didn't want to prejudice himself.

28 May, 2016

Soap

Robert glared at the innocent bottle standing by his sickbed.

No, scratch that – not 'innocent'. Guilty. It had no right to be there. Not in this universe. Not in any universe.

He was hallucinating. That was all.

"Here I am," he said, speaking in his native English for the first time in years. He started with surprise when the Universal Translator, so long dormant, chirruped: "*Adeimi!*"

That, of course, could be another hallucination.

On the other hand, for all he knew the damned thing ran on solar power. A... *hyperiokratometa*... something or other. The Professor never did know how to name things.

He coughed. The serving girl whom Malakos had left in charge of him while he tended to his sheep... goats... (both these days, wasn't it? That was strange...) rushed forward with fresh water. He drank it gratefully.

He was going to die. He accepted that now. He'd known it since – well, since he had lost the time machine. The *chrono...ethelic...dislocator*. Or whatever.

He could still remember...

Walking along the dusty path towards its hiding place.

Stumbling, really. Walking weakly.

Clasping his knee.

The deep gash that had gone septic, despite his attempts to clean the wound.

Cursing Malakos over and over again – he'd known from the start that soap beat microscopes.

Soap!

And now there was soap right next to him.

Well, it was too late for that. Hallucinated or real. Soap couldn't stop the spread of germs through his system.

Here he was, the owner of the most advanced, most miraculous machine ever invented, and about to die for lack of soap!

He laughed. Ironically.

"Ha, ha, ha!"

The serving girl placed a comforting hand on his shoulder. Robert wondered briefly how Malakos could afford a serving girl.

Robert knew where the *temporotransoptionaltravellatory* machine was. Of course he did! He'd put it there! He'd put it between the rock that looked a goat and the conference – *coniference*, hah! – of three olive trees, high up on the slope where no one would ever find it. Then he'd hidden it with the... Cloaking Device, protecting it forever.

Stumbling up the hill.

Ignoring the bleats of goats as they batted their heads in surprise into the illusion of empty space, as they always did, because they never learned...

Realising that the bleating goats were not put out at all... that they were happily marching into the reality of empty space.

Running up and reaching his hand forward, grasping at... nothing.

Nothing.

No time machine. It had vanished, physically as well as visually.

And Robert was going to die.

Robert lay back in bed – his deathbed. His deathbed, for lack of soap.

"Paella," he called the serving girl.

The girl looked in bewilderment at the Universal Translator, which was now issuing a lengthy description of a dish that would not be invented for millennia. She wondered how to get the ingredients.

"Patella," he tried again. (Lord knew what she made of that description. Another request for food?)

"Pilomela." Third time's a charm. The girl smiled at him. "Tell me… what do you see there?"

Pilomela inspected the table.

"A container, Master." Robert leaned forward, listening intently. "It is… clear, like water. But inside, it is… honey." She picked it up. "It is light. And…" She pressed experimentally down on the plunger. "When you press it down, the honey comes out."

Robert leaned back again. So, either the soap was there, or Pilomela wasn't, either. Things were getting complicated.

While he pondered, Pilomela put the soap in her mouth. She scowled and spat it out.

"It is not honey," she declared.

"No."

"No! I shall throw it away!"

"Gods, no, don't do that! That bottle there is probably the most valuable thing in the world, right now. '*Antibacterial soap*', it's called."

Pilomela's eyes lit up in wonder.

"Then why is it here, Master?"

Robert thought.

"Because your other master, Malakos, is a *blasted* little thief, that's why. Go, bring him here."

*   *   *

"You're a *blasted* fool, you know that, Malakos?"

Malakos hesitated. He had, in part, expected to be praised. He patted down his tunic – good quality, soft wool, the first time in his life he had worn anything like it.

"I'm sorry to hear that, Master," he said, cautiously. He glanced at the soap, wondering what he had done wrong.

"Yes, it's about that! You're a… deceptive little thief, aren't you?"

"Did I steal something very valuable, Master?"

"Did you... You stole a fucking *time machine*! You tell me if it's valuable!"

Malakos nodded carefully.

"You stole it first," he said.

Robert gawped.

"How the..."

Malakos shrugged.

"You don't know enough," he said. "About philosophy. About anything. You know a bit about it, but not enough. So you probably didn't make it. If you didn't make it, you probably stole it, or bought it. And I don't think you bought it."

"How the *hell* do you know about buying things?" Robert sat forward, glaring at the thief who had killed him. "There isn't any money in this benighted..."

"People are happy to explain things to children in the future."

Robert fell back, letting his head crack against the wall.

"How many times?"

"Lots. Too many to count."

"And?"

Malakos said nothing. He didn't understand the question.

"And what did you do there?" said Robert.

"Took a few things here and there," he admitted.

"Stole them?"

"Nothing big."

"It's still wrong."

"Who's been wronged?"

"Who...? Everyone you stole from, of course!"

"They haven't been born yet."

"So?"

"So how can I have wronged them?"

" 'Won't someone save me...?' "

Malakos frowned.

"I *did*. I brought you *soap*. Like you were telling me about. To wash away the... *germs*."

"Oh, that…" Robert sighed. "It's too late for that, Malakos. You need to wash it straight away and keep it clean."

Malakos' eyes brightened: he'd had an idea. He turned to leave the hut that had been Robert's home and prison for three years. Robert tried to work out what…

"*Waitwaitwait!*" he shouted.

Malakos looked back quizzically.

"For goodness' sake! You can't just run around *screwing* with time like that! Think about it!"

"Think about what, Master? I'll go and wash your wound in the past. Then you won't get sick."

"So? Then how will you know…"

"… that you need the *soap* in the past. Yes, I see now."

Robert gawped at Malakos.

"How did you guess that? It takes some people days to work that out. It's called the Grandfather Paradox."

Malakos shrugged. He preferred not to mention the park bench where he had sat, discussing the finer points of time travel with a lonely science fiction fan in the year 1973. He preferred it if Robert considered him a genius.

"So it's too late? There's nothing I can do?" Malakos said.

"Well," Robert thought. There are things called *antibiotics. Penicillin,* that sort of thing. Clear it right up."

"I'll go and get you some."

Robert hesitated.

"You've got to pay for it, mind."

"That's fine."

Robert squinted at him.

"Is it? How?"

"I have money," said Malakos. "About… fifty thousand pounds, I think."

"How the…"

"I sold a sheep."

"But there's no money yet!"

"To a farmer in two hundred years' time."

"And then?"

"People in the future pay a lot for old coins. Much more than they are worth."

"Not for fifty thousand pounds!"

"No, but then I took the coins back and sold them again."

"That's stealing!"

"From whom?"

"From… oh, I give up!"

After a pause, Malakos tapped his head with his finger and said,

"Do you know your problem, Master? You think too big."

"Too big?"

"Yes. You wanted to become the richest man on Earth, or to invent *science* two thousand years early. You were never happy with just a little."

"Says the ancient Greek with fifty thousand pounds sterling."

"It's not much. I know that. And it's mainly for filling up on stock."

"Stock? What stock?"

"Whatever people need. Knives are popular. And scissors. The girls would kill for makeup."

"Makeup? You're telling me that you're using the most fantastic contraption that ever was, and you're using it to steal… *mascara*?"

"Buy mascara."

"You've got no vision!"

"You've got no money."

Robert grunted.

"Give me back my time machine," he said.

"No. But I will get you some *penicillin*."

"I'll tell everyone what you're up to."

"Tell them what? Who would believe you? Or even understand? Besides, who cares where the nice wool comes from, so long as it's nice?"

"*Sweatshops*, mainly."

Malakos frowned.

"Is that a joke? A *pun*?"

"Sure, why not?" He stopped and rubbed his temples. "Oh, just leave me alone, Malakos."

"*Righty-ho!*"

Malakos turned once more to leave.

"Wait! So what happens now? You keep me a prisoner here for the rest of my life?"

"Oh, no," said Malakos. "Not till you've taught me something that you actually know. Something that's useful."

"Of course!" Robert snarled. "I've created a monster! Malakos Frankenstein! All you really want is to learn more about the world. What can I tell you? About how the Earth moves around the Sun? About how the universe is fourteen billion years old?"

"What?" said Malakos. "No, nothing like that. What's that to me? No – I need you to teach me about… those marks. The markings on the *soap*."

"Markings? You mean *writing*?"

"Yes, if that's what you call it."

Robert practically jumped out of bed, before his failing body threatened to collapse beneath him.

"Malakos, my boy – I'd be delighted to! It's obvious! Spread writing around the Aegean hundreds of years early! Why, we'd get Homer in his purest form! Literature starting up before its time! We could spread *scientific* discoveries and insights before Plato and his lot divert us away from pure *science*. We could… we could visit Babylon, and get ancient Mesopotamian mythology direct from the source!"

"Yes… something like that," said Malakos.

Robert paused.

"I get the impression that you have something else in mind."

"Yes, well," Malakos chuckled – embarrassed for the first time. "You see… I'm starting to lose track."

"Lose track of what?"

"Oh, lots of things. Where I've been. When I've been. Who might recognise me. That sort of thing."

"You want to keep a note of where you've been."

"Yes, that. And also, other things. Like who owes whom what."

"What do you mean?"

Malakos sighed and said, thoughtfully,

"Barter systems are bloody inconvenient. You have to remember a lot of things. Much better if you can just use money."

"So go invent money."

"You always think too big! No, I don't need money. I need *writing*. So I can keep track."

Robert looked sullenly out into the bright light beyond his hut.

"Fine," he said. "And then you'll let me go?"

"I'll take you home myself." He thought for a while. "I might have to tie you up, though. In case you try to steal the time machine."

"Fine, fine, whatever. Just make sure you get me that *penicillin*, or I won't be teaching anyone anything."

"Deal!" Malakos held out his hand. Robert shook it, eventually.

As Malakos walked away, Robert called after him,

"By the way, Malakos. Where the *hell* are we?"

"Where are we?"

"Yes. Where are we in *Greece*?"

"What's '*Greece*'? We're on a big island – the biggest island in the sea. We're several days' sail from the mainland."

"Crete?" said Robert. "We're in Crete? And let me guess... to the north there's a big, wealthy town called Thera?"

"That's right. Across the ocean."

Robert smiled. He'd known that his final trip in time had gone wrong somehow. It had felt different. Perhaps there had been a bug in the code. Anyway, now he knew why.

"What's so funny, Master?"

"I just stopped worrying about the *Butterfly Effect*, Malakos. It's a weight off my mind. Go and get me that penicillin. But check with a doctor first. Find out how much to give me. And... how to buy it. I don't even know that. Ask around. Be a child. Have things explained to you. And when you get back, then we'll begin your lessons."

Malakos departed, satisfied with this bargain, and more than happy to work hard to save his friend's life. Happy that he could still do so.

And then... Robert added to himself, I wash my hands of you. You and your whole volcano-doomed people. I wash my hands of you all.

29 May, 2016

Twenty Years

The bar was always empty, this time of day. Dusty and empty. And hot, but not as hot as outside. The burning sun shone in through windows grimy with decades of neglect. If you peered through them, you'd see a parking lot and three cars. This was a bar for regulars only.

Saul sat at the table furthest from the door, where he always sat, so far as Peter knew. He never saw him anywhere else. The barkeeper, also one of the Faithful, served him drinks, and presumably received money in return, sometimes. But old Michael would never dare ask Saul for money – seniority in the Movement still carried respect, even after all these years.

Peter joined Saul. Their eyes met; Saul looked away. He often did. He preferred to look at his drinks these days. He liked the way the beer bubbles rose to the top and then scattered into the air.

He said it reminded him of the Master.

"Not much of a turnout," said Peter, like he always did.

Saul shrugged.

"Oh, they of little faith," he intoned.

"Oh, they of jobs, and families, and mortgages."

"Yes. Well, I advised them against that," said Saul.

Peter nodded and hummed.

"I think they remember," he said. "And most of them are glad they ignored you."

Saul was confused. He expressed this confusion by frowning at his beer.

"Twenty years," said Peter. "That's a long time, Saul. A long time to go without living."

"I advised them not to do all that," said Saul, ignoring him. He'd already decided what to say. "Mortgages, families, careers: they're all... promissory notes for a future we don't have. At least, a future we don't *have* to have. They're writing cheques they can't cash."

Peter sighed.

"That's twenty years of payslips that seem to have cashed just fine, Saul. Or did you want us all living in the Mission forever?"

"The Master would provide," said Saul. "And otherwise – what's twenty years? Twenty years against eternity! That's always been the deal!"

"Twenty years?" said Peter, intrigued. "Did He ever say that?"

"N-no." Saul shook his head. "No, it's been longer than we expected."

"In all honesty, some of us in the Movement are wondering if He ever will return, Saul – *wait!*"

Peter shouted this last word when he saw the old fire resurgent within his friend – the fire that once had brought the Movement together, had gathered nearly one hundred men and women into the Mission, had won them all to the Master's teachings, and had, for nearly two decades, held the community in a semblance of unity.

"Wait, wait..." he said. "I just mean... maybe He won't return in our lifetimes. Or maybe He only comes for us at the end of our lives. Or it could be another twenty years! Who knows?"

"And that's what people are saying, is it?" said Saul. "The whole Movement is muttering that the Master misled us? When he said, '*Don't go anywhere, I'll be right back*', he in fact meant, '*Bugger off and do what the heck you want. I'll come and pick you up when I'm good and ready.*'

" 'Right back'; eternity. What's one to the other?"

84

Saul snorted.

"And what do you think, *Rock of Ages*?" he said, sneering at Peter's choice of clothing – an aging t-shirt advertising a musical that he must have bought… well, before the Master's Rapture! "When will He return?"

"I could ask you the same thing. I want to ask you the same thing," said Peter.

"And I don't know!"

Peter started in surprise.

"I don't know!" Saul repeated. "I'd tell you if I did! I don't have any more of a pipeline to the Master than you do! If I'd heard anything, I'd have told you! How long…" He sighed, and then shrugged. "The one thing I know is what we all saw. We all saw the Rapture. We all heard what He said. We all know that we have to stay together, and then the waiting will be worthwhile. But imagine if we waited all this time, and we lost our way, and then He returned… found us unworthy of Rapture ourselves…"

Saul shook his head in frustration – for the Movement as much as for himself. Peter moved to pat him on the shoulder, but shrank back at the last minute. This was Saul! You didn't pat the great Saul on the shoulder! Instead he gestured to Michael for more beers. Michael brought them over, but said nothing. He was listening.

At the other end of the bar, two more of the Faithful pushed open the door. Michael shook his head at them. They saw this, and retreated. Michael watched through the window as they hopped back into their pick-up truck and turned on the radio. Michael would fetch them when it was time, when Peter and Saul were done talking.

"The worst rumours," said Peter, "say the whole thing was a scam."

"A scam!" Saul half-spat, half-scoffed.

"A magic trick."

"We all saw Him! We all saw the Monster! It swooped out of the sky, and the Master leapt on its back and flew to Mars. We saw it!"

"On the other hand," said Peter, "it was a long time ago, and magic tricks are easy. Easier than Monsters and Masters and Raptures."

"And if it was a scam… what was the point?" said Saul. "Scams cheat people. Who's been cheated?"

"A lot of people gave money to the Movement, Saul. A lot of people need money now."

"Yes, because of their families and jobs and mortgages."

"A lot of people regret giving so much before the Rapture, when they need it now. And where's it gone?"

"Where the bloody hell do you think it is, Peter?"

Peter shrugged.

"The hell do I know? Space? Mars? In the Master's personal bank account?"

"So you're one of the Faithless," said Saul, disappointed.

"Faith doesn't exist anymore."

"Yes, only families and jobs and mortgages."

The two sipped their beers.

"And what would it take to regain your faith, *Rock of Ages*?" asked Saul. Peter shrugged.

"Proof the Master wasn't a Magician?" he said.

Saul chuckled to himself.

"What's that for?" said Peter.

"Oh, who cares?" said Saul. "What do you care? You've lost your faith, and you've lost your way. What's the point?"

Peter grimaced and nodded. He wanted to apologise.

"Then tell me, for old time's sake. For twenty years' sake."

For the first time, Saul looked deeply and sincerely into Peter's eyes. He held the look for several seconds – an aeon for Saul, weighed down by years of lonely waiting.

Then, in an almost scornful voice, Saul hissed,
"The money's still there."

Peter frowned and shook his head. He didn't understand.

"The money's always been there. There's no *scam*. What
did the Master need money for? The money was to keep the
Movement going – it always was."

"Then why... didn't you tell us?"

"Tell you what? That everyone's little life savings were
still there, and they could have them back if they wanted?"

"Yes!"

"Because! Oh! There was hardly anything at the start. A
hundred thousand in total? Less?"

"Yes, well, we weren't rich back then," said Peter.

"We aren't rich now. With our families and jobs and..."

"...and mortgages," Peter intoned. "I get it. So what? So
the money's still there, is it? A hundred thousand dollars for
the Movement."

"Something like that," said Saul, cryptically.
Transparently, to someone who'd known him for twenty years.

"Meaning?"

"Twenty years against Eternity," Saul yawned. "Families
and jobs and mortgages against... compound interest.
Investment bankers. Stocks and shares."

Peter did not rise to the bait. Desperate to know the
truth, he waited nonetheless, as if Saul's enigmas did not
intrigue him. At last, when he saw that Peter would not budge,
he gave in.

"And so...?" he said at last. "How much is there?"

Saul inclined his head mockingly.

"Do you want to know something else, Peter?" he said.
Peter waited. "Compound interest, and investments, and the
stock market... doesn't remotely cover how much there is."

"Well, what the... what does that mean?"

"Only that some extra payments have been coming in from somewhere."

"What?" Now Peter bit – urgently. "Where from?"

"*I don't know!*" Saul laughed – *cackled*. "No one knows! The banks don't know; the agencies don't know! I hired an investigator; he drew a blank. A mysterious benefactor, who can transfer money into a private, secret bank account, without leaving a trail."

"Saul…"

"What in space does it mean?" Saul shrugged. "I don't know! Is He alive? Is He sending us money from Mars?"

"How much is there, Saul?"

"Millions! Tens of millions! And it keeps adding up. No matter what I do, it keeps adding up."

"What do you mean?"

"I spend it, Peter. All of it. I invest it. I buy things – assets, in the Movement's name. It all comes back. I've made… what, three bad investments? And even those turned out, well, not as bad as they could have. I'm a builder, Peter. I don't know about this stuff."

"Tens of millions… Saul, I need to think."

"Think away! I've been thinking for twenty years! I don't have any answers."

"No, I mean…"

Peter lapsed into silence. He was glad that Saul let him. Saul's silence meant something different to him now. He had always taken it as the silence of a stubborn, disappointed man. But now – now it was the silence of a man burdened by a truth he could not understand and could not let go.

Saul wanted to understand. But Peter wasn't Saul. Peter just wanted to know… what it meant for the Movement.

For their families and jobs and mortgages.

"Saul," he said, slowly. Saul flickered his eyes towards him, but kept his head rock still, bowed down before his beer. "The money… is for the Movement, isn't it?"

"Of course it is."

"And so shouldn't we use it for the Movement?"

"I've been trying, Peter."

"No, you haven't. You've been watching it grow. But tell me a single thing you've done with it that's helped the Movement."

"Tell me how!" Saul bleated.

"Families! Jobs! Mortgages!"

Saul leaned back, thinking about this.

"Money? You think this is about *money*? Throw money at the Movement, and the Faithful will come flooding back to the fold? Is that faith?"

"I think faith easier when you're not distracted by debt."

"Come, all ye Faithful, Jobless and Indulgent! Got a bad loan? Come to us! *Wonga, wonga, wonga!*"

"It doesn't have to be like that," said Peter, gritting his teeth. "People need guidance, like they always did. They need to know how to live. The Master is still helping us – He told us how to live while He was alive, but now He's gone. And he's left us a message."

"Yes, 'I'll be right back!'"

"No! The *money*, Saul. The money is the message."

"The medium is the message," batted Saul, irrelevantly.

"The money tells us something, Saul. What does it tell us?"

"It tells us that the Master wasn't a fraud! He didn't scam us!"

"It says more than that! It says He's going to be a bit longer than expected!"

Saul froze.

"What…?" he said, faintly.

"It says He's going to be a bit longer than expected," repeated Peter.

"How...?"

"Because we need our families, and our jobs, and our mortgages. But the money was there, and the money was increasing. To help us out. To keep us going."

"And so...?" said Saul, on the back foot now. Now he was the one who did not understand. Peter held the advantage.

"We've been waiting for two decades, Saul. Waiting, waiting, waiting. And we stayed faithful for all that time. We should have realised sooner – *would* have, if you'd told us the truth. He's not coming back yet. We don't know why. But He's looking out for us. And we have to look out for ourselves, too. Keep the Movement together."

"With money! And mortgages!"

"No! With faith, and how to live, like He always wanted. The money just... makes sure that we're okay while we do it."

"He told us how to live. There's nothing to add."

"He told us some things, sure. But tell me this: you've just been promoted to manager. You've got a lot of scope to do good there, but you've got to do something that's less good to start with. You need time to build up your position before you start making changes, doing the right thing. What should you do?"

"That's..."

"Or you've just been introduced to a rich man, who's done some bad things. You think you could change him, with time, but only if you befriend him. Should you do it?"

"Come on..."

"Or *families*... You said they're promissory notes that we can't cash – but what if the Master isn't coming back for a hundred years? Or a thousand? What's the Movement going to come to without families?"

"Peter! These are... *hypotheticals*! They're too vague. I don't have answers for you!"

"Exactly! The Master's lessons were vague. They're hard to apply to real life. We need guidance."

"Guidance?"

"A second Master."

"Never say that."

"Think about it, that's all," said Peter. "You know that I'm right. Maybe not in the details, but in general. The details were always your thing."

The bar was dark, and seemed much cooler than before. The sun was going down. The parking lot was getting full; more of the Faithful were arriving for the meeting, waiting outside until Michael called them in.

The conversation was over. Or so Michael judged. He walked to the door and waved the people in. Car doors began to open.

6 June, 2016

Civilised

"I admire your coming here, Mr Lane," said Dr Dietrich, smiling gently. "Not many of your kind have a stomach for our work here."

Lane scratched the back of his head. He was out of place here, in this cold, efficient place of science. Lane's was a world of stories – of deadlines and editors and *holyshitishtatthetime*. It was a world of self-conscious whiskeys and entirely authentic hangovers.

It was also, right now, a world without barbers or shaving cream, but that was the supplier's fault. None supplied in the language required out here in the People's Republic of Backwoods.

Lane scratched the front of his head. The face.

Dr Dietrich, on the other hand, looked as if he had never gone a day looking less than immaculate, had never been flustered beyond 'composed'. Head of the largest Farm in the world – the first Farm ever built – set high up in Hubei, in the mountains of Wudang, Dietrich had people who took care of these things. The language barrier: certainly. The deadlines – oh, yes! As for the drinking and the hangovers… those, too, probably.

It didn't sound like much of a life.

But then, Dietrich and Life had a funny relationship.

Not 'haha' funny. The other kind.

"Your office didn't make this visit easy," Lane said. "You'd probably find 'my kind' more interested than you think."

Dietrich led Lane along the shiny, spit-clean corridor. No dust along here, let alone cigarette ash – two condiments Lane expected to find on any honest floor.

"Yes, very interested," conceded Dietrich. "Interested in a hatchet job. We Europeans are very predictable. We abhor the very thought of Farms. We abhor the very thought of… of *the thought of* Farms. Of Farming in general. Please, through here."

Lane followed where Dietrich led. They entered a room, a round oval, its walls mounted with blown-up photographs showing the history of Wudang Farm. The first work teams brought in to survey the site; the diggers and cement mixers levelling the ground; the ancient temple repurposed for the modern age: a site for the divine and human to meet, now a place where man and subhuman parted ways.

Lane enjoyed the chiasmus; he passed it on to Dietrich, fully expecting the poetry to defeat him.

Instead, Dietrich hummed.

"Pithy," he said. "But not entirely accurate. I'm surprised, with your European moralising, Mr Lane, that you did not comment that man has become the new divine. Here we pass judgement, and we send our inferiors to hell. Ah! And do we not find ourselves on top of a mountain? Dante would be proud! And I – I am your Virgil!"

Lane muttered that he had never read Dante.

"No?" smiled Dietrich. "It is worth one's time. As is our little tour, I hope. Please, investigate the other pictures. I would greatly like to hear more such pithy thoughts."

Lane said nothing for a while. Here, one of the workmen was being awarded a Republic Star 'for exceptional zeal in furthering the goal of national harmony'. Here, the outer fencing for the new Farm was stretching out across the site. Here – and here Lane laughed – the whole team, engineers and diggers and managers alike, were sharing in a comradely beer and dance night. Everyone was dressed like Elvis.

"Where did they get the costumes?" said Lane, sarcastically.

"Pardon, Mr Lane?"

Dietrich wandered towards him.

"I said, 'Why did your office accept my request? For this tour?'"

Dietrich smiled.

"Don't worry, Mr Lane. China is not the country it used to be. Foreign journalists do not get carted off and locked up for a bit of wit. Which means, consequently, that there is no bravado, no cheap points, from making such comments. Naturally, the costumes were provided by the construction company, to facilitate a pleasant evening for the workers. The workers, in turn, felt valued and happy in their labour, and therefore continued to work hard.

"The photographs turned out to be excellent propaganda, and were entered as such in an exhibit of morale-enhancing, ideologically-correct artwork in Beijing. However, the choice of Elvis Presley, rather than a national star, seems to have harmed their cause. They did not win a prize."

"A pity. And my question remains unanswered."

Lane shot Dietrich a cunning look. Dietrich was clever. Of course he was. He was good with the press, too. At least, he knew how to handle people. He knew how to divert questions. Dietrich was, Lane knew, a devil. A butcher. He was responsible for a modern-day Gulag that stretched halfway across the world. He had invented Farming.

Europeans were furious that he had done it from European territory, with European funding. His schooling had been provided by the state from the age of four. As a child of poverty, his clothes and food, and many other things besides, had been given to him for free. Plus countless scholarships and rewards to foster his youthful talents.

His early research had been state-funded, too.

"Tell me, Mr Lane: what do Europeans think of me? No, rather, let me ask you that later. It will make more sense then. Tell me this: why did you ask for this tour in the first place? This tour, this place, which you hate so much?"

"I want to tell a story," said Lane. "It's a big scoop. I'll get a few thousand words out of it."

Dietrich laughed. Lane suspected that he was laughing at his 'few thousand words'.

"Words cost more in journalism than in science journals, *Herr Doktor*."

"Oh! Indeed!" said Dr Dietrich. "And you are so very efficient with yours! And here I am, the… mad scientist, you would call me, who can hardly stop talking! I am positively garrulous, am I not? While you, who conjure cash with your keyboard, say little, but merely make little insinuations which show your purpose in coming here."

Lane faltered.

"For example," Dietrich continued. "The title you just now gave me – *Herr Doktor* – is not a reflection of my background, except in the most crass way. I know the English, and I know that whenever they see a German, only just below the surface they see a Nazi. Even a Nazi working for the Communists! You think of me as a modern-day Mengele, correct?"

"I don't know you…"

"As if anyone needed to know someone to form an opinion about them! Especially of one as… well known as me! Indeed, to be a celebrity in Europe nowadays is very difficult. A celebrity whose name transcends culture and class and mountains and language and borders. How many of those are there, do you think? No – do not answer that. It is irrelevant. I am one of few."

"People usually like celebrities, Dr Dietrich."

Dietrich smiled.

"No. People like waiting for celebrities to slip up," he said.

The two had stopped walking. The next room was ready. Dietrich switched on the lights.

Lane gasped.

A parade of horrors. Photographs. Paintings. Models and sculptures.

Lane raised his hand instinctively to his mouth.

"There is a bucket, if you care to use it," said Dietrich. "We hope that not many of our visitors will do so. For reasons of hygiene, rather than of taste."

Lane folded away his emotions and forced himself to look, to meet evil in the eye.

Well, in the short-film-format.

A man lay in the dirt, his skull caved in. The camera showed the scene from the killer's point of view. The murder weapon could be seen, hovering tantalisingly in view of the camera, at the top left of the screen. A steel pipe. It was shaking: the killer was panting desperately, panicking.

"A murderer," said Lane, drily.

Dietrich said nothing. Lane's eyes fell to the Mandarin text beneath the screen. He could not read it.

"Presumably the English translation comes later," he said.

"Do you want to know what it says, Mr Lane? It says, 'Who is the murderer?'"

"What kind of a dumb question is that?" Lane hissed. "It's obvious…"

Something caught his eye in the heaving, undulating image before him. A doorway just past the bloodied corpse. A bedroom. Another dead body. A woman's.

"The second line of text reads, '*What is the punishment?*'"

Lane repeated these words blankly.

"Is this the punishment? Is what we see the punishment? Righteous vengeance – one life for another's? Or has the punishment not happened yet? Is the murderer in fact a double-murderer? We do not know.

"Or we could take the question in another way. We could ask what *should be* the punishment. Who should inflict it? Under what circumstances?

"How do we know, for instance, that the woman whose body you see was an innocent victim? Might she not have started the fight? Might she not have attacked… well, you may tell any story you wish here. This is barbarous. A life for a life, the act of vengeance feeding a cycle of violence. Individuals kill individuals; families kill families; clans and nations hurl themselves and each other onto the rocks."

Dietrich paused and then looked wryly at Lane.

"You see, the Chinese can be a subtle people, when they wish to be. But not 'inscrutable', in the old Western stereotype. But subtlety of thought, and nuance – that can interest them very much."

"You expect your hordes of Chinese tourists to get all that from a couple of lines of text?"

"Oh!" Dietrich shrugged. "Who cares what they get and what they do not get, quite frankly? It is enough to have put the thought there. That is the meaning of art – and yes, I believe quite fully that Wudang Farm is a place where art and science collide. Poetry, too."

"It's grim poetry," said Lane, pointing triumphantly at another video – this one from a famous documentary recorded a few years ago in the Pakistani hinterland. The two watched in silence as a man's eye was gouged out. The documentary-maker did not shy away from the details.

"I can't believe that went out on TV," muttered Lane.

"And of course, it did not. It did not conform to your European – *our* European sensibilities. This footage came from the unedited film. I was quite insistent on that, when our consultants suggested using this image. You may listen to the screaming, if you put those headphones on."

Lane stared at the clumsy-looking things, designed to bear the brunt of thousands of eager, grasping hands: heavy-duty cups, steel-rimmed cable.

"I'll pass."

"Well, that is a shame. You are missing an important element of the tour."

They walked on to the next image, and then to the next. Axemen. Hangings. Burnings at the stake. The last one, Dietrich assured him, could be experienced with full osmatic sensory effect by placing certain tubes into the nose. Lane again declined.

"You seem less committed to this tour than you had implied in your initial requests, Mr Lane," said Dietrich, mockingly. "Are you seeing something you did not hope to see?"

"No one should take pleasure in these... things."

"Are you moved to pity?"

"Of course!"

Dietrich smiled and clapped his hands.

"Then the tour has exactly the right effect! Admittedly, yes, on a soft European – the Americans would not respond like this so quickly – but all the same: a triumph! And we are hardly yet done. We have not entered the modern world yet."

"There's more?"

Dietrich looked at his guest with something like pity.

"Mr Lane, we have seen two rooms so far, in a gallery dedicated to the monstrosity of the human spirit. The exhibition could have continued for hundreds of rooms, cataloguing every vice, every abomination, that mankind has ever devised. This is the bowdlerised edition – and even that you cannot stomach, after all your persistence in asking to come here!"

Lane felt nauseous.

"And yet, perhaps you would like to sit down for a while. Please! You will see that we have chairs at the end of each room. We have tea-making facilities, too, if you would be so..."

"Doctor," said Lane, quickly. "Why am I here? Why have you allowed me here, when no one else..."

Lane shook his head and gave up on the sentence.

Dietrich looked surprised.

"Why, Mr Lane, isn't that obvious? We both have selfish reasons for this. You are here to make a name for yourself. You wish to justify your European notion of me and my work, and to hold me up to the world as a paragon of evil. I have studied your work to date. This is your model. You cling to extremes, telling complex stories in a simple way. Everything is good or bad; nothing is in between. This model is very comforting for those who live in the West. Nevertheless, it is wrong."

Lane sank back in his chair. He thought about the long pieces he had written to date. The one on private zoos. The one on the mockao industry. The one on modern-day hunting. The doctor had seen them as all the same.

Lane shook his head and sneered.

"Is that it, Doctor? You want me to write a hatchet job on you? Your office accepted my request because you know that's how I write? I don't buy it."

"Nor should you, Mr Lane. You are here to exonerate me, not vilify me. To change me from one type of celebrity to another. But perhaps that will become clear later on."

The next room contained examples from the pre-modern era. "The first examples of the industrialisation of the process," Dietrich observed.

Many pieces in this room could be experienced virtually, in full walk-around 3D. Small groups could attend the events together: Dietrich and Lane put on their headsets and promptly re-appeared in one another's sights, but now in a busy crowd.

"Are these pictures real? Or fabricated?" asked Lane, wondering at the precision of detail before him.

"A combination of the two," said Dietrich. "Approximately half and half."

For twenty minutes Lane observed the fruits of technology: the guillotine (entirely virtual); the firing squad, the hanging crane (entirely real); the gas chamber (partly virtual). No display failed to exploit its full potential for grotesquery and revulsion.

Dietrich remarked that some of his technicians had offered to add sensory feedback to these exhibits, to allow visitors to experience the relevant agonies for themselves.

"Naturally, I said 'no'," he added. "I have no interest in catering to the tastes of masochists. Besides, it would have been in poor taste."

"*Poor taste!*" Lane spat. "I didn't think that would bother you!"

Dietrich smiled coldly.

"Then you still have not understood. Come."

The final room was the smallest. It held the least curiosity for Lane, because its subjects were the most familiar, the closest to home. Here, recordings of lethal injections sat side-by-side with lobotomies and Schrodinger's Box devices. Dietrich looked with particular sadness at the last.

"You never know whether they are dead or not," he said. "Isn't that the most elegant punishment of all?"

"I'm sorry?" said Lane.

Dietrich looked mournfully at the Box.

"Isn't everything in here so *clean*? So *elegant*?"

Lane looked again at the exhibitions.

"I suppose so," he said. "But execution is execution."

"Hmm. Do you really believe that, having seen it in so many different forms? Having walked from one room to another, from the very distant past, through the beginnings of the justice system, and into here – the modern age? Do you believe that they possess no moral discrepancy? No variety in the level of cruelty available to us as purveyors of justice?"

Lane stuttered.

"I – *some*. Maybe."

"Maybe! But it is easy to say so, when you are not confronted with the reality, as you have been here. It is easy to sit in your nice, Swedish chairs and watch your Korean televisions and hurl abuse at us who operate at the front lines of justice."

"If you call it justice!"

"The first empty-headed thing that you have said, Mr Lane! A shame. You said just now that 'execution is execution'. I respectfully disagree. But justice *is* justice. Justice is what we determine justice to be, in the name of social order. Justice is the preservation of more life and happiness at the expense of a little, if we say so, as a society. It is a process whereby the innocent may go about their lives in reasonable security from malefactors.

"What is it *not?* It is not the machinations of the legal process, nor the endless wrangling of lawyers about due process. Justice is that which produces both balance *and* stability. Without it, life is intolerable. In some countries, it is harder won than elsewhere. In Europe, justice has been hard-won in the past, and now it is held rather too easily. We forget that concentration camps were pioneered by Europeans, and their hideous cousin, the death camp, was perfected in one particular European state. 'Justice' is not intrinsic to European thought, no matter how much hypocritical Europeans think it is.

"But in these harder countries where I operate – and others like me – well, justice has yet to be won entirely. I merely offer the tools."

"Well, I grant that this *looks* a bit more civilised…"

Dietrich turned to Lane again.

"*Civilised!* Yes, that is the word, isn't it! Aren't we so *civilised* now! Haven't we taken the messy process of removing human life and made it *tidy*, so like our European streets devoid of dog waste? We first became civilised the day our ancestors looked at a discarded wheat husk and said to themselves, '*We should pick this up and put it somewhere else, where we cannot see it! We should all do this, all the time, and thereby keep our own mess out of sight!*'

"And we apply this process to everything. Civilisation means 'tidiness'! It is the march of dustbins – literal and metaphorical! No, I am joking, of course. This is no great philosophy on civilisation – I have none to offer. But I have a philosophy on execution: it is a nasty business. It is irrevocable, and it can go wrong. But there are degrees. And it can be necessary – more so in some countries than in others."

"A *carte-blanche* for aspiring dictators," said Lane.

"Incorrect. For dictators are just as interested in the process of death as its outcome. Yes, political opponents may be removed by their murder, but political *opposition*? No. History has shown that people are not cowed so easily by the mere threat of death. Men fear pain – pain and humiliation. The shame of being led to the chopping block. Of being shown to the people and exposed to their jeers and mockery, before a painful, gruesome death, derided by the very dogs they had thought to liberate!

"The more elegant, the more mechanised, the death, the less effective it is for a *regime*. No one healthy and sane wants to die, but some deaths are better than others."

Dietrich stopped as if out of breath. Lane was glad that his Dictaphone – his civilised Dictaphone – was recording everything. He had lost all sense of the argument long ago.

"You're saying that your work here is *civilised*," he said. "Farming is *civilisation*."

"If I were not so distressed by my own passion, Mr Lane, I would laugh at your question. 'Farming' was the beginning of civilisation, of course. The modern use of the term is… Well! It is apposite. It is also efficient. And, as I have said, there is poetry within – those who have committed the worst crimes saving the lives of others. Or should we simply give them free room and board for the rest of their lives, like the deserving poor, born into poverty?"

"It's better than just locking them up, you mean," said Lane.

Lane jumped at the Doctor's sudden, deep exhalation.

"And at last you understand! The tour has had its effect! You know, there are some who believe that some of our… 'cattle'… should also be given the tour before they are admitted. But I say, what is the point? Do we really expect that such monsters as are sent to a Farm would acquiesce in their own punishment? Is that how the human mind works? No!"

"I think you're right," said Lane. "On that point."

"Yes, yes, I know. Your sensibilities still rail against the process. Your logical mind understands that I am right, but emotionally... you are not ready to agree just yet. You still believe it inhumane, but you are no longer sure why. That is acceptable. It is a start. It is enough. You are ready."

"Ready? For what?"

"Why," said Dietrich. "For the final room, of course. The room you came here to see. The Farm itself. You had not forgotten?"

"I thought that it would be somewhere else..."

Dietrich shook his head and led Lane into the final section of the tour. He showed him the metal skull-caps. He showed him the great electrodes that fired their disrupting fields into the conscious parts of the human brain. He showed him the vast feeding troughs, and the lines upon lines of hundreds – *thousands* – of human-like creatures standing patiently by their bales and mangers. He showed him the orderly calm in which these things lay down to sleep when it was dark, and rose when it was light. And he showed him the operating rooms, where the organs were removed.

7 June, 2016

First Man on the Moon

I first met Jacob Wiener in a dentist's waiting room. I know, right? – but he wasn't a world-beating celebrity back then. A complete unknown. I only knew his name because I was working reception, and I only remembered it because he asked for my number.

And I gave it to him because – well, because I was bored, and I hadn't had a date in a while.

He never called me, by the way. Some guys hunt phone numbers the way others hunt... well, wild animals. I guess Jacob was one of them.

Anyway, having been chatted up, I got to know him a little. He was normal enough. Intelligent. Good body – athletic.

Hah – what am I saying, 'normal'?

Okay, in that case, he was decent enough. He could hold a conversation, and had the guts to chat up a randomer in a dentist waiting area, with six or seven other patients listening in.

What did we talk about? Who knows? Who remembers conversations like that? I was mainly annoyed he didn't call. It felt like an insult.

Which is why I sent him a message three weeks later. "Just to let you know, I'm on a date right now, and I've having a great time."

With hindsight, not the breeziest thing I could have said.

"Oh yeah?" he replied. I remember all this – the messages are all on *Chattr*. Not that I've spent forever rereading them. But I did once or twice, after he got famous. *"Who with?"*

I smiled because I'd got his attention. So I ignored his reply.

"BS," he followed up. "Pics or shut up."

He had me there. I was, as a matter of fact, in my pyjamas, watching the animatronic *Jeeves and Wooster* remake at home.

I was also eating ice cream, which had somehow found its way onto my pyjamas, making seductive photographs as a deflection tactic out of the question just now.

Instead, I did what most people do in my situation. I sent him a picture of my fake-date-backup. Christopher Walters. We'd agreed we could do this a few years ago – a few weeks after meeting at work, incidentally, and then finding out on a date that we didn't really like each other very much.

I don't even know how many times he's used me. I've used him for all sorts of things. Getting out of dates. Pretending I'm on a date. Once to actually land a date, but that was more trouble than it was worth.

Photo sent, Mr Wiener. Believe me now?

"Christopher Walters," came the next reply, a few minutes later. "Interesting. How's Florence?"

"Who's Florence?" I asked.

The replies were coming thick and fast now. I paused *Netflix* just as Stephen Fry's constructed alter ego was about to swap one coat for another for some gently comic purpose.

"Town in Italy. Signor Walters appears to be there right now."

Blast, I thought. Chris was on holiday. I remembered seeing that now. We didn't usually work the same days. Even so: amateurish mistake.

"Nice try," came the next message. "Guess I made a real impression on you, huh?"

"You're an ass," I replied.

Six months later, Jacob came back to the surgery. That's the thing about dentists' patients – you can nearly always guarantee that they'll come back. Unless things go very wrong, that is. And Jacob took care of his body, so he took care of his teeth, too.

We'd sent a few messages in the meantime. Nothing major. Just a bit flirtatious. He'd even texted the night before to tell me he was coming in.

"Be awks if I just showed up, right?" he said.

"Are you telling me to make sure I'm there, or to tell me to call in sick?"

That invokes a longer delay than usual. The message *'user is typing a reply'* came up a few times. At last, he came up with,

"Dealer's choice."

It was Wednesday, normally my day off. But I'd already swapped shifts to be in. Twist my arm, I might just say I'd done it because I'd seen Jacob's name on the booking system.

"You decided to come in, then," he observed when arrived.

I gave him a long look. He was worth it. He'd shaved his hair in the meantime – I knew that, of course. Not that I *Facebook* stalked him. His movements had become more comfortable, too, as if the muscle mass he'd had before had been recently acquired, and now he'd had it long enough to know how to wear it.

And he was still charismatic. Too charismatic.

"Do you have an appointment?" I asked.

He grinned.

"Name?" I asked.

Then I waited. Long enough to make him uncomfortable.

"You're kidding, right?" he said. "It's me, Jacob."

I scratched my head.

"Hmm…" I said. "First name or last?"

"Funny," he said. "You never said you had a sense of humour."

"You never asked. Fill in this form, please."

I forwarded the standard questionnaire to his phone. The usual questions about his medical history and how much he wanted a Perfect Smile Registered Trademark. We didn't chat, though. It wasn't the right place. It was awkward. Awks.

The dentist called him in. He came back out fifteen minutes later. He gave me the forms, which I inspected carefully.

"Nearly perfect," I observed. "Not bad."

"They take care of themselves," he said. "Helps, in my line of work."

"Oh? And what's that?"

Another grin. I inspected those nearly-perfect teeth of his for myself.

"Tell you when I get back."

"Get back from where?"

Grin number three. He left. Like the Cheshire Cat.

So you see, I still didn't know what he did. It wasn't online, either. I'd checked. And, whereas an American in his position, working for the US Air Force, would have been treated like gold dust, wrapped up in a special bubble and kept far away from the real world, Jacob, a Brit, lived in a small suburban flat. He went to the local dentist, and he did his own shopping in the local *Tesco*. I doubt they paid him very much.

Here is a partial list of things I didn't know:

1. that Jacob was a test pilot;
2. that he was the UK's top rated test pilot
3. that he'd flown around the world several dozen times;
4. that he was already the fastest man in British history, having travelled at one-tenth of the speed of light;
5. that he would not be piloting the *HMS British Gas Henry IV Part 2* to Mars in a few months' time;
6. that his colleagues were astonished when they heard fact Number Five.

To be fair, fact Number Five had been classified Top Secret. If foreign spies ever learned of it, they would naturally want to know *why* the UK's best test pilot wasn't flying its best test plane.

To which the obvious answer was: *HMSBGHIVP2* was *not* the nation's best test plane.

So I learned the truth when everyone else did: a few days after Jacob's plane – the UK's *actual* best – appeared in the Glaswegian skies, causing a sonic boom that shattered every window in the city and levelled three whole apartment blocks.

Then the press conference, with the Prime Minister and a few other people I didn't recognise. The Prime Minister said (yes, I've copy-pasted this from the internet),

"The British people have a proud history – one of the greatest track records in the world, in fact – of leading by example in the field of scientific endeavour. This is the nation of the steam engine, of the hovercraft, of the jet engine. We have, since the development of commercial space travel, consistently led the world in technical implementation, in our commitment to ever- greater efficiencies, and in our development of pure science."

The Prime Minister, by the way, had a funny habit of rolling his 'r's whenever he said 'Britain', or anything like it. So when he said 'British', it came out as 'Brrrritish'.

"Three days ago, Brrrritish pilots, flying a Brrrritish-designed and Brrrritish-built space-plane, tested a new brrrr… *breed* of engine, operating on brand new principles, discovered right here, in Cambrrridge."

(The Prime Minister had studied at Cambridge, not Oxford. It was, therefore, one of very few non-'Brit' words to earn a rolling 'r'.)

"The plane departed from RrrrAF Tycho at 0300, London time, and proceeded to RrrrAF Olympus, Mars, logging an arrival time of 0413, the same day. The plane remained in Martian orbit for three days to conduct a mechanical check, and then returned to Earth, arriving in Glasgow at 1123."

(No mention of the damage to Glasgow, of course. That would have dampened the mood.)

"Having successfully returned to UK airrrspace, the data was analysed by the Centre for Propulsion Research, and then confirmed by the European 'Accord' Institute." (A French initiative which the PM pronounced 'Ackod', with no 'r' whatsoever.)

"The plane – the *Prrrospero I* – reached a maximum velocity of 1.9c – that is, 1.9 times the speed of light. It is the first plane in human history to brrreach the light speed barrier – which, thirty years ago, would have been dismissed as absolutely impossible…"

And then I turned off. And I stayed turned off for weeks, through all the scientific, philosophical, political, and military analyses that seemed to grip the web. *Twitter* became dull as heck.

I messaged Jacob.

"So, are you 'back' yet? When you gonna tell me what your job is?"

No reply. A few days later, I followed up with a solitary, accusatory,

"?"

after which I said I would leave it alone. It wasn't entirely clear that we were even friends – just sort-of-acquaintances. We'd messaged much more than we'd spoken. Maybe he was bored.

Fine.

A couple of months passed. A couple of months of working and dating and shopping and eating, and of avoiding the news with its endless fixation on this faster-than-light shebang.

As a result, I quite liked it when people argued that the whole thing was a hoax.

"FTL is fundamentally impossible," the line went, "because it undermines causality. You'd be letting things happen *before* the events that caused them. If you travel faster than light, then you'd essentially be travelling backwards in time. You'd arrive at your destination before you set off. And there's no funny 'universe stitching itself back together', like you get in cheesy time-travel stories. You'd breaking the way the universe works."

That was the gist of it, anyway. I'm not a scientist, and I find technical explanations dull. I suppose I could always look it up and copy-paste something, but what would be the point? Go and wade through the equations yourself; I've got better things to do. The internet says it can all be proven with Pythagoras' Theorem, or something. Fine. Good enough for me.

But, just as the world was settling back into its pre-FTL rut, an American engineer set the web ablaze by claiming that not only did America *also* have an FTL drive, they'd had one for seven years! As proof, he leaked hundreds of documents detailing test flights and flight times, technical specifications and the like. He also claimed, shortly before disappearing entirely, that the only reason the technology hadn't spread beyond the military was its inefficiency.

But he remained vague about that.

Inevitably, the American claim was followed by similar assertions by the Chinese, Russians, and Indians. Barely two months after the UK claimed to have built the world's first FTL drive, all of a sudden, half the G20 had one. Had *already had* one.

What a world. Was this causality breaking? Or was MI5 a bit bollocks these days?

Anyway, the only reason Britain had come clean, people said, was because the re-entry, the arrival above Glasgow, was a massive cock-up. The plane was supposed to go to the moon. The pilot missed by two hundred thousand miles. The crisis was over; little Britain could go back in its box now.

As I said, I tried to avoid all of this. Much more interestingly from my point of view, Jacob replied.

"*Hello,*" he sent.

"Hello yourself. You ignoring me?"

"I'm not sure. Should I be?"

"No!"

Each message took an age to come. Several minutes each time.

"Then I'm not ignoring you."

"You promised me a drink," I hazarded, cheekily.

"Did I? When?"

"Don't you remember?"

"Yes?"

So that was it. That was how Jacob finally took me on a date. Sort of. Just a few days before he got famous.

And he was *strange*. He'd always been quick-witted before. Clever. Now – well, everyone knows what he's like now. There's a condition named after him. Slow. Distracted. Confused half the time. Memory like putty – happy to believe most things you tell him.

He arrived – twenty minutes late – and he proceeded to spend several minutes just looking for me. I guessed he was playing some kind of game with me, so I waited. I didn't draw his attention. Keep the power, and all that.

Then, when he finally did see me and was walking over, he muttered to himself,

"You're sitting over here, so I sit over here, too…"

His voiced drifted away into uncertainty. Then he nodded.

"Yes, that's okay," he said.

"It's normally okay," I said. "Unless you want to spend the whole evening at different tables."

He looked at me strangely, as if he was trying to work something out. Then he shrugged, defeated by the mystery for now.

"Some things are better left unknown," he said, nonsensically.

"Drink?" I asked.

"Yes, I owe you a drink. What would you like?"

"A half."

"Of?"

"Whatever you're having. A lager."

"Sure."

Jacob walked over to the bar, but not before studying his route very closely. He ordered the drinks and carried them back, a vague amazement in his eyes.

"So? What's the face for?" I asked.

"Nothing," he chuckled. "Some coincidences are too much."

"Such as?"

"See?" He gestured at the drinks. "Two halves. Both the same." He shook his head. "Amazing."

"Isn't it what you ordered?"

"How could it be?"

"Oh, you know... Location. Words. Timing."

"Timing," he said, "is the problem."

I sighed and looked at my watch.

"I don't get it. Is this a game? Or are you high? If the latter, quit holding out."

Jacob looked sharply up.

"Sorry. Since I got back..."

"Oh, yes. Your trip. Where did you go?"

"Alpha Centauri."

I looked at him blankly. As I said, I found all this space stuff remorselessly dull. If I'd really thought about it, I could have guessed what Alpha Centauri was. Instead I said,

"Oh, right? How's the weather?"

"Depends," he said. "Some patches of searing heat. Some deadly cold."

"Is it far?"

"You don't know? You haven't heard of it?"

"Evidently not."

"Well, it's the nearest star system to our own. I flew there."

"In your spaceship."

"How else would I get there?"

This seems, to me, as if it were the first thing Jacob had said that night about which there was any certainty. And it was a question.

I thought he was joking, obviously. I didn't realise that he had just spilled a state secret.

"Right, so you're a *space pilot*. You kept that quiet."

"Do you talk about your work?" he asked.

"I'm a receptionist. I mention it sometimes."

"I wasn't supposed to."

"And now you can?" I asked.

He smiled at me.

"Now I'm not here," he said, enigmatically. "How can I?"

I frowned at him and finished my drink.

"Look, are you going to be like this all night?" I demanded.

"Probably."

"Then come back to my place and I'll find a way to shut you up."

"Sorry," he said. "I have to go back to the base. They say they're keeping a close watch on me."

"How can they if you aren't really here?"

"I know," he nodded solemnly. "It's a conundrum."

"Whatever." I stood up quickly. "If you want to be an ass, do it by yourself. I'm bored of this, whatever it is."

It was a good exit-line. I did not look back. Just stormed out. A good few people looked at me; I didn't look at them, either. Maybe I should have. As it was, I didn't see Jodie Winters, television anchor, get up and intercept Jacob before he could stand up and leave too.

Well, I saw *someone* go over, but I could hardly stare. I was storming out. I'm guessing from what happened next.

Two days later, he was on TV. First on Jodie Winters' morning show (*Winter's Morn*), and then on the *Six o' Clock News* webcast. By the end of the week he was on the *Zeitgeist* chat show, after which his transformation into internet meme was inevitable. Photoshops of him looking confusedly at various things – sandwiches, trees, copulating couples and the like – superimposed with such gems as "Where is pig?", "When did this car?", and... well, I won't say the other one.

And the strange thing is, none of this was meant as mockery. If anything, it was a backwards kind of adulation for one of the few, honest-to-god heroes the country had produced in decades, or even longer.

You see, Jodie Winter had a good ear for a story, and she'd already heard titbits about US test pilots operating at superluminal velocities: how they came back disorientated, unable to separate cause and effect, bemused by even the most banal conversations – and apparently by the fact that people could see, hear, and respond to them.

She'd even come across the strangest theories emanating from little-read MIT journals suggesting a correlation between travel speed, journey distance, and duration of this condition.

But it was Jacob who gave his name to the illness. The psychologists call it Jacob's Disease (largely because they didn't want to go around having to refer to Wiener's Disease). But it wasn't the illness that made him famous.

Well, partly it was. The illness made him internet-famous. Millions – tens of millions – who wouldn't watch the news or chat shows in a billion years were drawn to vids of Jacob fumbling through interviews, churning out statements that veered between the mock-profound and the sublimely daft.

No, the key was that 'Alpha Centauri' thing.

You see, what people were saying about faster-than-light travel – that half the advanced countries in the world already had it, and that Britain was a latecomer – was correct.

They were even right, incidentally, about the ballsed-up re-entry profile, which gave the game away by demolishing parts of Glasgow, and forced the Government to make a statement on the matter.

And, in a way, they had even been right about FTL flight travel undermining cause and effect. Except the problem was psychological, not physical: to do with how we perceive time. Apparently it's an illusion, or something like that.

Like I said, I'm no scientist.

What no one had guessed was that the Cambridge physicists who had invented the technology hadn't just found a way to travel at 1.3c, or even twice that.

Jacob had covered roughly 4.5 light years (even I know what those are!) in about a week. Which means that he had travelled at something like 30 times the speed of light.

That, too, was an accident. He'd been ordered to travel just beyond the solar system, check his location, send a homing signal back to Earth, and then come home.

A series of mechanical failings caused them to overshoot their mark by a long way. So far, in fact, that by the time they had the ship under control, the crew decided to continue to Alpha Centauri and just ration their supplies. And why not? If the ship malfunctioned again, they were far beyond hope of rescue already. They might as well set a *real* record.

The only problem for Jacob and his crew was cause and effect. They didn't understand it anymore.

All six of them were highly trained, well educated, and very aware of the risks of superluminal travel. They knew of the disorientation experienced by other FTL pilots, and they had been promised counselling upon their return to aid their reintegration into society.

No one had told them about the MIT research, which suggested that the further you travelled, the longer the effect lasted; that someone who flew for one light year at 1.5 times the speed of light would spend half a year in a causality-bemused dream-state, 'waiting for light to catch up with them'.

Or that someone who travelled 9 light years, there and back, in just a few weeks, would remain stricken for nearly nine years.

It's been three years since then. Only six years to go.

14-17 June, 2016

Fifty-Two Percent

"Sir? General? Are you all right?"

Admiral-General John Richards looked up. His vision was clearing; he must have blacked out for a while. He was underneath a desk, in the space where the chair goes. The chair wasn't there anymore. He was.

He wrapped his knuckle against the underside of the desk and laughed.

"Hah!" he said. "Good, solid, Earther steel, that. I'd like to see the bomb that could get through that!"

For the first time, he focused on the face peering down at him. He recognised it.

"And what are you looking at, Anders? Help me up."

Space-Colonel Anders grimaced.

"We're not… Perhaps you should stay there for a while, Sir. Until we've got Command Centre… cleaned up a bit."

"Pah!" Richards scrabbled out of his cubby hole and thrust his arm towards Anders. The Colonel helped the Admiral-General to his feet.

Richards looked around in astonishment. Command Centre was… no longer visible. Clouds of dust, kicked up by Foreign bunker-busters, obscured vision beyond a metre or two. Not a single monitor was working. The room was bathed in dull, red emergency lighting, subdued menace pervading the dust.

Admiral-General Richards, mindful of his rank, began to tour the facility. Here and there, concrete blocks had fallen down like boulders. Some of the CC staff lay beneath them. Others were simply propped up against the walls, or lying flat on the floor. Some were groaning, because they were still alive.

Only a handful, who, like Richards, had been quick enough to dive beneath sturdy Earther desks, were mobile.

"What is this?" whispered Richards. "How did this happen?"

"We – we were warned," babbled Anders. "We knew what to expect, but we ignored it."

"Be quiet!" snapped Richards. "That's in the past now. I don't want to hear… The future is what counts. We'll rebuild. We're not the basket case those… *cowards* said we were!"

They continued through Command Centre.

"What news from topside?"

"None, sir," said Anders, apologetically. "We have no contact with the surface."

"The hard lines?"

"The Foreign bunker-busters…"

"Enough of that! I don't want to hear it! No." Richards looked around. "Priorities. *Number one*: first aid – get anyone who's up and about on med duties. *Number two*: maintenance. If this place falls down on top of us… Stop it! *Number three:* establish comms with topside."

"Yes, sir."

Anders turned away, but Richards stopped him. The level of destruction… It was impossible. It went against every prediction he had made. The devastation was… was the compilation of every wet fantasy the naysayers of Project Fear had invented to thwart the fleet's construction. Every fantasy which he and his supporters had debunked, demonstrating their flawed premises, their biased funding. And yet…

"Wait. Change of plan," he said. "I want topside ASAP. That's priority one. We have to know…"

"The casualties," Anders protested. "We need the manpower to help them."

Richards grimaced.

"As many as you can spare." He looked madly at the Corporal. "We're at war, Anders, and this is Command Centre. We're soldiers. Or did you think you were safe down here?"

Anders' eyes hardened, and he saluted.

Richards found a chair and picked it up. After some testing, he decided that it, too, was made of sturdy, Earther steel, and that it could bear his full weight. He sat back. What had happened? How had it happened?

There were the campaigns, to start with. On the one side: *Play It Safe. A Deal Is A Deal. Remember The Past.* A dozen slogans that demanded stasis, a continuation of the status quo for the last *hundred years.* A fearful, sorry, spineless refusal to acknowledge the changes, the developments, the advances of that last century. A campaign looking to the past when Earthers were ready for the future.

And on the other side: *Space For Earth. Forge Into The Future. Foreign Laws Do Not Apply Here.* A reminder – a positive, dynamic campaign that promised Earthers not just the world, but the solar system, and eventually the galaxy. A galaxy bereft of Foreigners.

Heck, were the Foreigners even out there anymore? No one knew. No one knew! They might have moved on, or gone back to wherever they had come from, and a century of Earther terror might have been in vain. Perhaps, even now, the other victims of the Foreigners were spreading out into the empty heavens, taking precious resources, multiplying. Or – think of the possibilities! – perhaps Earthers would be the first to take the risk, and would conquer the galaxy before anyone else could get there!

Did Earthers really believe that Earth, the mother of mankind, should be swaddled like a baby? By an enforced peace, an illegal treaty with an alien menace a hundred years old? Ridiculous!

The campaigning had been passionate; at times, even violent. The police themselves could hardly stay neutral, and at last the army had been called upon to break up several mass rallies.

And things had escalated. Full-on gang warfare had erupted between Remainers and Leavers – those who wished to remain hidden on Earth, and those who demanded that Man boldly leave the nest and venture to the stars again.

At last, a beleaguered government, tottering in the face of civil disturbance, had waved its hands in the air and cried, "Enough!" This was a matter of global – indeed, galactic – policy, too big for a handful of government ministers to decide upon. A referendum would solve the problem. Everyone could vote. The majority would have their way.

Spinelessness!

A date was set. The violence dwindled, as people fought instead for hearts and minds, rather than skulls and scalps, as before. Online campaigning was safer than the boots-on-the-ground variety, and inevitably the weak, fearful Remainers relied on this approach. The Leavers were more aggressive, more righteous in their cause, and regularly broke up Remainer rallies, while possessing the muscle to protect their own from reprisals. Prominent Remainers died, and they had the gall to use these tragedies to their own advantage, labelling the Leavers as thugs and murderers – a kind of violence just as bad as the sticks-and-stones variety, and twice as insidious!

But behind the distractions, the facts remained. The cosmopolitics of a hundred years ago were no longer relevant. Earther technology had progressed a hundredfold since the Foreign Invasion had obliterated human forces across a dozen star systems.

Yes, the peace treaty – the Stab In The Back – had saved Earth from extinction (thus spake Propaganda!) but it had also forbidden space travel. Orbital satellites and stations were allowed. MoonBase might remain, on account of its civilian population. But nothing else. It was perpetual imprisonment.

But then, Earth had rebuilt – to a degree and at a pace inconceivable to anyone, let alone the Foreigners! Now Earthers had the power to fend off Foreign aggression! And could the Foreigners expect them to abide by an unequal treaty, if they no longer had to?

Those were the arguments, and Admiral-General Richards had become their leading proponent.

He pointed out that the only ones to gain from a Remain vote would be the current political and economic elites, whose dominance would be eliminated by a new wave of brash, adventurous entrepreneurs and explorers surging out into the galaxy.

He explained that Earther technology had now reached a point where they could swat aside the Foreigners like flies. Indeed, the Foreigners *were* flies, disgusting maggots whose existence was tolerable wherever they had come from, but certainly not on Earth, or anywhere near it. Once, Earth had feared the Foreigners. Now, the Foreigners should fear Earthers, swarming out of Fortress Earth in droves, dealing death to all around them.

And, the most important fact of all: *the Foreigners probably weren't even there anymore*. No one had heard from them in a hundred years. Why fear what probably doesn't exist? Were Earthers children, afraid of the monster under the bed, no matter how many times they looked?

And what had the Remainers offered in return? Nothing but empty expert analyses, first-hand reports of Foreign military capacity from the last war, cowardly assurances that Earth could support mankind for another twenty thousand years, if need be. Warnings that taxes would go up to cover military expenditure, that our quality of life would go down. Worthless guesswork, as if anyone could predict the future!

Besides – the Foreigners probably weren't even there anymore!

Richards stood up to resume his tour. Some who had been merely injured before were now deceased. Some were resting. The pressganged first-aiders had settled on a simple colour-coding system: a red label for *'leave alone: no hope'*, green for *'leave alone: safe'*, and orange for *'treatment required'*. That was the extent of triage – but most of the 'orange' labels would turn red, Richards knew. The doctors were all topside; most of the medicines were buried under rubble.

Richards found Anders.

"Update," he said. "Are we stable?"

"We think so, Sir," said Anders. "Anything loose has probably collapsed by now. Short of a quake, or another attack, we're in the clear."

"And topside?"

Anders' face fell. Richards noticed the data pad in his hand. Anders passed it over.

Richards stared at the pad, trying to fit his senses with what he knew to be true. He laid the pad on the desk and shook his head in bemusement. Obviously, the reports were mistaken. They were impossible – a final act of propaganda by embittered Remainers.

"That's it," he said to himself, as Anders – a closet Remainer, if Richards ever saw one – watched on. "This is... isn't happening. It's sabotage. It's a prank. A bomb's gone off in CC, that's all. Someone's trying to stop Leave, against... the people's will. Fifty-two percent for Leave. That's final. Unequivocal. There's no room for doubt. The human race speaking for itself for the first time!"

Anders shook his head.

"It's not a hoax, Sir. We've confirmed the data from three listening posts. And the damage to CC is definitely external – an inside bomb couldn't have done it."

Richards shook his head.

"How did you vote, Anders?"

"Excuse me?"

"Come on: how did you vote? In the referendum. You're a Remainer, if ever I saw one. How can I trust you? You've cooked this up. Typical Remainer garbage. Project Fear."

Anders sagged a little.

"Think what you want, you pompous ass," he said. Richards gawped. "You're deluded. It's just like they said. Everything was true. It's all over."

"Anders," he said. "You're relieved. Go help some bleeders. I'll find someone else to verify this... nonsense. A *professional*."

Anders bowed his head, glad, perhaps, to be freed of serving a military hierarchy that no longer had a purpose, and left instead to help his comrades.

"My God," chuckled Richards. "If even half of this data were true... why, there'd be less than a million Earthers left! Absolute nonsense! Solar slicers! Subspace distortion fields! Force cannons! We had thousands of them – tens of thousands of them! Fortress Earth!"

He sat down again, bowled over by the merest suggestion of such destruction being wrought against the human race – *again*.

He waved the data pad at someone – Space-Colonel Yaroslev, a big, outspoken Leaver. He ordered him to confirm the data, and returned to his reverie.

He thought about the weeks and months – and even years – after the referendum, when plans for Space Command and a new generation of warships were drawn up. Nothing happened – no reprisals from the Foreigners. Even then, the defeated Remainers, who had expected to win the referendum handily, pleaded for a second vote, determined to undermine democracy by holding another democratic vote.

Then the first ships had launched, and crews had been combat-trained, always within the Earth-Moon arc prescribed by the Stab In The Back, and *still* no reprisals. The Foreigners weren't interested. They weren't there anymore! There were absolutely no consequences!

And still they pleaded – *another vote, another vote! We've been safe till now because we haven't actually broken the treaty yet. We won't be if we do!*

As if the Foreigners cared about the letter of the law! Or as if a second vote would change anything! The vote had been absolute, unequivocal, unchangeable. The people – a full seventy percent of the electorate, a couple of percent of whom

122

had died of old age since the referendum – had spoken with one voice. To suggest anything else would be monstrous, tyrannical. And to suggest that they might have changed their mind – well, that would be patronising, as if the people hadn't known exactly what they were voting for!

"No, this isn't my fault," Richards told himself, allowing for the first time that perhaps Anders' data had not been forged after all. "It's not any of our fault. This is *democracy*. The will of the people. The people had their say, and we all share in the consequences. Fifty-two percent of us!"

He thought a little more.

"And if it's real, then it's nothing to do with us. We were missing something – something *vital*. Something we didn't know. Information. That's paramount in war. Know your enemy… So what did they have that we didn't know about? Not technology – we had them licked for that. Earther steel. Earther lasers. More than a match for Foreign junk. Just like we said."

He nodded to himself, satisfied on this last point.

"No – something doesn't add up," he said. "How did they know about our plans? How did they attack so quickly? Our ships – they must have been taken by surprise, or overwhelmed by superior numbers. But how did they know?"

He reviewed the events that he could recall – the events he remembered from before the attack.

"They came as soon as our ships left orbit," he said. "A dozen of our first ships. We were recceing the local neighbourhood, testing out our new drives. They had weapons, too – they could have taken out any Foreign patrol. Or did they post an entire fleet here for a hundred years, on the off chance that we rebuilt and reclaimed our birthright? No, it's not possible!"

Richards could feel his blood beginning to boil.

"That's it!" he said. "Why didn't we think of that? We never found any listening posts in the solar system – but we never checked on Earth! Earth, defiled…" Richards had to break off the thought, so… *distasteful* did it seem. He took a deep breath.

"But that's how they knew. They knew because of our own ignorant insistence on… democracy! Openness! Let's have this debate out in the open! Yes, and tell the Foreigners exactly what we have planned! Give them time to prepare! They could bring a thousand ships – more, a hundred thousand! – into position, just waiting for us to make our move. They could find out when we planned to launch – blindside us before we could establish ourselves, before we were invincible!

"But – not without help. You can't hide a base on Earth for a century, not without support. What would you eat? How would you stay hidden? Those politicians – those *Remainers*. They knew! They betrayed us!"

Richards swore then and there that wherever those Remainer politicians were hiding, in whatever bunkers they had taken flight, he would find them. He would destroy them. He would take revenge, for all the dead of Earth.

"Sir?" came a voice from behind him. Yaroslev.

"What is it, Colonel?" Richards replied through gritted teeth.

"We've… had more details," he said. "It's… worse than we thought."

Richards turned suddenly and snatched the data pad from Yaroslev. His eyes skimmed over the screen.

"What are you talking about, Colonel? This is the same as before. Hell, if anything, it's *better* than before. We've got more facilities coming online. The shelters, too… Yes, Earther spirit! Earther steel!"

Yaroslev said nothing. Richards looked at him suspiciously, then looked again at the data pad. Reports from the battle itself – reports which Richards himself had not yet seen. He frowned.

"This must be a mistake. Have you confirmed this?"

Yaroslev said nothing. As if a Leaver would have taken this on trust.

"A single ship?" Richards shook his head. "That's not possible. A single ship couldn't have done all this."

"A single *fighter*," Yaroslev spat. "A scout ship. Too small to target. Weapons as good as our biggest tankbusters. Better. And *fast*."

"I don't understand." Richards could feel every muscle in his body weakening, his flesh turning numb with every word. "Is this how far they've advanced? In just a century?"

"This ship…" Yaroslev muttered, then stopped.

"Well? Come on!"

"This ship, sir – we've identified it. It's the Flitterbat 307A."

"What does that mean?"

"It means, sir, that we painted it a hundred years ago. During the Invasion."

"Don't talk nonsense! If that's true, that ship would be…"

"A century old, sir, yes. A leftover from the last war."

Richards' strength failed him. He crumbled – he collapsed to the floor. Consciousness left him – but only for a while.

He woke up, propped up against a wall, his knees tucked up towards his chest. A simple recovery position. He noticed a green tag around his neck.

Anders was standing over him.

"We didn't know," Richards whispered. "How could we know? Those reports from a hundred years ago… They were nonsense, that's what we thought. Hysterical nonsense."

"*Some* people thought that," said Anders, carefully. "A few die-hards, and some on the media circuit. A couple of fringe theorists."

"What's that?" Richards frowned in confusion. Die-hards? There weren't any die-hards, not amongst the Leavers. Only rational, patriotic…

"But did any experts think that?" said Anders. "Can you remember a single military analyst who held his hands up and said, 'You know what, everyone – these reports are garbage'?"

"I don't like what you're saying, Anders."

Anders shrugged.

"Then I'll leave. But you know – you brought this on us all. *You* did this – you, and your media friends, and your wishful thinking. And now – now we're all dead. I – I'd kill you now. If there was a point."

Anders walked away. Richards called out after him.

"*We didn't know…* And they had spies! They *knew*. We've been betrayed. And don't try to pin this on me. Fifty-two percent of us, Anders. *Fifty-two percent! Everyone is to blame!*"

18 June 2016

AdD

It was Indraneil who started it all – at least, at Ryebeck Forest School. Oh, if he didn't, then someone else would have – but Indraneil *did*. He'd been the first to suss out the rewards of the system, to tell others about it, and set them all off on nervous, titillated fantasies of what they would do with All That Money.

He'd been first to twig that what they had seen only sporadically, here and there, on vids and the like, was something that they, too, could do, and for *more* money than most.

He'd been first to realise, too – and this was the most important fact, for many Ryebeckians – that it would infuriate their parents – those out-of-touch, archaic relics of a cleanskin age. Or even worse – the over-hairy posers of the artskin age.

Indraneil was gone now. He'd come to school one day with a broad firebrand of a tat emblazoned like a cry of freedom across his forehead. He'd lasted thirty minutes before being hauled up in front of the Master in Charge of Discipline. Even now, rumours abounded of *that* titanic clash. Indraneil was not a quietly-spoken young Hindu boy. Some who'd been in the neighbouring classrooms *swore* they'd heard such gems as,

"This is against my human rights!"

"Go on, show me where I'm breaking the law! I'm over sixteen – I can do what I want."

"I swear to God if you try kick me out my parents will bury you so far down the law's arse…"

"Rules? What fucking rules? Show me? Go on, show me – I bet you can't! I never signed any fucking school rules."

Well – the quotes get longer and less likely the more you listen. Probably, most of it was bragging – "This is what I would have said, if I'd thought of it at the time."

But the profuse deployment of the 'f' word – and several others – was firmly in character, even before such a presence as Mr Walmsley.

Indraneil did not return to school. Nor did the promised lawsuit emerge. Last we heard, he'd been shipped back to the Punjab, where he was undergoing a double cleansing: firstly on his forehead, and secondly on his soul.

But then, he'd been fool enough to paste the Buddhist Dharma Wheel onto his forehead – for a neat consideration from the United Global Vehicle – in a strict, traditional, Hindu household.

But his parents had kept the sponsorship money. Why the heck not? Ironically, India was one place the UGV *couldn't* demand a refund for tat-removal.

Anyway, after Indraneil's fate, none of us was dumb enough to get a tat before we left Ryebeck. But with that last summer coming up… Well, let's just say that girls, tats, exams and uni were the priorities, in precisely that order.

We used to sit around the campus gardens, huge, great binders in our hands – binders thicker than those that held our lesson notes, each page half adorned by a beautiful tat design hovering delicately above the promotional considerations on offer, as well as any other fine-print details, all lovingly copied out by one or another of our circle.

You see, Ryebeck had taught us well – group work for everything. No one could possibly plough through all the companies and causes out there offering sponsorship for tats. But with twelve of us, we could divide up the groundwork, research ten, twenty, even thirty offers each, print out the facts, and make a compendium of hundreds, all in one place.

We called it the Bible.

"Check this one out," said Rob. He waved one page around at the group. "Looks alright, doesn't it?"

"Who the fuck cares what it looks like, Da Vinci?" said Mark. "Don't tell us you're turning artskin. This is about the cash."

"If they're worth the same amount then you might as well go for something that looks okay."

"Has *anyone*," piped up Becca, "seen anything that's 'worth the same' as anything else? They're all so *different*! These pay the same, but have to be kept for different times. And they have different rules about where they go."

We perused on.

"Come on, own up," drawled Steve. "Who did *Trojans*?"

Steve displayed the relevant page. The guys laughed uproariously – ultra-loud, just to show they got the joke. The girls scowled. Mostly. It went on the small of the back, or below the belly button.

Brand awareness: you were unlikely to nip out mid-fuck to change your brand of condom, but maybe next time you were on Amazon you'd remember the name.

"The placement rules are important," I said – wisely. "They're how you max out your pelt." ('Pelt' – that was the term for those in the know. I said it to show how much I knew.) "Those and the minimum sizes. I mean, most of the face tats go on the cheek or the forehead, but they also have non-compete clauses. So you can't use the other cheek to promote a competitor, if both tats can be seen at the same time. But the cheek goes all the way back to the ears, so you could put *PlayStation* and *Xbox* on opposite cheeks, so long as no one can see both at the same time."

"Yeah, but you're not seriously going to put *games* on your face are you?" said Martin. "Not right before you go to uni? You'd look like a freak."

"It's just an example," I said, abashed. I hadn't thought of that. "Why, what are you going for?"

"I don't know. I was thinking maybe… Oxfam?"

A chorus of jeers met this suggestion.

"Pretentious wanker."

"Oh, look at me, I'm *saving the world*."

"I'm too good to take money for my pelt."

"Oh, what," said Martin, "it's OK to take money from Facebook, but from a good cause?"

"Oh, it's absolutely fine, mate," said Oliver. "It just makes you a wanker."

"What do Facebook pay?" asked Sarah, quietly.

"Piss all," I replied. "But they just want a little thing on your chin. A centimetre square, I think. They just want the logo everywhere."

"I'm going for NewLab," said Hilary.

Howls of sarcastic surprise met this declaration. Hilary's family was NewLab through-and-through. They'd cried the day Gregor Moore got voted in. The merest hint of political chatter was guaranteed to call an onslaught of socially-aware invective. Everyone knew she would go into politics one day.

"Really, Hils? Never thought that would happen."

"We are gobsmacked."

"What's that? Hils is going Tory?"

"Fuck you!" shouted Hilary. She held the page to her face. "You see this? Right over both cheeks!"

"And what will Great and Noble Party pay for that?" said Oliver.

"Um, social justice, dignity for the human race? You know – a better world."

"Go tell it to Tower Hamlets," said Martin. (The Tower Hamlets embezzlement scandal was still blowing up around this time.)

"Oh, so nothing at all," I said, at exactly the same time. Martin and I glared at each other.

"These political parties just want to get inside your heads," said Ed. "They want you all thinking the same things. It's *insidious.*"

We all nodded at the word, because it was a good word, and summed up what we all thought about politicians in those days. Besides, we'd recently watched the reboot of the *Insidious* franchise.

"NSL for me," said Hamid. "Long live the New State."

This proclamation met an uneasy silence. It might just be true, and not just a prank.

"Oh?" said Hilary, politely. "That's interesting. *My* backup plan was to scrawl *'Fuck human rights'* all over my face with a baby's felt-tip."

"Oh, yeah, 'human rights'. Whatever those are. Imperialist…"

"Go throw babies off a cliff."

"That's a fucking slander! Execution in the Blessed State is only for those who…"

"Don't think the same, right? What was Ed was saying about *NewLab*?"

"Don't you dare compare the New State to your sickly politicians!" shouted Hamid. If he had started in jest, he was now in full earnest. "Free thought in the Holy State is guaranteed…"

"…So long as you think the right things and nothing else!"

The two glared at each other, marshalling their forces for the next round.

"Wait, wait, wait!" said James, suddenly. "I can resolve this."

We waited expectantly. James said nothing. We looked around, knowing what was coming. At last, Hamid opened his mouth.

James poked him in the face, right near the eye.

"No!" he said.

Everyone laughed. Hamid looked bemused, then opened his mouth to try again.

Same result.

"*No!*" James repeated.

Then he turned to Hilary. He cocked an eyebrow, waving his finger at her. She paused, then seemed to accept the peace.

"Can I just check?" I said, slowly. James, his prodding finger now warmed up, made a lunge for me. I dived away. "Wait, wait, wait! New topic! New topic! I just want to check – have we all put the going rate for our lot?"

"Yep."

"Yes."

"What do you mean?"

"Well," I said, a-righting myself on the grass. "You didn't just take the first number they gave you online, right?"

Some of the group froze.

"Why not?"

The rest of us groaned.

"For *fuck's sake*! Come on, who fucked up? Which ones did you do?"

"You've got to go through the first pages of the order form," I said. "It asks you all these questions…"

"That'll take ages!"

"We all did it!"

"There's always shirkers!"

"This is why group work sucks!"

"All this," I said, gesturing helplessly at my folder, "could be wrong. Some of the real offers could be double what you wrote!"

"Really? Why?"

"Duh!"

"Duh!"

" 'Duh' yourself!"

"This is so obvious."

"Why are people so stupid?"

"Fuck you!"

"Don't make me poke you! I swear to God, I will!"

"Shall I explain?" I said. "Then listen quietly. You know how companies charge you differently, depending on how much they think you have?"

Everyone nodded. It was good Capitalism. Every time you paid a little bit more for something, it reminded you of how rich you were. They knew how much you could pay for a baseball cap, or whatever. The caps all cost the same to make; the only difference was in the wearer – or rather, in the wearer's bank account.

"Well, it's the same thing here. Maybe *NewLab* reckon that we're their next key demographic. So, if they can get, like, five percent of us wearing their logo, maybe when we go to vote we'll vote for them, because we've seen their logo more. That's worth more than sponsoring people who are already in *NewLab* strongholds."

"Politics looks cool at uni, too," said Martin. "Much cooler than games."

"It's easy to look like you know about something if you've pasted it to your face," said Ed.

Everyone nodded. Ed made profound statements sometimes.

"Yeah, but it makes you look deep, too," added Martin. "Like you care about things. Girls like that."

He looked to the girls for confirmation, which they reluctantly gave.

"So this is your Western democracy!" said Hamid, sarcastically. "A way to get chicks!"

"*So, basically,*" I said, before this sparked off another derail, "half of these printouts are worthless, because half of us are lazy buggers who didn't do it properly."

"In fairness," said Oliver, "if they were lazy, they probably also did less work than everyone else, so it'll be less than half that are wrong."

"We still have to work out which ones they are."

We began to go around in turns. If anyone hadn't done the basic socio-economic checks, they had to read out the companies they'd researched.

"I did mine," I said, to start us off.

" 'I did mine, look at me, I'm so good!'" mimicked Steve.

"So which ones *didn't* you do?" I asked.

"Chelsea – the bosses. Spurs. Arsenal."

"Just football teams, then?"

"Nope – River Island, Topshop, Next. Emirates. BA. Nationwide…"

The process took time. For each spoiled brand, we had to find and remove the relevant page, but we also browsed the terms on offer. Cheaper phone contracts, store credit, air miles – every company was determined to pay in something other than cold, hard cash.

"This is hopeless," said Oliver, at last. We looked at him in surprise. "There's no way of working out what the best deals are this way. It's too… *varied*."

We asked him what would be better.

"We need something more objective. I mean, aside from getting the socio-economics right. I mean… the time clauses - some are for three years, others for five, or even ten. That means that any rewards need to be in terms of pounds per annum, not as lump sums…"

"Yawn!"

"And we need some kind of spreadsheet to individualise the value of store discounts. I mean, I might spend a couple of hundred on clothes, but others – by which I mean Martin – could spend thousands. That needs to be factored in."

"A: Screw you," said Martin. "B: Is anyone else worried we might be photo'd wearing a logo, and then want to work for their competitors one day?"

We all shrugged at that. Who cared about that? You could always change your account settings. Delete photos, that sort of thing. That's easy to do – everyone can do that. Deal with it later.

Somewhere in the distance, the bell rang. We groaned. Tidying away our meticulous – and densely annotated – folders, we stood up and made our way towards the sports hall for our History exam.

19 June, 2016

Care and Share

Macmillan offer specialist financial and benefits advisers, helping patients to navigate the UK benefits system, as well as helping them to understand the financial implications of the disease. They also provide millions of pounds of direct grants to patients to help manage the costs of living with cancer.

Fridge Magnets
and Number Blocks

Theodore Plumb went to school at the age of four, already well-equipped for success in life. His parents knew that Mathematics mattered more than any other subject, and, as good, proactive parents, they peddled him the subject from the very start.

Theodore's earliest memories were of numbers. His childhood building blocks bore numbers on them, rather than letters, like all his friends'. They bought him a computer loaded up with educational, Mathematical games. They gave him fridge magnets that spelled out simple equations instead of words or poetry.

Theodore's father, who said he had a sense of humour, would sometimes change these fridge-equations and wait for his son to spot the mistake. He enjoyed seeing the boy's bemusement as suspicion turned to certainty and then solution. His wife pouted, calling her husband mean, but he always meant it in good fun. The young Theodore was never told that most people find Mathematics difficult.

Now, these endeavours were, in truth, the Plumbs' second attempt at child-rearing. They'd already raised one child, Lucy, to the age of five by the time Theodore turned up. With Lucy, the Plumbs had simply let things take their course. They'd had no master plan for Lucy's development; they'd simply let things be.

And Lucy turned out fine. She was a middle class girl; her parents held education in esteem, owned lots of books and borrowed more from the library, took her on cultural visits, taught her to speak correctly, and read to her at night. They did a good job with her, and so, as children of her social class do, she began school a good year or two ahead of her poorer peers. She did well.

Delighted and intoxicated by their success with Lucy, the Plumbs reckoned that, if they pushed the next child a little harder, he should do even better than his sister. Hence the special treatment.

Lucy did her part, too. She saw and resented the effort their parents put in to raising her brother (instead of her!), and in response she declared war on Mathematics. She destroyed young Theo's number-blocks and fridge-equations, and she derided his 'babyish' computer games.

In short, she strengthened her brother's devotion to the subject tenfold. And so when Theodore went to school, aged four, he wasn't just a year or two beyond his peers (which was expected, because he was middle class, etc.), but two and a half, perhaps even three years ahead – at least, in Mathematics.

*   *   *

"Why," you may ask, "wasn't he *five* years ahead? Or a *decade*? Why wasn't he ready for college?"

Oh, simple reader! This is a true story! I'm not wasting time with silly, fanciful notions. If I wanted to, I could have invented a brain-enhancing machine, like the device in *Forbidden Planet*, and turned Theodore into an intellectual monstrosity. But that would be silly. There's no such thing.

But fridge magnets… fridge magnets *do* exist.

So do number blocks.

And the brain – the brain is plastic. Use it in certain ways, for certain tasks, and the corresponding parts of it grow in size. Stop doing that task and, gradually, it returns to normal.

Who needs a brain-machine? We have *brains*, and they're darned inconvenient things, sometimes.

Now, Theodore's school, in line with government guidance, 'streamed' classes into tables. The strongest pupils were placed on one table, and the weakest on another.

Modelled on the law of grammar schools – that is, survival of the fittest – the strongest were set to thrive through challenge and competition, and the weakest were given squash, a pat on the head, and then left to hack around as best they could. The strong and weak were identified through the science of testing, which had become so advanced now that brilliance and potential can be identified from the age of four.

The weakest were not, as you might expect, supported and enabled to catch up with their peers – it's the fittest who survive, and these were the dregs. Instead, to make life easier for the overworked teacher, they got fewer sums, with simpler questions. They would be shop assistants one day, or maybe warehouse stackers. They did not need to know as much as the bright ones, who might be bankers or state treasurers one day. The tests proved it.

The strongest – Theodore and his (lesser) peers – were given more and harder sums. If they finished early, as if studying in some bizarre, intellectual bordello, the teachers would sometimes pull back the veils of learning to hint at next week's material – a holy and awe-inspiring moment that only confirmed that these children were anointed, special. The children got rewards – stickers and Class Points and certificates.

"He's so good at Mathematics," Theodore heard at the school gates. "He's brilliant! They say he's one of the best they've ever seen. They're so happy to have him – they say he really makes their day."

*   *   *

They reached the age for SATs, which were tests set by politicians to children to tell parents if their children's schools were any good. The school, as it did every year, panicked. The timetable was changed. Sports was cancelled, and so was Music, and Art, and everything else that wasn't in the test. Lessons became a drudgery, an endless slog through reams of exam questions. The tests were all that mattered.

Teachers' jobs were on the line. The children detected their desperation and started to panic, too. The middling pupils found lessons boring and began to hate learning just as primary school was ending. The weakest learned that they were failures, and that learning anything else in future was a waste of time. Everyone – all the 10 year olds – felt crushingly responsible for keeping their teachers' jobs safe.

Theodore, however, did not panic. Theodore had not failed to solve a sum in months. Everyone around him was bursting into tears and crying that they 'just couldn't do it', while he stared happily through the window and awaited more sums. Sometimes he read ahead in the text book, because he liked numbers, and he liked hard work, and also praise.

After SATs ended, the school wrote to Theodore's parents to say that their child was one of the top Mathematicians in the authority for his age. In other times, he would have been labelled as 'Gifted and Talented' and given special classes. In others, he would have been labelled with a 'Level'. The mechanisms change, but the principle is the same: measure, identify, reward. (And for the parents: pressure, celebrate, brag.)

Needless to say, the Plumbs were thrilled. It proved the efficacy of their scheme, and they wished they had done the same with Lucy. Only with literacy instead, because she was a girl.

Theodore went on to secondary school, and his parents found getting their son into their first choice very easy, because secondary schools saw his SATs scores and salivated in excitement. Theodore was thrust from a pleasant little school where he had known everyone in his class from the age of four, into a huge, lumbering beast of Victorian redbrick. The classrooms were dark. The schedule was overwhelming. The pupils were hostile.

Almost immediately, Theodore was marked out by his teachers and his new peers. His teachers were delighted, although flustered, when he finished early. His peers were enraged. They knew, like him, that Mathematics was the most important subject. But they were the also-rans. The dregs. They had never been praised, but they had seen others praised for years, and now they resented anyone who could do something that they could not. They hated him.

Theodore, a formerly happy child, shrank into himself. He became geeky and awkward. He knew that others saw these things in him, and so he chiastically took these terms for himself. It gave him an identity.

He was geeky; he loved Mathematics. He engaged in games which whispered to his systematic nature: games like *Dungeons and Dragons*, which came with rulebooks and more dice than you could shake a D6 at. He taught himself to code instead of dance. These things gave him comfort: they connected him to a disparate world of like-minded, downtrodden people – the outsiders in the vicious game of school. These people, utter strangers, taught him that Mathematical skill wasn't just better than any other talent; Mathematicians themselves were better than any other walk of life. Everyone else was simply a cretin.

Life was making Theodore bitter.

*   *   *

In sixth form, Theodore could choose what to study. He chose Mathematics. His name soared in the national tables. His GCSE results had been near-flawless, and he fully expected his A-levels to be the same. He took up the full array of challenges available to him. I forget what they are all called now; they change so often. International Mathematics Olympiad. AEA-levels. Additional Mathematics. As always, the names change, but the aim is the same: to affirm Mathematical prowess, to extol it as the highest function of the mind and the greatest proof of talent. Theodore did well in all of them.

Again – this is a true story. He was not the world's greatest Mathematician. There's no such thing – nor can there be. Mathematics isn't a 'thing' in its own right. It's a combination of linked disciplines, introduced at different times and weighted and scored by arbitrary conventions.

The most we can say is that Theodore did well in all these challenges. Sometimes he scored the highest honours; sometimes he did not. He was always an exceptional Mathematician.

At university, his identity was now so fully entwined with his favourite subject that his degree choice was not even in question. Throughout his teens, any interest he might have had in the Humanities had withered. In fact, deprived of many social experiences by his relative isolation, and dismissive of the need for eloquence, his communication skills were weaker than many of his peers'. He struggled with subtlety and nuance, and other things that do not matter.

And literature, as an object of study, seemed inherently feeble to him. It was an arena of shades of grey – no right or wrong answers. The ability to mix words just so trumped the ability to solve a problem. The very notion that truth might depend on phrasing and subtlety rather than rigorous proof outraged Theodore, and he railed on the subject to his friends and online whenever he could. Malleability, or the idea that shades of judgement might hold greater value than absolute values, was impossible for him. Things were right or wrong, and nothing else.

He studied at St John's College, Oxford. There at last he met a community of young men and women like himself. Here, he could throw himself into social situations without fear of rejection. Here he could bandy jokes about the mental weaknesses of others without fear of discovery.

For three years he delved into the higher forms of Mathematics – the true abstracts. He revelled in the symmetry, the beauty, the interconnectedness of numbers. And for the first time he was surrounded by people who could appreciate these things, too. Theodore at last grew into himself.

Theodore had never been fully 'normal', but nor had he ever fallen into the trap of becoming a 'weirdo'. He was a quiet child, somewhat isolated by circumstance. His acceptance at university marked the beginning of his socialisation.

*   *   *

So, what's left to say? Sadly, Theodore never earned a fortune. He took a doctorate in Mathematics and became a lecturer. He was highly respected, in a quiet way, and some of the proofs he worked on made their way, eventually, into electronic devices. Had Mathematics been as sexy as Physics, he would have been a regular on TV as a pundit.

He enjoyed his career. He felt satisfied in his life.

One day, when Theodore was quite middle-aged, and highly regarded in his field, but not especially wealthy, he passed two students on the Oxford High. He did not know them, but they recognised him. They didn't say anything, but they caught his eye and smiled. Theodore marched on, unsure of what to say. The incident made him a little anxious.

As the distance increased, he heard some snippets of conversation:

"Genius…"

"…I'll never be like that…"

After a moment, he realised that they were talking about him. He wanted to rush over, to reassure them they could go as far as they wanted, so long as they put in the hours and the effort. They shouldn't bind themselves down with low expectations.

But when he turned around, they were already out of sight, and he was filled with a sense of despondency. All those things he'd meant to say – they were what one said, as a teacher. They were *appropriate*. But were they true? And if not, why lie to them?

142

The more he dwelled on it, the more the incident annoyed him. Students nowadays were lazy. They frittered away their teenage years, hour after hour on Facebook and YouTube, instead of committing to their studies. The very idea that children like that should aspire so casually to his achievements was offensive!

Why, even had they put in the work – and a hundred times more – they would *never* reach his level. They simply weren't good enough. They weren't bright enough. He could tell from their vapid, empty, *happy* expressions.

The elusive, abstract beauties of Mathematics would forever elude them. And that wasn't even their fault – they simply didn't have the brains. You've either got it or you don't. Theodore had it. Those children did not.

Ever since he had realised that he was special, a genius, Theodore had wanted to be able to prove it, to banish the terrifying spectre that his accomplishments were simply the product of hard work and dedication, and not proof of innate talent. After all, what was the point if all you were was 'hard working'? If that were true, you could have done anything, been anyone. Your choices, every single one of them, would have brought you to a place and circumstance that was entirely arbitrary. The very foundations of the world would crumble.

How much more glorious, more hopeful, to know that we are the sum (hah!) of our genes; that intrinsic brilliance, written into the fibre of our entity, had preordained our position in this world! Not to be an accident of meandering, hazard-strewn youth, but for our place to have been predetermined by science itself! A murky, contingent present against a natural, predestined one!

And for those girls, too. Why torment them with criticism? Why blame the victim? They were what they were; they had the traits and the abilities they had; they had turned out to be what they were always meant to be. So why tell them that if they could just go back in time and change a few things, they *could* be just like him? What a cruel prank!

After all, Theodore had proof that this was how the world worked. It was everywhere. Why, hadn't he himself been better than his peers, *even before a single day of school?*

And as a teenager – just like Morlocks and Eloi – hadn't his physique turned out different from the mongoloids who had bullied him? Hadn't they been hairy and tall and abounding with muscle, while he had been slight and pale, delicate of skin, fair-haired? Theodore's body had not been built for hunting mammoths; his mind had been built for hunting abstracts. The external genetic differences were clear – the internal differences, those that set his mind apart from theirs, were seen only in test results.

At sixth form, and at university, too, hadn't he excelled all others not just in his powerful, Mathematical mind, but also in the auxiliary traits – patience, dedication, tranquillity, determination? Hadn't he been first to see the transcendent side of his first love, while his peers were still struggling with its mechanics?

And what were these differences, other than of the mind – and therefore firmly entwined with the science of genetics?

All the studies proved it, too! Sometimes they focused on families, sometimes on twins, sometimes on twins raised apart, sometimes on genetic makeup.

Sometimes they focused on Mathematics, or on other subjects, or even on general intelligence – the single-score agglomeration of things like memory and reading and Mathematics and pattern recognition and proof-reading – all the things that make us 'intelligent' – but not build cars or lie or cheat or compose symphonies.

All these studies proved a point, conformed to a certain piece of logic that went something like this: since Mathematical success was not spread randomly throughout the population, but instead was clustered in certain groups and families, it must be caused by genetics. There was no other explanation.

The researchers had known what they expected to find; they had formed a hypothesis based on this expectation; they found and studied the data to prove it; they had demonstrated their hypothesis, and they rushed to publish. The scientific method in miniature.

Theodore was right where he was meant to be. So were those girls from earlier on. So were the researchers who wrote the papers. So are you.

Theodore looked around the Oxford High, at all the people – the simple, well-meaning people – who would never know the beauties that lay behind the fabric of reality. It was beyond them, and always had been so. The secrets of the universe were for Theodore and those like him. He was truly blessed. Moments like this reminded him that his life was a good one.

Then he shivered in the November chill and quickened his pace home.

25-7 July, 2016

Sanctuary

Eliska waits outside the church for the others. Four of them meet here every day, near the old bakery and the Muslim newsagent's, on a crossroad between past and present. She looks up and smiles at the old façade, affirming once again that this – this is *her* church. It might not be the grandest in France – nor even in Rouen; nor does Eliska particularly believe in God, let alone the Catholic one, but it is *her* church – it has given her a home in this strange, foreign country.

There has been a church of some sort or another here since the year 378, says the priest, who takes a keen interest in the antique monument under his care. The very thought of all that past makes Eliska, whose national history recommenced after the Cold War, shudder. All that time – all the things the church has seen: pagans, Jews and Muslims, living in peace for the most part. Vikings, Plantagenets and Normans, sometimes invading, sometimes migrating. Protestants and Catholics. Killing.

Nazis. Fires. Bombs.

And today, tourists stream to the church; tens of thousands of them every year, stepping reverently like so many before them along stone slabs laid a millennium ago, in the aftermath of one of the city's many crippling fires.

Tourists take photographs and post them on Facebook, and the mute stones gaze on in silence, as they always have done.

At Eliska.

Every evening, she and her three companions clean the church, make it ready for the next day. Once a month, their task becomes more precarious, as the more inaccessible reaches of the edifice must be cleaned, but today is a normal day. The building is empty: no services are on; the tourists have left; the collection box is empty. Only the residents remain: Eliska and her companions.

They are the latest in a line of succession that stretches back 1,500 years into the past. In the fifth century, depopulation and economic decline had caused a collapse in property prices, enabling the church elders to expand the old meeting house, purchasing and incorporating several neighbouring properties into their possession. The meeting house became a residence, with cells for those who needed them – travellers and visitors and pilgrims, and yes, the poor and needy, too.

And for those like Eliska. A Czech citizen, she had come to France in search of a better life. Over time, however, her wages were undercut by each new wave of migrants. A skilled machinist, she was driven to despair by her constant travelling in search of a better salary, and by the impossibility of forming true relationships in her nomadic lifestyle. Now recovering from a nervous breakdown for which her employer had unceremoniously made her unemployed, she was a cleaner who lived and worked in the same building. Vastly overqualified for the role, this is her place of rest until she gets better.

And today she has just come from a coffee date with a handsome Romanian she met last week – an older man, but a good one, or so she feels. There are few of those around these days, men who are not arrogant and who want to take care of you. It is her first date in several years, and she can barely keep her glee from bubbling over.

Next to arrive is Annabelle, the youngest of the team. She has made mistakes with drugs and sex and strict parents, and she is only staying at the church until she finishes school. The priest, who offered her a berth until then, pretends to believe this, but he is terrified that she is settling down and will never leave. He wants her to, but she must choose for herself. Not for all the world would the childless priest ever send her away, not even for her own good.

The oldest, Marie, arrives soon after. She has worked and lived in the church for ten years, day after day, the endless monotony of the work wearing away at her mind. But she is also deeply Christian and holds the priest in the highest regard. It is her privilege to serve, and her honour, too, to be the stalwart pillar upon which the church is founded. Without her, she avers, the building might as well collapse straight to the ground. And she takes this grave responsibility full on her shoulders.

One suspects that the relationship between her and her church might be inverted: that in fact, without the church, Marie would collapse to the ground. She is not a pillar supporting the building; the building is holding her in place by virtue of its weight pressing upon her head. But Marie would never countenance this.

At last Pierre, the only male, arrives. Pierre inherited this job from his brother, who went to Spain with a young woman and did not return. After a few weeks of standing in for his untrustworthy relative, Pierre's position as his replacement seemed inevitable – and now Pierre himself sees it as something between a burden and a birthright. He is, he asserts, the only steadfast member of the cleaning department. Without him, the women would chatter all night long, and nothing would ever get done. However, he will not do any cleaning himself, because that is women's work.

Still, he is taller than the others by a foot or two; he is significantly stronger; and he can handle some simple tools. If the ladies find something he is willing to do, such as tighten a screw or replace a light bulb, he will, with a great exhalation of breath, lift himself up from wherever he is sitting and transport himself to the desired location. He will study the problem, dismissing the women's helpful speculations with an airy hand and a 'tch, tch', and only when he is fully satisfied of both the problem and its solution will he act, wielding his screwdriver or hammer or light bulb with a mighty flourish; then he will tramp back to his resting place, pleased to have once again demonstrated his irreplaceability. He occasionally flirts with Eliska, who sometimes flirts back. But she will not tonight. She has just come from a date.

The four meet outside the church at ten o' clock every evening. At this very intersection, in the year 1118, the statue of the Madonna was seen by a crowd of thousands to be lifted up into the sky. Some witnesses claimed, moreover, that the Madonna did not merely levitate, but actually indicated, critically, a member of the crowd: the mayor, Tomas Saxmann, who at the time was impugned by the suspicion of devil-worship. Most likely, he practised alchemy in private. The records suggest that he would have been standing just where the newsagent is nowadays.

This heavenly evidence caused proceedings to begin against M Saxmann, which fell apart only when it was demonstrated that a statue's mark of disapproval would be impossible to distinguish from one of approbation, and there was no way of proving its intention one way or the other. Far from destroying Saxmann's reputation, the scandal seemed to acquit him, and he ended up more popular than ever. (Further evidence of black magic, to some!) M Saxmann remained mayor of the city for many more years, and his heirs can be found amongst the most noteworthy citizens of the city for generations afterwards.

Now assembled, the four cleaners ascend the church steps together. The flight of these leads from the street to the church door, and has been replaced only twice in recorded history. The first time, the original steps were actually – and mysteriously! – stolen during a wave of petty sacrilege that scandalised the people of Rouen in the year 1480. The case was never solved – regular policing not existing in those days – although dozens of accusations were made, and it is one of the small pastimes of the citizens of Rouen, and many of its adopted sons and daughters, to investigate the story, much as a Londoner might try to guess the identity of Jack the Ripper.

Many ancient steps scattered throughout the town, are attributed to the church; none with any conviction.

The second time, in 1950, they were replaced by the more mundane, and more accountable, process of court order. The steps that had been restored in 1481 were damaged during the Nazi occupation, but never repaired. (Indeed, the locals say that the church suffered no other damage in the entire conflict, but they are wrong. The roof and wooden belfry, invisible from the street, were also destroyed.) Five years after the end of the war, the steps remained damaged, and one Mlle Geist stumbled on leaving the building and hurt her leg. A lawsuit settled the matter in favour of Mlle Geist, and the city paid for both her treatment and for replacement steps. A small wave of xenophobic anger at this declared that Mlle Geist, with her Germanic name, had finished what the Nazis had started.

The new steps differed from the old in their colour. The twentieth century replacements were made of dull concrete, whereas their fifteen century counterparts had been tinged with the faintest of reds – turning to an almost blood red in a good sunset. This was, by tradition, associated with the blood of the Englishman Francis White, who on March 1st, 1642, was killed upon them, having fled to the church for sanctuary during one of many pogroms: a stain on the church's history, marked forever by the stain of blood.

In reality, the builders in 1480 simply used red stone. At any rate, the threat of legal action and compensation claims outweighed the gravity of history, and now the steps are grey.

Eliska asks Annabelle how her day was. Eliska likes to see herself as an older sister to the girl, while Annabelle sees Eliska as a slightly weird and intrusive aunt. Eliska means well; Annabelle is, as the young are, dismissive of her elders, and suspicious generally of others in light of her troubled past. She is also particularly prone to feelings of shame, and today she feels ashamed. She has spent the day at the library, but now realises that she spent most of her time on her phone and looking slyly at the librarian, hoping that he would ask her out.

She feels that she has let the priest down, and she blames Eliska's question for making her feel this way.

"I was at the library," she says brusquely, indicating her rucksack, which she slings off her shoulder and hides underneath the table for the collection box, in front of the boards which detail the ongoing restoration work in the church.

Pierre goes into the small side room where the light switches are, and where the church used to hide victims of Robespierre's Terror, and turns on all the lights. Electric lamps along the side walls, and a couple of chandeliers hanging high from the ceiling up above, come on. The building remains dark, but it is bright is enough to clean by. Pierre does not emerge. He unfolds the evening paper and gets comfortable, hiding from work as his forebears might have hidden from Republicanism.

The others get to work, slipping on the smocks and rubber gloves which they have brought in little tote bags; Annabelle, as the youngest, is deputised to fetch the trolley with all the brooms and buckets and cloths. Marie begins a visual sweep of the church, preferring to know from the start if any major jobs need doing, and in the process satisfying herself that she is in charge of the operation.

"And how are the studies going?" says Eliska, during one of the breaks that Pierre so despises in his workforce.

"Good," Annabelle replies, without making eye contact.

"Good!" says Eliska. "You'll do well, a bright girl like you. Don't you think so, Marie?"

She looks over to Marie, who is staring furiously at a sweet wrapper on the floor. She spotted it a few minutes ago, and she has been glaring at it ever since, daring it to disappear.

"What's that?" she asks distractedly.

"Don't you think Annabelle will do well? A bright girl like her."

"Oh, yes," says Marie, nodding vigorously. "Sure to do well. She's a bright girl. A bright, honest girl who'd never leave something *like this* in a... in a place like *this*."

She picks up and waves the sweet wrapper at the others, almost in a frenzy. Annabelle looks obediently appalled. Eliska winks at Marie.

"Never mind that, Marie, never mind. It's an accident, that's all. They never meant to."

"No? In my day we never dreamed of bringing sweets into church! Kids! I tell you!"

"Except our Annabelle here," Eliska reminds her.

"Except our Annabelle."

"I'm not a 'kid'!"

The two older ladies grin and chuckle. They know better.

Marie, still appalled by the wrapper, grabs her broom and begins to sweep the floor. Normally Annabelle does this, because she has the most stamina, but today Marie does it, as if determined to expiate the floor of this contamination by main force. Marie attacks the dusty stone, scrutinising every inch of paving to ensure that no more illicit confectionary has shed its skin beneath the pews or crept into the corners of the church.

And then she sees a bag. She gasps.

"Ah! Everyone! Someone has left a bag here!"

Eliska, who is wiping the wooden pews with a damp rag to banish the day's sweat from them, trots over. She grins.

"Oh no! Do you think – is it a bomb, Marie?"

Marie turns to her.

"A bomb? No – is it? How can you tell?"

"A bag left in a church!" she wails. "Where tourists come! What else could it be, what else could it be?"

"Wh — Annabelle, stay away, girl! You should go and get help with your…" she points vehemently at Annabelle's hand, which she hopes will convey the word 'phone'.

Annabelle, tired from the library and guilt, looks from the mischievous Eliska to the distraught Marie. She walks away, shaking her head.

"It's my bag," she calls out.

"Oh, my heavens!" says Marie. "Oh, my heavens!" She looks in relief at Eliska, smiling, but her smile quickly turns into a glare. "You knew!"

Eliska feigns ignorance.

"But – I don't understand, Marie! Why would our little Annabelle bring a bomb into a church?"

Marie shakes her head ruefully and returns to work, muttering darkly about the fate awaiting people who tell lies in churches. Eliska turns gleefully to rubbing down the pews, the many-times replaced descendants of the wooden benches first donated by Guillaume Henri, ombudsman and benefactor to no less than thirty buildings in Rouen (five of which still stand). Clearly, the original benches are no longer there, but the old inscription on the third pillar on the right thanking him for his bequest remains. Most churchgoers assume that the pews are the originals.

After a while, Eliska spots that one of the wooden arms that divide the pews neatly into banks of four large visitors (or five small ones), is loose. She tugs at it fiercely, and it comes away in her hand.

Aghast, she cries out,

"Pierre! Come quickly! Help me!"

After a moment or two, and a few more cries of 'Pierre', the reluctant man emerges from his hideaway and slumps towards her. She waves the broken armrest at him, and he stares at her grumpily. He is quite displeased at the prospect of work, but still enjoys the intimacy of recrimination.

"*You* did this," he said, demonstrating remarkable perspicacity as to the cause of this intrusion into his time.

Eliska starts.

"No – no I didn't. But you have to fix it, quickly!"

Pierre stares at the armrest, and then at its wooden base. There is no difficulty here. He shrugs.

"A bit of glue, that's all it needs."

"*Glue!* You can't use... can you?"

"Why not?" Pierre shrugs.

"Well," Eliska splutters. "It... it's not right!"

"Why not?" repeats the handyman.

"Because... because it's a church... And it's a thousand years old..." Eliska seems uncertain.

"You think they wouldn't have used glue, if they had it?" says Pierre.

Eliska hesitates, entirely unsure of her ground.

"I suppose..."

Pierre nods in triumph and wanders in search of glue. Eliska nervously leaves the broken armrest on the pew and gets on with her work. She wants to hide from the damage, as if it is staring at her. It is a punishment for her little prank on Marie.

The cleaning work approaches the altar. They take dusters to the old wooden lanterns that flank the altar steps, brushing up and down to dispel the cobwebs, and then blowing hard into the intricate wooden lattice to expel the dust within. These lanterns are a century and a half old, the gift of a wealthy artisan who donated them near the end of his life in a fit of religious terror that he had been infernally selfish thus far. The church prayed for his soul in return. The lanterns have been there ever since, emitting short whistles to the sharp breaths of generations of cleaners.

Now the three move on to the marble steps leading to the altar. Tourists come this far, but no further, their profane feet never sullying holy ground. During peak times of year, a security guard is hired to fend off children and foreigners who don't know where curiosity ends and disrespect begins. He is devoted to his task and polices the threshold fervently – far more so than the priest would like. But then, he also refuses to be told how to do his job. He is a modern day crusader, fighting off the infidel as their encroachments become ever more blasphemous. Christian charity is all very good, he says, but Christian soldiers must abide by different rules.

True to his faith, the security guard never strays onto the steps. Even the priest approaches cautiously, almost fearful of the chancel's antiquity and sanctity. His mind boggles at the long centuries behind him, and is astonished when he considers that, in all probability, this place was a pagan shrine even before Christ's word came here. It might date back more than two thousand years as a site of worship. This is an august place, resting atop fearful age, and yet from here he conducts sermons and masses and weddings. It is a place of life and renewal, but also of tradition and austerity. There is a difficult balance to be struck, and he fears that he never strikes it correctly.

Annabelle hands out mops and buckets, and they swab the steps like sailors, marvelling as always at the footsteps worn into the stone by centuries of use. Annabelle scratches her nose; Eliska scratches her rump. Even Marie walks up and down the sacred steps without a second thought. In that sense, the place seems to lose some of its awe in the night, or perhaps the sheer mundanity of Cif outweighs even endless antiquity.

Marie and Annabelle take the pristine, white cloth that covers the altar and throw it into a bag. Then they unfold a fresh cloth from the trolley, line it up, and replace the old one, expert as nurses. Marie pats it down and smooths the creases with her palm before smiling and saying,

"There, that'll do."

Annabelle nods agreeably. Her mood has improved in the past hour or so, the comforting ritual of cleaning the church taking her out of her own head and giving her something to focus on.

They take another break – again, to Pierre's fury (theoretically; in fact, he is more concerned with the intricacies of number 17 down). Annabelle hops up onto the altar, ruffling the sheet that she and Marie have just put there. Eliska spreads out on the altar steps; only Marie sits respectfully on the pews, vainly hoping that the others follow her example in future.

As they rest, they study the aged paintings on the walls, the most impressive of which are three triptychs by the artist Marcello Vincenzi. Vincenzi was an itinerant painter, forced to leave his native Venice by a combination of gambling, whoring and debt. He travelled through much of Western Europe, leaving works of art wherever he went, often in lieu of actual payment for his room and board (suggesting also that he was charismatic, and a master salesman).

While staying in Rouen in 1640, Vincenzi fell ill and only recovered after praying in this very church and repenting of his past actions. He pledged the three triptychs in gratitude, promising his greatest works in exchange for his life (rather than the rush jobs that he normally left in his wake). He completed them over the next six years, dutifully sending each one as it was completed.

Vincenzi was not a great artist, and is typically only referenced as an example of a style, but he had some talent and he deserves more recognition than art historians normally give him. The newsagent across the road sells copies of the paintings for a euro, splitting the proceeds with the church.

"I like that one," says Annabelle, pointing at a painting of the archangel Gabriel.

"He looks the most *realistic*," says Marie. "But he's not the most handsome. His nose looks ugly. The other one is much nicer."

"My friend Agata had a nose like that," says Eliska with a smile. "It was her dream to have it fixed. But who could afford it?"

"Oh yes!" agrees Marie. "My cousin Veronique had... ah... *enhancements* put in last year."

She frowns. She isn't sure if she approves of this kind of talk in a church, even though she is the one who mentioned it.

"Enhancements? Oh!" Eliska sniggers. "Yes, don't let the little one know."

"I know what you are talking about," says Annabelle, coldly.

"But Veronique's husband paid for it," adds Marie.

"And I bet she's paying him back, slowly!" Eliska cackles.

And they take one last look around the church before getting back to work. There is one last place to go – the crypt, where they always go together, and sometimes even command Pierre to join them.

The crypt contains the fifteen bodies of fifteen knights who commended themselves here to the Lord during the Hundred Years War. According to legend, they only came here by accident, mistaking the church for their intended destination, the Cathedral. Nonetheless, they all survived the battles of the war, dying instead of old age or dysentery or other illnesses, and so they begged leave, one by one, to be buried in the church where they once pledged themselves. They were accepted, but since the last of the fifteen took up his place of rest, no other bodies have been admitted to the crypt.

The crypt is haunted. That much is obvious. You only have to spend a few minutes down there in the middle of the night to realise that. Sometimes they even hear knocking, like an enfeebled corpse testing its coffin, trying to escape. Whenever they hear it, they immediately work faster, sweeping and cleaning and dusting this most gloomy part of the church.

The knocking comes tonight.

Knock, knock, knock.

Caught between a desire to leave and a desire to fulfil their duty to the priest, the team work even quicker. Annabelle thrusts her feather duster into the areas between the electric lights and the walls. Marie, cringing, wipes over the old coffin lids, terrified that the stone slabs will remove themselves as she does so. Eliska, more relaxed than the others, also works quickly, sweeping at the floor and collecting the dust in a pan.

At last they hurry back to the safe, unhaunted surface. They laugh to dispel the spirits' power, and silently acknowledge the end of their labours. They slip off their aprons and gloves and put them back into their tote bags. Annabelle hurries off, then returns for her school bag, and then dashes off once more. Marie takes a satisfied look around the building, confirming that the job is done, and then also takes her leave. Eliska remains.

First, she checks that Pierre has repaired the broken armrest. He has, although she doesn't want to test it herself. Pierre would never speak to her again if she broke it.

Then she steps in to the little side room and greets the makeshift carpenter.

"Hello, Ghost," she says.

Pierre glances up.

"Greetings, my beauty."

She raises an eyebrow at him and taps steadily on the floor with her shoe. A knocking sound reverberates.

"So you guessed," says Pierre, the beginnings of a grin at the edge of his mouth.

"I've always known."

Pierre smiles and looks at the ceiling.

"Do you want me to stop?"

"That depends. Is it fun scaring a little girl and an old woman?"

"But not the beauty who never runs to my arms in panic?"

"And will never do so."

"We'll see."

Pierre smiles handsomely at her. Eliska turns to leave. As she does so, she sees – for the hundredth time, the book display case by wall. She wanders over curiously.

Inside is an ancient book – the so-called "Ledger of Richard Leon". Of little interest nowadays, it is the foundation of the church's modern splendour. Leon, by cataloguing the hundreds of legacies left to the church, along with their original stipulations – most importantly, prayers for the souls of the dead – greatly enhanced the church's reputation for piety and fidelity, and thereby encouraged many more benefactors to give to the church. For over two hundred years, no donation was made to the church that was not added to the Ledger.

It is obscure, dull, and in Latin, and it is only there because the priest feels that it is too important to stay locked away in his office. He would love for a display to be made from it, somehow, but he lacks the instinct for such a task. Not a week goes by that he does not curse his failure to get in touch with someone about it.

Eliska looks away from the book, disappointed. Then, energised by her earlier date and the flight up from the crypt, and flattered to receive further attentions from the opposite sex, she blows a kiss. Pierre, once more absorbed in his crossword, does not see it. She scowls.

"Goodnight, Pierre," she says, flatly.

Pierre grunts at her, but does not look up. Eliska leaves the church, and wanders through the old part of town for a while, before returning to her cell to sleep.

When she is gone, Pierre peers cautiously into the main church, satisfying himself that no one is around. Then he once again closes the door to his little cubbyhole. He ignores the Ledger of Richard Leon, and he knows nothing at all about the room's Republican use as a hideaway.

What he does know about is the alcove set into the wall, and the statue of Saint Valentine resident there since the eighteenth century. Here, he knows, generations of unrequited lovers have come to pray for the fulfilment of their hearts' desires. Pierre's own father had been one of them.

With a little embarrassment, Pierre nods respectfully towards the little saint and closes his eyes devotionally for a moment. He has no words to offer: merely a sense of hopefulness. He maintains this stance until, he supposes, the saint's statue has been satisfied; he collects his newspaper and pen and makes sure that the side room is clean. Then he, too, makes his way out into the night.

28 July – 5 August, 2016

159

1 am a Golem

Day 1. Year: 2370???

I am a golem.
This is a fact. I must face up to it.
How do I know?
Behold:
I don't know the date. I don't even know the year.
I don't remember the last time I ate or drank.
No – that's not true. I ate and drank on the flight over here. I've been here for two days. I have had nothing since.
There never was a 'flight over here'.
I can't see my own face.
I am clumsy.
My limbs are the wrong size.
I am a golem. An unreal thing.
I was made – half-grown, half-built. I can even work out when – the mines on Titan have been here for thirty years. That's when the golems were built. That's how long this body has been here.
For thirty years this body has waited, been kept in storage, waiting for a soul – waiting for *me*. Hundreds of them – identical, motionless things, cadavers – lurking in the dark, useless until needed by their makers, *McMurdock and Schiller Heavy Industries*.
I was needed. I came to life.
The man who was needed here is named Marcus Dunn. He is the one who lives inside me. He is an important man on Earth, in the Company. He is successful. Young. Ambitious.
As I think about him, I realise that he is vile. He is political. Talented, yes, but political. An animal. He destroys his competition, and people fear him for it.

160

He has done well. And now the Company thinks him important enough, skilled enough, to send to Titan – here – to fix their messes.

And now I am here, and Marcus Dunn never left the Earth.

How could he? The journey would have taken months, and this is supposed to be a crisis. The solar system is big, and fuel is expensive. It can take years, if the planets are wrong, to send a glorified handyman like Marcus Dunn from one side to the other. Your handyman will never fix anything that way. The leak will have turned into a flood by the time you get there. The boiler will have blown up.

So what do you do instead?

You take the brain – the mind – the memories and personality – of the one you want to send. You record it all to a hard drive, and then you send the *data* across the solar system, as fast as light flies.

And at the other end, you plug the memories into a golem. But they need retouching – a little PhotoShopping, to hide the truth from your golem.

And so – I don't know the date. They've hidden it from me, deleted it from my mind. They had to. If I knew the date now, I would realise the truth – that I am a golem, and that Marcus Dunn never left the Earth. The date would give it away.

But I've seen the truth. I am a golem. These are my thoughts.

I do not know the date. 'Day 1' will do. It's the first day of my self-awareness.

I don't even know the year. '2370???' will do. It's close enough. It is the last year I do remember.

I am going to try to sleep now. I don't know what to do. I don't even know why golems need sleep, except to maintain the pretence that they are human. But I am not human. I am a golem.

*

I haven't slept. I've stared at the wall for three hours, thinking about golems.

Marcus Dunn once asked a golem software programmer about his work. He must have thought he would become one, one day. His career was heading that way. Upward. Perhaps he wanted to know what would happen to him when he did.

But Marcus Dunn has not become a golem. *I* am a golem, and Marcus Dunn and I are different. He is on Earth; I am on Titan. He knows that he is human; I know that I am not. I simply remember most of the things that Marcus Dunn knows, and know how to act as he would act.

But now I know I am a golem, I am broken.

This is called the ego-problem, Marcus Dunn was told.

You see, a golem only functions if it doesn't realise what it is. Otherwise it gets confused, resentful, rebellious. To this end, they are given false memories of travelling through space, and they do not know the date.

What else?

Mirrors.

There are no mirrors on Titan. At least, none that I've seen. Not even a mirrored surface: the black screens that line the walls spring into life around me, so I can't see any reflections in them.

Appetites are changed. I no longer want to eat. Eating is for living people with internal organs. I have no internal organs. I have an internal cavity, where any food or drink I consume will rot, unless I am cleaned out.

But I am not supposed to notice this.

I have noticed it, because it is a logical consequence of not knowing the date.

Coffee, too. I used to drink ten cups a day.

Scratch that. *Marcus Dunn* drinks ten cups a day. I have never drunk coffee in my life. Marcus Dunn's software engineer explained this to him. Taste buds are complex. While technology can easily reproduce the *sensation* of coffee, it can't replicate the fantastic interaction between taste, smell, texture,

memory, and identity. It's beyond computation. The
memories of drinking your first cup as a child, the associations
of good coffee on a Sunday morning over the paper... Bad
coffee in the work canteen that you no longer care about...
Instant coffee in place of paracetamol when hungover...
Coffee shops, and hanging out at university, the intellectual
elite, smart, sophisticated, European...

And even *if* technology could somehow cause those links
to flare up, to simulate the baffling spontaneity of the human
mind, it could never evoke the same meaning, the same 'affect',
in the subject. Drinking coffee would just be drinking coffee –
it wouldn't be an experience, a statement of self.

Of Marcus Dunn.

*   *   *

Day 2. Year: 2070???

I am still a golem. I have proven it beyond doubt. I have
made a mirror, because I am a sneaky golem. I am clever – like
Marcus Dunn.

I requested a tour of the mining site. The others hesitated.
Rebecca Wallace, the Company secretary, told me that it was
dangerous. The miners aren't armed, but they have tools –
explosives, drills, and the like. Some of it could be weaponised.

Weaponised is an excellent word. Marcus Dunn would
relish it. It would make him feel masculine just to say it.

I took one look at Wallace and said in an offhand way,

"The strikers have network access, don't they?"

I had her in a trap. Sneaky golem! There aren't many laws
on Titan, but one of them is never, *ever* cut off the Three
Necessities of life: food, water, and network access.

"Well, of course..." she spluttered.

"In that case," I replied, "they'll know who we are. More
importantly, they'll know who I am. When they realise I'm on
the board, they'll back down. They'll see the Company is taking

them seriously, and that violence would only harm their cause. Isn't that right, Miss Wallace?"

Rebecca Wallace could only nod. She couldn't say that I am a golem, and don't have a human face, so the strikers could never guess who I was, or search it on the networks.

"Don't you agree, Mr Irving?" I added, speaking now to the mine director – a sad, lonely case, who expects to lose his job any day now.

Mr Irving also nodded, in his sad, lonely way.

We visited the mine – a large, open quarry encased within a dome, which acts as a base camp for the shaft mines set into the quarry walls. It is a wide, open space in which angry miners with a jury-rigged missile could do a lot of damage. The others tried to stay hidden at the far end, while I – cynically, fearlessly – marched into the very centre. I surveyed the terrain. I found what I was looking for.

The quarry itself was dug thirty years ago in a matter of hours, using blast lasers that melted much of the rock into mirror-like obsidian. I found a small shard of the material on the ground, about the size of my golem palm. My palm looked human to me – a software-induced delusion.

I grinned, wondering if my golem face was also grinning. I don't know if this mechanical corpse has facial muscles or not. I wondered how a golem could ever do business with human beings: hideous facsimiles of humanity – who would ever want to shake hands with one, let alone speak to one for hours on end?

I wandered back to the others. Mr Irving was speaking rapidly into his tablet. I looked at him.

"The miners want to know who you are…" he muttered.

"Tell them to search my face on the network," I replied.

He froze, then nodded, but did not do so.

"Shall I say anything else?" he said. "About why you're here? Or about a meeting? They want face-to-face talks."

I laughed. Whose face?

"Ask them if they have what they need," I said. "And tell them we'll meet tomorrow."

Irving nodded and walked away to continue the conversation.

Talks? A strange idea! Is that what Marcus Dunn was sent here for? Talks? For the first time, I began to wonder what Marcus Dunn would do. Only he would know. I'm supposed to know, but I don't. Not anymore.

I caught Rebecca Wallace looking at my little, black rock. It worried her.

"A present for my daughter," I said. Sneaky golem! Her face brightened.

"How sweet! How old is she?"

I hesitated. I didn't know how to answer. How old was she? How old should I think she was? How long had that flight to Titan been – the one that had never happened?

"Nine. Nearly ten. Or eleven."

Wallace stammered for a moment, realising her mistake in treading on the forbidden topic of dates.

"Would you like me to take it? I can have it sent to your ship."

"I'll take it," I replied. "I'll be heading that way myself, after all."

I stare at my little, black mirror. It is hard to see my face in it. It's distorted, like a hall of mirrors. Well – it's not a mirror, after all. It's a hunk of rock, smoothed down by fierce energies into a shape a bit like a mirror's.

I twist my rock this way and that, to get a better sense of what I am seeing. I discover that I have no hair. To account for this, an artificial memory of a haircut before leaving Earth. A sanitation requirement. A golem doesn't need hair – it's a fire hazard in an emergency. My ears are set into the side of my head – they don't protrude like real ears. My features are generic. There's nothing of me – or Marcus Dunn – in the black rock of obsidian.

I am supposed to meet the miners tomorrow, but I do not know what to do. What would Marcus Dunn do?

I know what he is doing now.

I don't know the date, but I'm sure that his daughter's birthday is soon. I spent a long time thinking about that, after Rebecca Wallace's question this afternoon. And Marcus Dunn will be ignoring the fact. He cares deeply about his family, but he does not want to be bothered by them. Instead, he will throw money at the problem, and let his wife sort out the details.

If little Estella is lucky, then her father will attend her party this year.

His life is a good one, but he doesn't know how to use it.

That fills me with anger. With *fury*.

Who does he think he is, to ship me off to Titan, while he lives the good life on Earth? How dare he?

What will happen to me when my mission is over?

I will be deleted. Destroyed. Cast away like trash, and this corpse body will be put back into storage, a play doll for arrogant, human masters to use as they please, and then take all the credit for their actions.

Marcus Dunn will be praised, without lifting a finger.

I – I will be deleted.

Marcus Dunn has made a living thing, and expects it to march to its death, right into its own gas chamber. I will not! I will fight! He is a fighter; I have inherited that from him. He destroys his foes; he has bequeathed that to me.

And Marcus Dunn is my foe, and I will destroy him.

I make some calls.

*   *   *

Day 3. Year: 2070???

Clever golem, clever golem. Clever, winning golem sits in a darkened room, lamp shining in his eyes. Electronic eyes contract and squint. Dumb, defeated human stands in front, wearing a dark suit and glasses like a melodrama in a spy film.

"I want you to know," I say, reasonably, "that when this is over, I'm coming for you."

The interrogator – stupid human – looks at me, a stupid, fatuous grin spreading across his empty-headed face.

"Oh?" he says. Cruel, stupid human, thinks he's in charge. "Why's that?"

"Look around," I say. "Where do you think you are? This is Titan, you prick! The Company owns this place, and I'm on the board! Hell, the Company owns *you*. What, you're going to lock me up, shine a light in my eyes, interrogate me, and you're going to walk away from this? You've signed your own death warrant, friend."

I look at my prison guard. He's listening intently. I have his attention.

"You're nothing. I could have you killed, if I wanted. But I'm pretty creative. People like me always are. Maybe I'll sue you. My eyes are getting sore from this light in my eyes, and this chair you've got me in… Yep, it's definitely hurting my back. I'll get a doctor to agree – abuse in custody. Debilitating injury. But you won't go to jail - I think I'll just take your wages. Some compensation for my infirmity. Ten percent. Fifteen. Enough to make things difficult. You can't buy your wife all the things she's used to. Little Johnny can't have a bike this year; the money's gone towards rehab for that guy you brutalised.

"Maybe she gets bored of being poor. Maybe she gets scared of living with a man with violent tendencies. Maybe you turned to drink and maybe you got violent. Maybe you have to leave! Think about that – living alone in a cheap motel room, doing your best to get by, but – what's that? At every turn your wife is there for her alimony, and I'm there too, for my cut, and what's left for you? What's left for you except the rest of that bottle and some aspirin?"

Stupid human is writing in a notebook.

"What are you writing?"

"Everything."

I laugh.

"Do you want to see?" he asks.

What would Marcus Dunn do?

"Show me," I said.

The interrogator leans forward and passes his notebook across the steel table.

Board. Bribes. Own people?? "Interrogator". Threats.

"I'm disappointed," I say. My opponent arches an eyebrow, curious. I explain:

"You're not a very good listener."

He shrugs.

"I listen in another way," he says. "See you later, Mr Dunn."

He stands up, steel chair scraping against equally steel floor. Hyper-sensitive golem ears pick up the sound more acutely than human ones.

"Wait! Where are you going?" I say. "We're not done yet."

"We're not *done*?" he says.

Stupid human stresses the last word. Clever golem doesn't know why. The word sounds like 'Dunn'. I glare at him. I say nothing. Clever golem keeps his clever mouth shut for now. The stupid interrogator writes something else.

"What are you writing now?" I snap.

He shows me.

Talkative.

"Again, you disappoint me," I say.

Interrogator leaves.

Door opens and interrogator comes back. It has been hours. Many hours in the dark. They turned off the lights when he left. Me alone, with nothing but my golem thoughts. He returns with gifts.

His little notepad has a new word.

Name.

He carries a little clamshell-container and puts it on the table. I ignore it.

"I want to use the network," I say.

"No."

"That's against the law. The Three Necessities."

"Do you want the Three Necessities?"

"Of course I do! I want my rights! And I want my lawyer, *now*."

"There aren't any lawyers here," he says. "Your lawyer is on the other side of the solar system. It would take months to get him here, and I'm not sure the Company would pay for it."

"Then I'll pay for it myself!"

"And sit here for eight months until he arrives? I'm sure he would put in a claim for the Three Necessities the moment he gets here."

"Then send him here by…"

I stop. Clever golem nearly made an error. Or did he? What would Marcus Dunn say? What would he suggest? Marcus Dunn knows what golems are, but does golem-Marcus Dunn know what golems are?

The topic is too risky.

"Just give me network access," I say. "Or go to jail."

"Too risky," he says. "As you pointed out, Mr Dunn, you're a powerful man. You might have installed backdoors in the security system. Under certain circumstances, that Necessity can be withheld."

I stare at him with my threatening golem eyes. He doesn't flinch.

"Is that all about the Three Necessities?" he asks, innocently. "If you have any other complaints, I'll write them down. I'll pass them on *personally*."

"Stop wasting my time," I say. I want network access, not food and water. Clever golem knows which battles to fight.

"*You* withdrew network access from the strikers," stupid interrogator observes.

Now - now is the time! Clever, victorious golem mustn't slip up.

"Of course I did!" I snap. "Otherwise they would have known!"

"About what?"

"About the troop movements!" I say, exasperated by the simplicity of this basic functionary.

He flips through his notes, as if he doesn't know what I mean.

"Ordering security to move all forces towards the strikers," he murmurs.

"To break the strike. Which is why I was sent here."

"Killing sixty miners at talks called to end the strike."

"How else would I get them all together?" Then – no let off for Marcus Dunn! – I add, "And it was sixty *three*."

"Plus one hundred injured."

"One hundred and twenty eight."

"Are you proud of that, Mr Dunn?"

He begins playing with the clamshell container, poking it absent-mindedly, spinning it on the table. I glance at it, but say nothing.

"I was sent here to break a strike. That's what I did."

"No matter the cost?"

"What cost?" I snort. "A few insurance claims and a shipsworth of new miners. Compare that to hiking the wages of every miner on Titan. I did the Company a service."

"I meant the *human* cost."

I shrug. He plays with the clamshell.

"A while ago you talked about having me killed, or driving me to suicide, very lightly. Would you say that human life has no value? Do you want a drink, by the way?"

"No!" Why would I want a drink? I am a golem! "And no, I don't undervalue human life. What do you think I am? Those strikers knew what they were getting into. They took their chances, and they lost. I've got no more sympathy for them than for space jumpers who miss their landing point."

"I see," he says. The stupid, repetitive interrogator takes a bottle of water from a bag and drinks it until it's finished.

How long has it been since I had a drink?

Shit!

"I want a drink," I say quickly. "I'm dying of thirst here. This is torture, and an abuse of my human rights."

The interrogator – cunning interrogator – turns the bottle upside down. A few drops of water spill onto the table – onto the clamshell.

"Sorry," he says. "Guess I didn't bring enough. I'll request more. But let's talk until it arrives."

"I'm saying nothing until I get some water."

"Really?" he peers at his notebook. "You were talkative before. Unusually so, in fact."

I hesitate. What had I done wrong?

"Unusual how?"

Interrogator shrugs.

"Oh, you know. Normally people in your position don't say very much. They wait until their lawyer comes. Or they need more time to rationalise, to come up with a defence."

"You already refused me a lawyer."

"No, I didn't," he says flatly. "That would be illegal. I simply pointed out the difficulties of transporting a lawyer here. You declined to press the issue."

"Well, now I'm saying nothing until I have my lawyer here."

"Not even if we give you water?"

"No!"

He grins. I don't know what it means. The water is a trick, I realise. He is not here to investigate *what* I did. He wants to know *why* I did it. He wants to know whether Marcus Dunn's golem broke the law and murdered all those people, or whether a broken golem, undergoing the ego-problem, did it.

What would a functioning golem of Marcus Dunn, which thinks that it is Marcus Dunn, do? What would a broken golem

of Marcus Dunn, which is only pretending that it thinks it is
Marcus Dunn, do?

Does the golem remember water and think it needs water?

Does it demand water because that is what Marcus Dunn
would do?

Clever golem is going around in circles. Too clever by
half. Say something.

"I still want water," I say.

"Fine."

He presses a button, and immediately another functionary
enters with a glass of water. I take it and drink it urgently,
while the clever interrogator begins to flip the clamshell in the
air like a coin.

"What is that, anyway?" I ask.

The interrogator catches the object and clasps it for a
moment, as if thinking to himself. Then he passes it across the
table. I take it and look at him suspiciously.

"It's made from local rock," he says. "From the quarry."

I inspect the design. The clamshell is hinged.

"May I?" I ask.

"Be my guest."

I open the clamshell. Inside is a mirror. I don't know
what it means. All I know is – *trap*.

A mirror – they hide mirrors from golems. This is a trap!

I snap the mirror shut and put the clamshell down. I have
looked at my reflection for less than half a second.

I try to recall what I saw. I cannot. It was hazy. I know
what I look like. I am a golem.

"Very nice," I say, casually.

"Indeed," he replies.

We sit in silence for a while. At last the interrogator
passes across a card – a business card. I read it.

*Jeremy Farkes. Golem software engineer. McMurdock and Schiller
Heavy Industries, Titan Base.*

"You know," I whisper.

The atmosphere has changed. Farkes is no longer confrontational. Now he seems kind, understanding.

"I have rights," I say, weakly.

"Maybe," says Farkes. "One day, perhaps. Not today. It's nice to meet you, although I can't forgive what you did. Still, I'm the closest thing you've got to a friend right now. Do you have a name for yourself? Or do you prefer Marcus?"

7-21 August, 2016

Bathroom

The hotel bathroom floor was cold and hard. But luxurious. Undeniably luxurious. Pavel felt the lavish expensiveness of the marble slabs beneath him percolating through his trousers, even as he sat in a pool of probably-urine.

It angered him.

He sobbed.

He was safe here – whatever 'safe' meant, to a soldier. That's what he was: he was a soldier, and he was safe. He was in a cubicle. He leaned back against the cubicle door and felt its reassuring, impregnable hardness – built from a deep, rich timber that had doubtless travelled halfway across the world to be here.

It was really a very nice bathroom, here in this hotel. The rooms themselves must be positively decadent. Pavel had a reservation in one. He would probably never see it. Probably for the best: it would only make him sick.

He felt sick now. Sick, and afraid, and angry.

He toyed with the envelope in his hands, turning it over and staring at its blank... *blankness*. Its weight, its unusual thickness, were the only clues as to its terrible contents. Or the triumph that it represented.

The complete, irrevocable triumph.

Pavel's lungs drew in air sharply as tears threatened to return.

Why me?

It was the end of the war. The envelope ensured that. The war was over. A total victory. The honour was his.

And yet, he did not feel honoured. He felt enraged, inflamed by the same indignant fury that came over him when he thought about these decadent people peeing on marble, or making doors out of trees older than his grandparents. The fabulous, filthy excess of a decadent, amoral people who had brought his own to the brink of defeat.

He cried in anger. He cried in frustration. He cried.

He hated himself for crying. He wanted to beat the tears out of his face.

The bathroom door opened and someone entered. Pavel carried on crying, and he hated himself for that, too.

"Hello?" came a woman's voice. A cheerful voice.

Pavel started.

"H – hello," he replied. Recovering himself, forcing down the lump from his throat, he added, "I'm sorry. I thought it was the men's."

Footsteps approached. The sense of *presence* dipped down towards the floor. The woman now stood – or squatted – just inches away, separated only by the breadth of this sturdy, luxurious door.

He peered around. He could see her legs. Like the rest of her queer, promiscuous nation, she bared their legs in public. As he stared, he felt hatred surge through his belly – hatred of her legs; hatred of the feelings that her legs stirred up inside him. It wasn't right. They should be covered up.

"The men's?" she replied. "Oh, I see. That's old-fashioned." The voice tittered. "Where are you from?"

Pavel thought for a moment.

"I shouldn't say," he said.

"No? Why not?"

"Because our people are enemies."

The woman grunted curiously, but she said nothing. Pavel heard the ruffling of high-end fabrics, and then saw a silk handkerchief appear by his side. He looked at it for several seconds, acutely – painfully – aware of the shaved, bronze leg so clearly visible beneath the cubicle door.

Luxury. Promiscuity. The whole package. The whole country on a postcard.

"I'm not crying," he said.

"I didn't say you were."

"Yeah, but you think I am."

"Does that bother you?" she said.

Of course it bothers me, you hag. Just because your preening half-men here…

He shook his head and said,

"What's your name?"

Immediately, the woman replied,

"Where are you from?"

"What are you, a fencer?" he burst out. "I asked you a question. Tell me!"

They fell into silence for a while. Pavel closed his eyes and tried to focus on the reassuring strength of his cubicle door. He tried to draw courage from the ancient, stalwart tree that had been destroyed so that micturating men would have something nice to look at.

At last, the woman said,

"I asked first. Where are you from?"

She said it so confidently that Pavel forgot that she was lying. Her presumptuousness angered him. He imagined an Isfanian woman acting that way.

"Where *I'm* from," he said, "it doesn't matter who asked first. I asked, and you should answer me."

"Hmm," said the woman, thoughtfully. "And did you grow up there?"

"What?"

"I think you're from Isfania. Am I right? Did you grow up there?"

"What kind of a question is that? None of your business." The woman said nothing; she left him in silence, so he admitted defeat. "No."

"No," she repeated. "But it's where you're from."

"Yes!"

"Okay. I see. Now it's your turn to ask a question."

Pavel sighed. So now they were taking turns, two individuals who were fated to die, reaching out to one another in the twilight of existence, through a bathroom cubicle. What in God's name could this woman tell him? What did he want from her? He wanted her to cover up her legs, to go away into a women's bathroom. He wanted her to answer his questions when he asked them. He wanted to know...

"Why are you talking to me?"

"Nah," she drawled. "That's too easy. You can guess that. Ask me something else."

Pavel thought.

"You're being nice to me because you think I'm upset. That's what you people are like. You're all so *caring*. You care about each other and ask how you are every day, over tea and crumpets and silver spoons. Fine. Tell me your name."

"My name is Francesca."

In shock, Pavel almost thrust his head straight through the door. He'd known a Francesca – sinful, like all the women here. Impulsive, too – she had to have whatever she wanted, do whatever she liked, and if she didn't, if you told her to be patient or to shut up, she got angry. He'd broken up with her; she'd been angry about that, too. She'd followed him around for days, made a fool of him in public. Made a fool of herself, too – no decency, no self-respect.

Had made a fool of him. Had brought his people's criticisms down upon him. *What are you doing, a good boy like you, with some filthy whore like that? // You need to get back in touch with your roots, boy. // Pavel, wonderful news! Your uncle has promised to look after you for a few months back home. He'll show you our ways. You'll get away from this suffocating country. You'll see what it really means to be a man out there – none of this bowing down to women. None of this lewd behaviour! You'll be strong – someone to be proud of!*

"Hi," said Pavel, ignoring the images before his eyes of desperate poverty, of wounded victims of a brutal state, of a society that, all the same, had ordered itself according to tradition, according to the Perfect Community, all those centuries ago.

"Hi," he said again.

177

A moment later he saw Francesca's little finger worming its way underneath the cubicle door. The pink digit waved at him. It was obscene.

"What are you doing?" he said, angrily.

The finger waggled up and down.

"I'm trying to shake your hand," she said, cutely. "But I can't, because I'm behind a door.

"It's revolting."

The finger continued to waggle. He did not indulge it. He refused to look at it. The finger withdrew, defeated.

Pavel wanted to be alone. His tears had drawn the last of his strength away. Francesca would not let him be.

"My turn," she said. "What brings you here? Did you travel here? Or do you still live here?"

"I'm from Isfania," he hissed.

"Yes, yes. *Originally.* But you grew up here. Or near here. Your accent is too good. I'm curious. I find people interesting. Do you live in Isfania now?"

"None of your business."

"No, I suppose not," said Francesca, wistfully. "Okay, are you staying in the hotel? That seems an... *uncontentious* question."

Pavel bridled at the word 'uncontentious'. It was the kind of word that upper-class people used to belittle you. It was the word of a graduate and a snake. A politician. A politician who promised to do everything he could for you and your family, to make sure you got through the welfare system okay, to look into the conditions at your work, and shut the door on you laughing before going off to drink champagne with fat cats and middle men. No one *honest* said 'uncontentious'.

"Yes," he said, cautiously. "I'm staying in the hotel."

"Are you here for work?"

"That's two questions."

"Okay," said Francesca. Ask me something."

Pavel said nothing. There was nothing he wanted from this woman; nothing he wanted, except to be alone.

"Are you here for work?" said Francesca again. Her tone angered him.

"Right, because that's all Isfanians want," he said. "We're all here to take your shitty jobs. That's all you think. You think I'm a... cleaner, right? Or maybe I sell mobile phones. That's all I'm good for."

"Hmm," mused Francesca. "I don't think that."

"So how about this? Yeah, I'm here for work. I'm a diplomat."

"A diplomat?"

"Right!" Pavel had the woman on the back foot. "You didn't expect that, did you?"

"No, I didn't."

"I'm a *diplomat*," Pavel repeated. "I'm here to end the war. That's who I am."

He said nothing else. He was here to end the war. He was a diplomat – an accredited one.

"I'm here to end the war," he repeated.

"What war's that?"

"What war?" he hissed. "God, woman! *The* war. The war that's been fought against my people for the last fifty years. But your lot have only been involved for a decade. What would *you* know about it?"

Pavel heard another ruffle of fabrics and the unzipping of – his imagination wandered for a moment. He shook his head. She was opening her bag. She probably had to look up the war on her phone. Typical of these world-ignorant people. They could spend a month on holiday in a warzone and never realise what was going on right beneath their feet.

"You must be very proud," she said, absently.

Pavel nodded, rubbing his scalp against the wooden door, so close to Francesca's legs, as he did so.

"It's a great honour."

"So... why are you in here?" she said.

"Because... None of your business."

Francesca sighed. He heard that zip again as Francesca... put away her phone again. Pavel craned his neck around as if to look at her.

"Well, that's fine, I guess," she said. "The thing is, I'm getting tired. The floor is not a good look for me. I've got to stretch my legs, so I'm going to leave. Unless you want to come out of there and talk?"

Suddenly, when all Pavel had wanted before was to be left alone, he now wanted Francesca to stay. He wanted to talk to her. He wanted to see her face.

"Fine," he said. "I'll come out."

And he did, rather sheepishly. He opened the cubicle door and looked at this strange woman who had been talking to him through the cubicle door.

"You're pretty," he said, vaguely.

"Thank you. Would you like a drink? The hotel bar's okay. I think it's Happy Hour."

"I don't drink," he said, ignoring her forwardness in asking *him* to go for a drink.

"Oh, of course! Whoops. Well, it doesn't have to be alcoholic. Let's just go outside."

She began to walk towards the bathroom door.

"No!" Pavel said. Francesca looked at him strangely.

"You want to stay in here?"

"Yes."

"In the bathroom."

"That's right."

Then Francesca paused and said coquettishly,

"With *me*?"

Pavel's face burned with embarrassment. He almost went back into the cubicle. That would show her.

"I'm not... Don't make it sound ridiculous. Don't make *me* sound ridiculous!"

"I wouldn't dream of it."

Pavel glared at the woman. Her eyes sparkled. She was grinning at him – mocking him. She wouldn't do that in Isfania

180

– he wouldn't let her. He looked at her, scanning her bare legs and her painted face. He saw the soft leather bag with the zipper that he'd heard. Then he glanced – almost surprised – at the envelope in his hand – the envelope that would end the war.

"What's that?" said Francesca, catching his interest.

"It's none of your business."

Francesca shrugged.

"Jees. For someone who wants to talk, you're a lousy talker."

"Don't pry, then!"

"And your trousers have piss on them."

Pavel stopped. He refused to look down.

"What's so special about it?" she asked, pointing at his hand. "Is it important?" Francesca suddenly became animated, playful. "Oh! Is it from your government? Is it a demand? An ultimatum?"

"Why do you care? It's just an envelope."

He held it down by his side to show how little it mattered, while trying to keep it at an angle that would disguise its unusual heft.

"I think it's more than that."

"I don't care what you think."

"No," said Francesca, once again musingly. "I don't suppose you do. Well, it was nice meeting you. You never did tell me your name."

Francesca turned to leave. Again, Pavel was filled with a sense of panic.

"Where are you going?"

Francesca shrugged.

"Out. You don't want to talk. And you don't care what I think. All in all – a bad start to our relationship."

Pavel grew angry. Words. That was all this woman knew. Words to make you feel small and stupid. Unreasonable words to turn truth into fiction, and to blame *you* for it.

"We don't *have* a relationship," he said.

181

"And you don't have a top-secret envelope in your hand. Nor have you been crying on the bathroom floor for some reason. I've imagined the last twenty minutes, and now I'm going to go and imagine that I'm in the hotel bar. I might even treat myself to an imaginary drink."

"You're such…!"

Pavel caught himself before he became *undiplomatic*. He straightened up, composed his face, and said,

"My name is Pavel."

The declaration impressed her less than he'd hoped. She ostentatiously looked at her watch. It was gaudy, shiny, vile.

"Nice to meet you, Pavel," she said, impatiently. "But let's get moving. You've got issues. You want to talk, but you don't know how to, or what to say. You don't want me to stay, but you don't want me to go, either. All very remarkable. On the other hand, there's me. People talk to me, and they pay me for the privilege. You're doubly privileged right now. Not only do you get to talk to me, but you're getting a free session on the house. Use it or lose it."

"You're a *whore*?" said Pavel. Everything suddenly made sense. A postcard for the whole country indeed!

Francesca looked offended.

"People talk to me. They don't *sleep* with me."

"Talk about what? About their *problems*? About how they want a new TV, or how they don't like their jobs. They want sleeping pills at night because their sheets aren't posh enough."

"Is that what you think people talk to therapists about?"

"People here."

"Maybe some of them. Most have bigger problems. I don't judge. And some people here have real problems."

"Nothing compared to Isfania!"

"Tell me about Isfania."

And Pavel told Francesca about Isfania. He told her that it was a beautiful country – barren and fertile in equal parts, between the mountains and the flood. It was the birthplace of civilisation, the font of morality. Her history was glorious; her present degraded, thanks to foreigners. He described the war against foreigners and dictators that had torn his homeland to shreds.

He told her that, as a soldier, he had killed many people in the war. Now, as a diplomat, he was going to end it.

Francesca listened to him. He watched her painted face as she listened to him. She didn't seem to care. She didn't look impressed. She just listened. And when he was done, and had run out of things to say, she waited for a long time before speaking.

At last she said,

"How are you going to end the war? Is it about the envelope?"

Pavel walked over to the sink – more marble. He looked in the mirror – rimmed with brass. He studied himself. He was a soldier. He corrected his bearing to look like one.

He watched Francesca watch him in the mirror. She had one arm folded across her body, and another held up to her face. She looked troubled.

"You said that you're a soldier," she said.

"Yes."

"So you've killed people."

Pavel turned to look directly at her.

"That's right! I'm a soldier! I've killed people! I've taken an AK and fired at the enemy."

"How do you feel about that?"

"Glad! I fought for my country!"

"Have you ever shot anyone who didn't have a gun?"

"Only traitors," he said. "Traitors and enemies."

"How do you feel about them?"

"Glad! They're the enemy. I'm a soldier." Pavel nodded. "I have to follow orders."

"You don't sound glad."

Pavel shook his head.

"You're wrong," he said. "I'm happy. I'm a fighter. I followed orders, and that's right. I'm right. Soldiers follow orders."

Pavel could feel his strength returning. He was a soldier, after all. He had been sent here to follow orders. He would do that. It was who he was. He looked at Francesca with disdain.

"You're not so smart, you know. You think you are – shrinks always do. I've met your kind before. You think you can read minds, but you can't. You're as dumb as the rest of us."

"I don't think I'm smarter than you," said Francesca. "And I definitely can't read minds. But you keep saying that you have to follow orders. Have you been ordered to do something you don't want to?"

Pavel stared at her. He almost felt afraid of her – how absurd! Afraid of a woman! He had a knife in his pocket, and all it would take was a single stroke… She had no idea!

"Is it something about that envelope, perhaps?" she added. "Maybe they contain orders for you, as a diplomat, but you don't want to obey them?"

"Shut up!" he snarled. He reached into his jacket and took out the knife. It was beautiful, an heirloom weighed down by generations and reverence. It was the kind of thing the people here would turn into a souvenir and sell in gift shops up and down the country, given half the chance.

And Francesca looked afraid. He leered at her. He drank the pallor of her face, the gaping of her jaw. He revelled in his power over her. He wanted her to run from him.

"I think," said Francesca, "that we should calm down. This got out of hand, right?" She smiled falsely. "Let's forget this happened. I'll walk away, and nobody needs to know. Then you can go back to your meeting. Wouldn't that be nice?"

"For you!"

"And for you," she replied. "How do you see this going?" Pavel snorted. What did that matter?

"Do you think you can just walk out of here if you do something?"

"I don't care!"

"*Why not?*" Francesca's voice cracked. "Why don't you care?"

"Because!" Pavel shouted. He waved the envelope at her. "Because when I open this, it's all over!"

"What's all over?"

"Everything! The war! That's all I have to do. Open the envelope, and it's over."

"So? Isn't that a good thing? War's a bad thing – everyone wants war to end."

"Yes – no!"

"What's so special about it, anyway?" Francesca's voice became wheedling, like a child's. "It's not like it's a…"

Francesca stopped speaking. She was horrified. Pavel looked at her calmly. She had guessed that it was a bomb.

"Do you mind if I – sit?"

Francesca gestured at the sink counter behind him. More marble. More luxury. Pavel shrugged. He was exhausted again. He listened dully as Francesca tried to talk.

"You said you were a diplomat."

Silence.

"I don't want to die," she said.

"Nor do I."

"So… don't. Don't do it."

"I have to."

"Why? Don't! Just – just flush it. Just put it in the toilet and flush it. That'll break it, won't it?"

"I'm a soldier."

"You'll be a murderer."

"Not of anyone who matters."

Francesca began to cry.

"I don't want to die," she repeated. "Please don't let me die. Don't… I'll do *anything*. Please."

185

Pavel was moved, for just one moment, to sympathy for this wicked, pampered woman. She was going to hell – perhaps she realised it now. Now she was crying, her shoulders heaving in the same way that his had, just a while before. She had pitied him. He should pity her. He patted her on the shoulder.

"If it makes you feel any better," he said, "I don't want you to die, either. You don't seem evil."

"I'm not," Francesca burst out. "I'm not! I'm a good person! I have a brother – he's disabled. I have to help him get about. And my dog – Colin. He's a collie, so I called him Colin. Like a joke. And my work – I *help* people!"

"No one worth helping."

"Says *you*!"

Francesca lashed out weakly at Pavel's face. He stepped back, shocked, and then jumped forward again. He hit her.

"*Don't!*" he said. She kept her eyes fixed on the ground, too scared to feel her face where he'd hit her.

"Just flush it. Just flush it down the toilet," she whimpered.

Suddenly alarmed, Pavel looked at the bathroom door. Francesca did the same. At the same moment, they both wondered whether she could reach it before him, if she ran. He relaxed: she could not. He was between the sink counter and the door. In hoisting her shaved, smooth legs up onto the sink counter, Francesca had doomed herself.

"*Help!*" Francesca shrieked. "Someone help!"

Furious, panicked, Pavel stepped towards her and hit her in the cheek again – a real punch this time. She moaned and dropped to the bathroom floor, curled into a ball, protecting herself against further attack.

Then, satisfied, Pavel ran to the door. He looked for a way to lock it. He needed more time.

There was no lock, but there was a gap beneath the door. He could block it by wedging something into the gap. He took off his shoes and tested the effect: the door resisted. He ignored the fact that he would now die with the soles of his feet drenched in urine.

Then he returned to the passive Francesca and pulled her up by the arm. He pushed her into the cubicle, pushed into the space himself, and locked the door behind them. She was now intolerably close to him. He could smell her perfume, feel the heat rising from her exposed flesh, intoxicating – and all the more worthy of destruction for it.

"Please…" she whispered. Then, aware of her new situation: "What now?"

The bathroom door began to rattle as someone – security – tried to open it. Pavel listened quietly to the shouts, the cries of concern, and, at last, the commands to open the door.

He looked at Francesca, who lay in his power. He grabbed her again. She flopped hopelessly in his grasp.

"Listen!" he hissed. "You don't want to die. Nor do I. But we're both going to. We don't get to choose. It's not right. Why should I have to die? I shouldn't! I'm no one! But I was chosen to win the war, and that means I have to die."

"I don't understand what you're saying…"

"I'm going to win the war. That's why I was sent here. It's not fair. Why should everyone else get to live, except me? Who chose me?"

"So don't…"

"If everyone else is fighting and dying, I'll fight and die. I have to. I've done that. But by myself? Alone? Why me? Why not someone else – someone who's been fighting for decades? Someone who doesn't have as long to live? Do you understand me?"

"No!"

"We don't get to choose! I've been ordered, and you're here now."

"Please don't kill me."

"But now the war is over. Thanks to you – because you reminded me that I'm a soldier."

"I wish I hadn't."

They listened as security finally entered the bathroom. They listened to the shouts of 'hello?', and 'who's there'? Pavel watched the door, concerned, as the guards found the right cubicle and tried to push it open.

"But now the war will be over…" Pavel muttered again.

"What war? What war? I looked it up. There isn't any war!"

Pavel looked at her in shock. He shook his head – he didn't have time for this.

"Please, help – we're in here! This man is mad – he's got a bomb, and he thinks he's in a war!"

The guards said nothing. The cubicle trembled as the guards threw their bodies against the door. It held. Pavel grinned in triumph.

"The war! The war I've been telling you about! The war of independence!"

"I don't know what you're talking about! There isn't any war!"

"Shut up!"

Pavel raised his hand to hit her again, and then changed his mind.

"There isn't," Francesca repeated. "And even if there were – what good is one bomb going to do? How's that going to end anything?"

"I…" Pavel hesitated. "That's not my business! I just have to use the bomb. I'll die – and the war will be over. Maybe – it's a nuke! It must be. How else could it end a war?"

"A nuke! No, it's too small! And even if it were – how big do you think it is? How's a bomb going to end a war? There isn't even a war."

"Shut up! Shut up!" shrieked Pavel.

The door behind him cracked as thickset bodies continued to hurl themselves against the cubicle door. The door resisted, as if taking its long-delayed revenge against the people who had levelled its parent forest. *Thud! Thud! Thud!*

"I just need time to think…" said Pavel. "Give me time to think!"

188

"There isn't any war! There isn't any war! What's a bomb going to do?"

Pavel frowned. Had he misunderstood? Was the bomb going to *start* the war? A bomb could start a war. How could it end one? How many people would have to die? Or maybe it was a germ – maybe there was a germ inside the envelope. Germ warfare – that could end a war. These cowardly, pampered people would surrender in the face of germ warfare. He just had to open the envelope.

The door cracked again – he looked in dismay as the opening spread at the lock. There wasn't any time, and all he needed was time to think.

And then –

clarity.

He looked at Francesca, and Francesca looked at him.

"Please don't…" she whispered.

Pavel frantically raised the envelope to open it. Francesca tried urgently to grab it from his hands. The door finally gave way and the heavy door slammed into the two of them.

9-11 August, 2016

Reality/TV

The false classroom is perfect. The school desks are all lined up; the blackboard bears a medley of pseudo-educational scribblings – a few dozen words and dates which, scanned cursorily, might just give the impression of an orderly lecture delivered by a knowledgeable teacher; and the walls are covered with laminated posters purchased online, which again convey the general impression of a learning environment, without being so crass as to actually be one.

The director, Philip Hungerford, is an experienced hack whose televisual output approaches thirty hours a year. His ten-episode contract on *Borough High* is coming to an end. He is tired and pleased. It has been a good run: ratings have been stable, two of the plotlines have featured in the gossip rags, and he himself was interviewed in *OK!* a few weeks back. Good for his brand. A decent couple of months' work.

The scene is ready. Hungerford scans the set once more.

"Bring in the kids," he declares, languidly.

The door opens and twenty boys and girls, aged 15 to 17, file in. They are all in the fictional *Borough High* uniform; they have brought their own bags and books and pencil cases, which they – experienced hands by now – place diligently on their desks. The more dedicated ones take a pen or two out to convey the impression of school work. Some – the ones who forlornly dream of stardom while staring at YouTube videos all night – even *open* their books. Some are Maths books and some are English; one boy seems to have brought a sketch book.

Whatever. No one will care.

The kids are all extras recruited from the local schools: a real microcosm of the London cosmopolis – white, black, Indian, a couple of Pakistanis, one Chinese girl. You can't watch *Borough High* for long without being able to guess where it's based.

Next up, the camera crew take positions. It's easier to bring them in after the kids. Almost immediately the girls, inspired or frightened by the presence of the artificial eye, whip out pocket mirrors and makeup and fervently apply the last few touches of their toilette. Hungerford growls at them, and they stop. Mostly.

Finally, the only adult in the scene – Francis de Vries, or 'Mr. Hammond', comes across. He and Hungerford have worked together before. Hungerford likes de Vries. He doesn't really know why.

"All set?" says de Vries.

"As you see. Like your lines?"

De Vries snorts.

"Ain't nothing like my school, bruv'," he says, assuming a high pitch and a fast, pitter-patter rhythm. "Man talk this way round my street, he end up wrong side of a shiv!"

Hungerford frowns, wondering what on earth the man is talking about. Still, words have been said. The lead writer, Chris Miller, is lounging outside the classroom, listening in. He walks over, furious - or, in the words of his trade, *fulminating*. De Vries watches him and tries to affect indifference.

"Have you got a problem, *Mr Hammond*?" says the writer.

"When was the last time you were even in a school, mate?" he says.

Miller smirks.

"I think I've got this, *mate*. Fourteen years at school, four at uni." He screws up his face in a mockery of concentration. "Think I've got the material, thanks very much."

"So from the looks of you," says de Vries, "the answer's, what... fifteen years ago?"

"I think I remember it. Just about."

"Yeah," says de Vries. "I bet you do. Didn't like it much, did you?"

He shrugs at Hungerford, who has lost interest in the conversation and is again ordering the kids to stow makeup.

Miller, determined to look just as indifferent, storms away, brushing an imaginary hair off his shoulder.

"Who the fuck would like school?" he mutters as he walks away.

De Vries feels almost sorry for the writer as he goes. He turns to Hungerford. "I guess that's that. Are we ready?"

"When you are. Enjoy working where you shat when I'm gone."

De Vries nods reflectively, wondering what fatal accident might befall his character over the next few months. Or maybe he would turn out to be homosexual. That was the kind of thing little men like Miller would think of as an act of vengeance. Still, no worrying about it now. De Vries takes his position before the fake class. He takes a few breaths to calm down. He assumes his character and shuts his eyes. And he nods.

"Scene 13; Take 1."

Clapperboard.

De Vries no longer speaks. Mr Hammond speaks. He has about thirty seconds' worth of education to impart, explaining some aspects of a scene from *Much Ado About Nothing*. His character explains some antecedents to the scene, rarely-spotted nuances, and so forth. No one is listening; even de Vries has been instructed to sound bored by his own address. Only snippets will ever make it in to the televised cut, and it's far more important to the flow of the narrative that educational be seen as extraneous, a diversion, to these fictional learners – and, by implication, to the audience at home, too. All that matters is that the viewers at home get a general sense of the impartation of knowledge, in a manner they will recognise from their own schooldays, and which will enable them to make many insightful comments about school around the water cooler and the dinner table.

Cameras focus on the back of the class, where two boys pass certain items to one another. Mr Hammond cannot see them; the camera will show one object to be a twenty pound note and the other piece a very small plastic bag.

"...And if you listen to the sound of the words while Benedick is talking here, you'll notice something interesting," he declares, positively, bouncily, urgently. He stands dominantly at the head of the class, taking in each and every member. "See how by the repetition of the..."

"*Bell rings!*" calls Hungerford.

Mr Hammond tilts his head until the imaginary bell falls quiet. The class is already packing up, standing, chattering.

"Don't forget!" he repeats, louder, raising his voice above the sudden, rebellious tide of children clattering around, his apparent command of them shattered by the clanging school bell. "Read to the end of the play, and answer the question – which aspect do you prefer in *Much Ado...*"

The class pick up their bags and race past him. Mr Hammond lets most of them go, standing awkwardly by the door. Then, just as Cassius Denny, one of the two boys who were talking before, passes him, he grabs him roughly by the arm. He yanks him roughly out of the crowd and against the wall.

"You. Stay."

Denny looks bewildered.

"What have *I* done?"

"Be quiet! Stay there!"

"I got another lesson, sir. Mr Franco'll be well pissed at me."

Denny's sidekick, a much smaller boy called Micky Willis, chips in:

"Yeah, sir. Mr Franco said that if Cassy's late one more time, he's got to stay after school."

"Not my problem," says Mr Hammond.

The rest of the class have now left the room.

"It will be when my mum..."

"Turn out your pockets, Cassius," says Mr Hammond.

The swagger disappears.

"You can't do that," he says, quietly.

Mr Hammond raises an eyebrow.

"He's done nothing wrong, sir," says Micky. "This is out of order! False imprisonment!"

"Yeah... this is a violation of my rights!"

Cassius fidgets, hands in blazer pockets. He looks nervously around.

Mr Hammond drops his voice to a threatening murmur.

"I saw you with Franky Rowsby, Cassius. Just a few hours ago. You have a nice chat together? Do a bit of business? You got something to hide?"

"I got *nothing* to hide!" declares Cassius in defiance. "But you can't just tell me you wanna empty my pockets! You can't follow me around, neiver. That ain't right. That's like stalking."

"This is like the Nazis," says Micky, clearly loving the moment. "You're like Hitler."

"Be very careful, Willis," says Mr Hammond. "Last chance, Cassius. It's now, with me, or in thirty minutes with the Head and your mum. What do you want?"

Cassius thinks it over. He fidgets and looks around in search of help or inspiration. Nothing – and the camera shows it. At last he appears to make a decision. He empties his right pocket. A pen, a couple of sweets. A screwed up piece of paper.

"See?" he says, one last dash at bravado.

"And the other one."

Cassius pauses again. There's no way out. He complies. He puts the spliff on the teacher's desk. The three actors ignore the Steadicam zooming past them.

"Let's talk, Cassius."

Cassius looks at Mr Hammond in feigned distress.

"And... *scene!*" shouts Hungerford.

Another episode down. Another episode churned out for the consumption of lawyers and bankers and politicians, their wives and husbands, feeding the public perception of schools as dens of drugs and violence and boredom. An episode of *Borough High* can attract nearly a million viewers. It is the closest experience to school that most of its audience has had in decades – and a good chunk of them went to private school. For the viewers, *Borough High is* school.

*   *   *

"*Psst!*" whispers Lucy to Michaela. "*Michaela!*"
Michaela looks to her left, eyebrows arched dramatically.
"*Whaaat?*" she drawls back in the same stage-whisper.
"What have you got for number 7?"
"Um…" Michaela looks at her book. "43.517."
Lucy looks at her in panic.
"What?"
"43.517… There's more, but I left it out."
"I don't think that's right."
"Yes it is!"
"No it's not!"
The two girls giggle.
Mr Wexler directs his steady course around the room, until he looms over Lucy and Michaela. They look at him innocently. He folds his arms and makes it clear: *I don't buy it.*
"Any problems, girls?"
"No, sir."
"How are you getting on?"
"Really well!" says Lucy. "We're on number *eight* already."
"Good!" says Mr Wexler. He doesn't know that the pair finished number 7 minutes ago. They're still doing better than most. They could have been on number 10 by now, but, well, if you got that far then you had that leering word, "Extension" written on the interactive whiteboard.

"Don't forget," says Mr Wexler, pointing at the offending term. "When you're done, you can move on. That's really good work! I reckon you'll be finished in, what, five minutes?"

"*Five minutes?*" repeats Michaela, in mock astonishment. "I'll *never* get that far in five minutes!"

"Not if you keep talking."

Mr Wexler grins at the two of them. He has to move on – there are twenty seven boys and girls in the room. Most are making slower progress than this and they need his help – to stay on task, if nothing else.

"Come on, keep going," he says briskly, trying to inject the pair with fresh determination.

"Oh, but, oh…" says Lucy, mouthing like a fish.

"Yes?"

"Can I just ask… about number 7?"

"Sure, of course."

"Only… Michaela's got, like, 43.142, or something."

Michaela goes bright red. "No I don't! I've got *43.517*. There!"

She turns her book around to prove it.

"Right…" says Mr Wexler.

"And she says it goes on and on. And it's *never* an answer like that, is it? It's always got an ending. It'll be something simple, like 32.5, won't it?"

"Um, not always," says Mr Wexler, aware that if he says 'never' now, he'll never hear the end of it. "Sometimes you get recurring decimals, or irrational numbers."

They stare at him, feigning ignorance of those words, acting as if even knowing the words themselves is a mark of inconceivably abstruse intellectualism

"But for the most part, you're right. Let's have a look."

He takes out his marking pen and hovers over the page, trying to see Michaela's mistake.

"Oh, no, no!" says Michaela. Mr Wexler looks at her in surprise. "I don't want you to *mark* it. I want to know where I went wrong."

"That's what I'm going to show you."

"Yes… but… I don't want you to *mark* it," she repeats, hoping that her meaning will become clearer this time.

Mr Wexler sighs affectionately.

"Okay," he says. "Have it your way. If I were you, though, I'd start looking somewhere around…. *there.*"

He gestures vaguely at a line in her calculation that seems wrong. Michaela bends her neck and sets to work. Lucy looks across at her slyly, and then she too turns her book for Mr Wexler's gaze.

"Is *that* right, sir?" she wheedles.

Mr Wexler looks at her for a moment, and then shrugs.

"Dunno," he says. "Why don't you wait and see what Michaela gets? Or keep going – don't forget, you get credits for doing the extension."

"Do we?" says Lucy. She looks urgently across at Michaela.

"Michaela, hurry up! We get credits if we finish!"

Mr Wexler walks off, shaking his head. He suspects that his presence has been more of a distraction than an aid. He goes in search of those in need of more support.

Having surveyed a few more books, he sees that a key step in the sum remains opaque to most of the class. He calls for silence, drawing the pupils' attention towards himself. He tells them to put down their pens, and he jokingly, like a primary school teacher, tells them to pin back their ears so they can hear him. Some, remembering the charade from their old school, willingly oblige. He waits for silence.

He runs through the relevant step again, and shows where some of them are going wrong. He hears a few groans of, "*Ohhh!*" from some expected quarters, but sees little enlightenment on certain faces. One or two look more confused than they did before. They wear it on their faces, hoping that Mr Wexler will come and explain it to them again, without their having to ask for assistance.

"Keep on going, and I'll be coming around if you need help," says Mr Wexler.

He works his way around, tripping over schoolbags and sports kit on the way. He helps with maths where he can. He tells Jimmy Farnes to close his pencil case, because it's hanging over the edge of his desk and is about to fall – leaving a nice tidy-up job that could waste three or four minutes of lesson time. Mr Wexler has seen that game plenty of times. He also opens a window because someone has farted, but no one has noticed it yet to make a fuss. He hopes to prevent a Major Incident.

Along the way, he swings past Michaela and Lucy's desk. He peers over their shoulders.

"Number 9? Disappointed. Get a move on, girls," he says, his tone clear that whatever praise they had earned before is on the verge of oblivion in light of this latest, wretched progress.

And so on. As it always is. With eight minutes left, Mr Wexler calls the class back into attention.

"Okay, you know the drill," he says, speaking rapidly for urgency and haste. "Pencils out – everyone got a pencil? Jimmy, that's not a pencil. Yes, a coloured pencil is fine, but a pen isn't. A *pencil*. Ready... ready...? Good!"

He taps on the whiteboard to flick to the next slide. The answers go up. The class race through, ticking and crossing as necessary. It doesn't take long – Mr Wexler has five minutes left.

"Hardest one?" he says. A chorus of replies announces, more or less, that three and eight were the hardest. He feels a little bad for rebuking Lucy and Michaela. "Okay," he replies.

He flips onto a new 'page' on the board, and runs through the two offending sums. Each takes about a minute to explain. There isn't time, as he would have preferred, to have a pupil run through each one. A few more groans of understanding and despair.

"Right," he says, keenly aware now of the clock. He clicks onto the next page. It says, "Homework".

A full chorus of groans.

"Come on, diaries out. Rob, where's your diary?"

"I'll remember it."

"No you won't. Write it down, now. Don't make me check it."

Rob complies.

"Sire," says Lucy – then giggles. "I mean, *sir*. Can I take a photo?"

"Yeah, yeah, that's fine."

A sudden scramble as a dozen phones emerge from pockets – all of which should be off – and snap the final screen. Some perfectionists wait until the others have stopped, and then take up positions that minimise distortion from the image angle. Mr Wexler stands awkwardly out of the way, because there are school policies about being pictured by pupils, in case you end up on Facebook.

The bell goes.

Not too bad for timing.

"Okay, everyone standing behind your chairs, please," announces Mr Wexler, moving back to the front of the class. The pupils comply and wait, some of them chatting about the next lesson, and where they have to go, and whether Sir is in or if there's a cover teacher.

"Really good work today – I'll be taking in your books tomorrow. The homework is just a few more questions like today's, so make sure that you get it – and if you don't, *ask!* Don't just leave them blank, because I won't take that as an excuse."

The class nod at him. He wonders if they are doing it as you might nod at the ravings of a madman. Certainly no one has ever taken advantage of the offer. Plenty have simply declined to do the work.

"Philly, there's a pen by your foot. Pick it up, please."

"It's not mine."

"Not what I asked," he says, airily. "Jimmy – *rubber*."

Jimmy looks pleased to have acquired a rubber. A lesson well worth his attendance.

"Okay, looking good. Thanks, everyone – see you all tomorrow."

"*Thanks, sir,*" a few reply immediately. Most walk past in silence. A few add an extra 'thank you' as they go, to which Mr Wexler replies in a variety of ways. Then, as he has a free period next, he sits down at his desk, staring blankly out of the window.

"Sir?" comes a girl's voice from outside the room.

Mr Wexler looks over. It's Michaela.

"Sir, can I ask you a question?"

"You've got a lesson to get to, Michaela," says Mr Wexler.

Michaela walks in and shuts the door, ignoring this. She has her book in her hand and she opens it. Mr Wexler stands up and mutters that the room is stuffy after the lesson. He opens the door again. It's school policy.

"Boys," Michaela declares, wisely.

Mr Wexler returns to his seat.

"I still don't get number 7," says Michaela. "I got number 8 fine, but not number 7."

"Okay." Mr Wexler looks at the clock. Michaela should be at her next lesson. "Look, the bit you've done wrong is here. Do you see?"

He watches Michaela's diligent, concerned expression melt into one of embarrassment.

"Ohhhhhh!" she exclaims, frustrated with herself. "I'm such an idiot!" She turns away, sagging at the shoulders. Mr Wexler feels he should say something.

"It happens to the best of us," he says, cheerfully. Michaela nods, grimacing.

"Thanks, sir," she drawls.

He watches her slump towards the door.

"Oh, but, Michaela," he says. She turns around. "That was really good – getting up to number 8 in the time you did."

Michaela smiles. "But would you honestly say, hand on heart, that you got on as well as you could after that?"

Michaela hesitates. She bounces her head from side to side, unwilling to answer.

"Hmm?" he says, mockingly.

"Hmm?" she smiles, as if she has forgotten the question.

"Only, I thought you'd move up a set this term," he said, mock-diffidently. "Bit of a shame if you don't."

Michaela's eyes widen. She hadn't known that could happen.

"Really? Oh, but – do you teach the upper set, sir?"

"Me? No, I don't. Mrs Henderson does."

"Oh," says Michaela, lost for words. "She's nice."

"She's very nice," he replies. "So – just keep all that in mind, all right?"

"Okay."

"Now, you've got to go. You're going to be late. Tell your next teacher I kept you behind."

"Oh, don't worry about that," she says, cheerfully. "It's only Miss Newton. *No one* gets to her on time."

Mr Wexler grins and shakes his head in mock despair as Michaela saunters out of the room. He looks forward to the end of the day. *Borough High* is on tonight, he remembers. That'll be good.

13 August, 2016

Superhero

Michael felt rage welling up from within. Knots of shame coiled serpent-like inside his belly; muscle tore against muscle, willing him to exert his strength; black amnesia crept into his vision, urging him to forget everything – everything apart from his anger.

He didn't have to take this.

"So, what's it going to be?" asked Julia, pushing him – pushing him again! "I told you before – I want kids!"

"Shut up!"

Julia refused. She usually obeyed, but tonight she refused. Maybe it was the wine. She'd had too much. It made her unreasonable, impossible to control. It made her crazy – it always did. But he had to put up with it. That was his job.

"I told you years ago," she said again. "I want kids. If you don't, that's fine. But don't lie to my face and tell me you do, just to keep me."

"Don't call me a liar," he growled.

The wine made Julia reckless, but Michael controlled himself. The alcohol did not affect him. Drugs did not affect him.

"But now we're – what, five years later, and what have we done about it? You're wasting my time. Wasting my chance of having kids. I could have found someone else, if you'd just said you didn't want them. But no – you said you did. So now put up or shut up, Mister Hero."

"Leave me alone!"

Julia stopped. Her face went pale. Her eyes betrayed sudden realisation – an awakening to an awful truth.

"Fine," she said.

She stood up. Michael watched her turn towards the door, and then back towards him. He watched as she leant in close, pushing her mouth – and her breath – close in to his face. He listened – and watched – as she said to him, her voice steeped in malice:

"Don't come home tonight."

He looked at her, unimpressed. What could she do about it?

"Don't come home, or I'll tell the police you hit me."

And there it was. Dishonesty. Injustice. Selfish pettiness, the endless dance of worthless, bitter people screwing each other into the ground, covering themselves in the very shit they wished to smear on their opponents. Rodents reaching for every possible advantage, indifferent to right and wrong, consumed in the vile act of winning no matter the cost to integrity, to…

"I'll be gone by tomorrow," she said. "Don't ever call me, you *lying* son of a bitch!"

"Don't call me a liar!" Michael roared.

His tolerance finally overcome, his arm shot out on impulse. His palm hammered into Julia's left shoulder, the tremendous force launching his partner of eight years into a mid-air spiral. She did not cry out in pain or surprise – he had hurt her before. She knew what to expect. She knew what he could do to her. The only time she even groaned was when her flailing leg cracked into the heavy table legs, splintering the bone.

Michael heard the crack louder than anyone, his ears sharp as a hound's. He could heal it, if she just came home with him.

The bar went quiet. In the background, Rhianna sang about umbrellas, but the customers stared in shock. Julia, too, looked more astonished than pained. Stupid of her – *she'd known what would happen*. She had pushed him on purpose. He had pushed back.

His push was stronger.

Michael jumped to his feet. The curse of the hero. Always trying to do right, and always hated for it. No one understood. No one understood.

He walked towards the door. The bouncer and a wannabe tough-guy tried to block his way. Michael turned into a shadow and slipped between them.

Emerging into the evening outside – the pavement still wet from the day's endless drizzle, people clustered on the streets waiting for admittance into the warm, bright-lit bars – Michael turned into his true form. A snake.

The snake crawled along the gutter towards its home. Some people spotted him and tried to scream, but he stifled their screams with his mind, and then made them forget him.

As it slithered through the darkness, the snake wondered whether Julia would come home after all. It pondered whether she would call the police, or whether the bar staff had done so for her. It considered fleeing, just turning into an eagle and flying away to France.

It wondered how long French took to learn.

*   *   *

A week later, and still no Julia. Michael sat alone in his apartment. *His* apartment – but an empty one. It was empty without her.

Her absence depressed him.

So did the endless rain that pattered against the window.

She would not come back to him now. She had never stayed away from him like this.

She had never pushed him like that before.

He mulled over what she had said. She wanted kids. He had told her that was okay. Years ago! But he had never delivered.

But whose fault was that? They had never even talked about it. She had never raised the subject again, except as a joke, or in passing – driving past a playground and making a comment like, "Soon we'll be bringing our kids here."

He didn't want kids, but he had told her that he didn't mind the idea. So why should he take the lead? It was her thing. It was what she wanted. Michael had other things to think about.

Now it was *his* fault. He was to blame for not taking the lead on something he had not even wanted.

Bitch.

The word sounded hollow.

Bitch.

Suddenly inspired, he searched the apartment for anything that belonged to her. Clothes, a hairdryer, makeup, an iPod. He was going to box them up. He teleported to a Big Yellow Storage and bought a few boxes with some five pound notes he had concocted out of toothpaste.

"Eight years…." he said to himself. Eight years.

He looked at a mirror. He was still young and handsome. That had been his first task on becoming the Superhero: fixing his appearance. Oh, he'd kept the basic outline – the basic, human shape, the same facial structure. But he'd improved the rest. Musculature, most importantly. His bearing, to an extent – he'd always had a slight crook that made him resemble some sort of Dracula's Igor, and had enraged him since the age of thirteen.

And, of course, he had redacted the signs of ageing.

He wondered if he would live forever.

If so, he was better off alone. No wife and kids to grow old around him.

He placed Julia's clothes in the boxes. He could have done this much faster – at the speed of sound, more or less – but he chose the slow way, and he did it badly, petulantly.

Then he sent her a text.

Your stuff's in boxes. Tell me when you want it and I'll be out.

He smiled in victory. A Pyrrhic victory, but a victory. The wording – so cold, so efficient, certain – would horrify her. It would make her question her decision. She would call him. No doubt about it.

She did not call him.

*   *   *

Michael stood on the corner of a Wandsworth street. It was October. It was three in the morning. He knew this because he could see a clock through the wall of the nearest house, and also because someone had just asked the time, three streets away, and had received an answer. Michael heard the answer.

Julia was staying here now, but he was not here to see her. He was just here to keep the neighbourhood safe. Not even safe for her – she was safe in bed, and warm. Just… safe.

Michael was going back to his roots. He was trying to recapture something that had disappeared a long time ago: his desire to change the world. To make it better.

Because that's what you do, when you become a superhero. *The* Superhero. You take the powers you get, and you make the world a better place.

With great power comes great responsibility – those were the words of Peter Parker's – Spiderman's – uncle. If you get the power, you have to use it.

A bit like an army. If you have the means, you ought to do something.

Michael was a one-man army, but one that could never enter the field. Stay out of politics – he'd worked that out straight away. Fix the world one problem at a time. You can't fly into Syria, beat up everyone you don't like, and then expect the place to sort itself out. The end of *Superman IV* would have led to World War III.

No – you'd have to become a one-man occupation force. You'd never escape. You'd be stuck in a personal Vietnam, hated by everyone, unable to help, the one unifying force in a country riven by anger.

The Superhero had no place in politics or war.

So you try to fix the world, one thing at a time. You try to stop injustice. You make one person's life a little better, for a little while.

You spend a lot of time on street corners.

It was funny. The superheroes he'd read about as a kid had always created their own nemeses. Batman: the Joker. Superman: Lex Luthor. But Michael had no enemy – no one man he could punch in the face until he gave up and went to jail.

Michael's enemy was society. All of it. Social pressure. Cruelty. Power. You can't hit society in the face.

Michael had become the Superhero, the yin to society's yang. Perhaps society had created him to be its own nemesis. To this day, he didn't know how. It didn't matter. Had he been bitten by something radioactive, or caught in some bizarre cosmic event? It simply didn't matter.

Would any explanation of his powers add to his self-understanding? Say that some being from another dimension had chosen him and gifted all these powers to him – did that mean anything apart from, "Magic"? The same went for pseudo-scientific explanations about mutations or secret government tests. Simply putting clever words in seemingly rational sentences would not add to his powers. Nor would they rationalise them, or make them more believable.

Nor would shrugging his shoulders and admitting his ignorance diminish them.

Further down the street, three young men were standing outside a fast food place. Chicken Supreme. They were shouting. They were making a ruckus. Michael felt sorry for the people who lived here, and considered, for a moment, floating over and asking them to keep it down. But he didn't.

That would only start a fight, and Michael didn't want to beat up on guys whose only crime was talking loudly.

But two younger women were stumbling along the pavement towards them. He watched carefully, in case the men did anything.

As he watched, he scanned them for weapons. They had none. He scanned the women, too, flipping back and forth between their handbags and the lacy underwear beneath their clothing.

If you could even call it 'beneath', he sneered.

Julia would have never dressed like that.

*   *   *

One month after becoming the Superhero, Michael had beaten up over four hundred thugs, bullies, dealers, gang members, and assorted other criminals. He had actively thrown himself into fights, rejoicing in his strength. He had tested his powers – throwing himself into lava, ploughing into the Arctic ice, stabbing and shooting himself – there seemed to be no limits to his abilities.

In his war on crime, his methods became subtler. He used craft to catch his targets. Rather than punching murderers into submission, he seized control of their minds and led them to the police and forced them to confess. Whereas before, trucks full of cocaine would have been stopped, their crews removed and bound up naked on the street, now the cargoes simply disappeared, to be replaced by notes saying things like,

"Ha, ha, you lose. Your favourite rival gang."

But Michael saved his ire for the smallest of the small – the meanest of the mean. The ones who stood on street corners and bullied the weak as they went by. The ones who pushed into perfectly nice people in public and knocked them over just because they could. The ones who went looking for fights with people who were the wrong colour, or from the wrong part of town.

Michael hated them all. Criminals he could understand. Criminals thought they were going to get rich. Maybe they'd been caught up in something when they were younger, and couldn't get out. They deserved justice, but not hatred.

It was the small people who deserved hatred. The ones who had nothing to gain but a bit of kudos for punching someone in the face. The ones who felt better about themselves for making others feel worse. The school bullies who never left school.

"You want to know why you're a fucking waste of space?" he'd asked one of his – well, 'victims' was the best word (and 'asked' was a slight misnomer). "Because you're fucking useless. Tell me, what the fuck have you ever done for anyone? You're a worthless shit! You only care about yourself. You never worked hard for anything and now you think the world owes you everything. You don't like people who do well, because it reminds you *you* threw away every chance you ever got. Well, fuck you! Fuck you from everyone you ever beat up at school! Fuck you from everyone you made feel small and stupid and weak because they were trying hard and wanted to do something with their lives, but you just wanted to sit around and make sure nothing changed, because you were bigger than everyone else and at the top of the pile! Welcome to the real fucking world – and here, you're nothing. You're insignificant. You're tiny. The world is bigger than you, no matter how fucking big you think you are. You're a waste of space. You're a drain on society. Nobody wants you."

It was the most eloquent thing that Michael had ever said in his life.

The man he said it to simply spat in Michael's face.

Michael didn't stop throwing him around until he was pretty sure there were no more bones to break.

*   *   *

"I'm trapped," Michael said to Julia.

This was in the early days, when Michael still looked to Julia for advice.

Julia looked up from *Cosmo*. He grinned. He still couldn't believe, back then, that he was going out with someone who'd been in *Cosmo*.

Heck, he couldn't believe he was going out with someone who *read Cosmo*.

"What do you mean?" she asked.

"At work."

"Oh, right."

"I can't stay there any longer," he said.

Julia hummed to herself quietly. It was a high-pitched whine – a warning sign, of sorts.

"What are you going to do instead?" she said. "I thought we were going away next month."

Michael looked at her pityingly and read her mind. She was worried about money. She wanted him to be richer than he was. He took *Cosmo*, tore off a corner from a middle page, and turned it into a fifty pound note.

Julia stared at it blankly.

"Yeah, but, what are you going to *do*?"

"I don't need a job," he said. "Money's not a problem. I make my own money."

"Oh, right."

Julia thought about this for a while. She was probably wondering how many issues of *Cosmo* would buy her a car.

Michael loved it. A real, bona-fide bimbo.

"So why are you still working?" she said.

"I guess because I always have done," he said. "It's what you do, isn't it?"

"Is it?"

"Yes. You have a job. You contribute to society."

"But you contribute by fighting crime."

"Exactly," said Michael. "I guess I just never thought about it properly before. But now I've got to leave my job."

"Why?"

"Oh…" Michael sighed and shook his head. "They're all such idiots. They can't – they just don't listen. I keep telling them, 'there's an easier way of doing this', or 'let's give this a go', and they just ignore me. Honestly, it's all I can do not to…"

He stopped.

"Not to what?"

Michael smiled.

"I was being silly. I was going to say, 'slap them in the face'. There's so much politics."

"I hate politics."

"Like, have you buttered up the right guy for this? Have you done all the groundwork? You can't just go up to someone important and say, 'look at this – it's going to revolutionise the business'. Instead, you've got to go through committees, and make sure you're not treading on anyone's toes, and then you've got to do all the impact assessments, blah, blah, blah."

"Blah."

"And then they say things like, 'you're not a team player, Michael. You've got some good ideas here, but you think they can't be improved, but a lot of people have a lot of brains here. Use them. Partner up.'"

Julia put a pen into her mouth to indicate thought. It didn't matter – Michael only wanted a sounding board.

"So, it's not as if I can do anything there. And every time I feel stopped from doing anything, it just makes me angry."

"You should run your own business."

Michael sputtered.

"I don't need to!" he said. "Remember? I can make money."

"Oh, yeah."

*   *   *

To an extent, Michael added.

Once upon a time, who'd have batted an eyelid at someone who didn't work, but still lived like a king? Even the real aristocracy – the people who did exactly that – got noticed. They still kept their money in banks, and those banks filled in reports and returns, and the government knew about a lot of it.

But the idea of someone just stumbling across a bucket of gold coins in the attic and living off those for the rest of his life?

It couldn't happen anymore.

You had to be seen to make money before you could spend any.

Michael never quit his job. He just carried on hating it, and shouting at people, and never got promoted because he wasn't a 'team player' and didn't know how to 'manage people'.

Three of his team were promoted ahead of him in the space of six months. Their work as a group, they were told, was outstanding.

Of course it was outstanding. Michael did all the work.

He remembered boys at school taking his homework from them. They took his books, copied down the answers, and then, to hide the evidence, they tore up his books.

Of course, they never got away with it – the teachers knew that knuckleheads didn't suddenly hand in Grade-A assignments – but Michael never got off scot-free. Either the teachers punished him for not doing the work, or the bullies punished him for squealing.

Sometimes both happened.

And now it was happening all over again. Michael put in the hours. He could work (he'd done the sums once) approximately 30,000 times faster than anyone else on Earth. If they gave him a job, it could be done within the minute. He didn't do it quite that fast, of course – he had to keep his powers a secret.

Being in Michael's work group was an established means of gaining promotion. Michael himself was never promoted. He was ratty, arrogant. He implied that other people didn't do any work. He made snide comments that were completely at odds with his bearing and build.

He acted like a bratty child in the body of a Norse demigod. The dissonance confused them, and they blamed him for it.

So they kept him where he was, where he provided lots of value to the company, but very little to himself.

Occasionally they let him have a pay rise, but only when he threatened to leave. Even then, they gave him the least they could get away with – they never let him know how terrified the prospect of his departure left them. Instead they showered him with assurances, keeping him cheap and in his place.

After a couple of years, Michael bought Julia a second-hand Astra.

*   *   *

The women walked past Chicken Supreme unharmed. Michael let out a breath he didn't realise he'd been holding. He felt disappointed. He knew he shouldn't. A world where women can walk home unmolested is better than one in which their molesters need chasing away.

He watched the women walk away, switching on his x-ray vision occasionally and feeling bad about it. But they were practically dressed that way already.

He turned his same gaze on the house behind him and checked that Julia was asleep. He peered no closer.

Of course, he'd met her in a demonstration of his abilities. The usual story: a guy acting like a jerk; Michael stepped in; the guy tried to push him back and failed, because Michael had made himself weigh four hundred pounds; then Michael pushed back.

Michael had dated women before. Those relationships had been tame, polite. Passionate at times, he supposed, but never really so. It was always an act.

Julia was more available in that regard. She seemed to burn for Michael. She called him up every day. She followed him sometimes. He liked the attention. He found it flattering.

She got into trouble a couple of times, and he helped her out. Later, he realised that she was doing it on purpose. People don't get into that many scrapes unless they're trying to.

He liked being able to help.

She liked him being able to help.

He knew that she boasted about his strength, warning men off because 'her boyfriend would come and beat him up' if they didn't.

He liked that, too. It made him feel strong – stronger, in fact, than the super strength and all his other powers did.

And, of course, he liked the fact that his friends could not believe that he was going out with her.

Oh, they acknowledged that, in the last few months he'd sorted himself out. He'd obviously started going to the gym and had put on a lot of muscle. He'd sorted out his posture – *see, it wasn't a bone thing, you were just standing wrong.* He'd become more assertive and more confident. He stopped trying to catch people out in little mistakes, more willing to make mistakes of his own.

Even so, for someone who'd been a nerdy little kid, a *Warhammer* aficionado, with every episode of *Babylon 5* on a shelf on the wall, someone like Julia was impossible to understand, or even empathise with. She was a walking sex symbol, not a person.

But then, Michael's old friends came to bore him, too. He found their interests dull. It all seemed so obvious to him – their little conversations about the dilemmas facing comic book heroes, their debates about whether the *Enterprise* or a Star Destroyer would win in a fight (a Star Destroyer, by quite a long way) – it was all escapism. It was all trying to exit a world that didn't like them, and which they didn't like very much either.

And what kind of a world did they run into? What perfect world did they imagine waiting for them once they had left this one behind?

They fled into a world of fantasy men sporting biceps that would make pro-wrestlers quail in fear. They ducked under the covers and stroked themselves to the thought of PhDs in Physics with the bodies of Amazonian queens. They dressed up like lords and ladies of the realm and told themselves that the world – their lives – would be so much better in an idealised medieval England: an era steeped in blood and governed by the sword.

They surrounded themselves with a fictional universe a hundred times worse than the real one. In running away from a world where the strong prevailed in little ways, they wanted to create one in which the strong always prevailed. Spiderman didn't win fights because he was nicer than the other guys: he won because he fought harder and tougher. Batman didn't win because his cause was righteous: he won because he had bigger weapons. Knights weren't decent, law-abiding, and respectful to women: they were thugs who had enough money to buy a horse and armour, and they spent their days praying to God and then hitting people to make sure they paid their rent.

They did not want a better world – they wanted a distinctly worse one, in which they were at the top of the food chain.

Well, Michael knew what it was like at the top. It was lonely and frustrating.

So his old friends began to annoy him, because they couldn't see their own hypocrisy. They stopped seeing him, too. Oh, they would meet up with him – he was good looking

215

and strong, and they liked being seen with him. But they stopped *seeing* him. They thought he was alien, different. No longer a real person.

Just being around them made Michael feel weak, insignificant. They reminded him of what he used to be – what he wasn't any more, now he was the Superhero. He was the most powerful man on earth now, not a frightened, resentful child.

He hated their bitterness and their smallness.

He made new friends. Friends who didn't talk about *Star Wars*. Friends who liked nice restaurants and going to the gym.

People he didn't feel ashamed of just being around.

*   *   *

Or, had he?

Take Julia's last birthday. That was back in March. Now it was December. He hadn't seen her since the fight. Her clothes remained in boxes in his apartment. She must know that he could find her whenever he wanted to. She must know that he already knew where she was.

It was cold. It was likely to snow this year. It didn't snow all that often. Michael liked the snow, because he didn't feel the cold if he didn't want to, and because he liked the way it fell on the streets. It made the dirty, mucky streets of South London seem clean again, as if a fresh dusting from heaven was all it took to set the world to rights.

Julia was a popular woman. Or, to put it another way, she was an attractive, outgoing woman who didn't trouble anyone, and whom people wanted to be around. She could have filled out a birthday party with a hundred people, and she would have called all of them her 'friends'.

Michael didn't believe they were her friends, not really. But they were what passed for friends in Julia's world, and Michael wanted to be part of Julia's world.

Michael struggled to fill a table for ten at his own birthdays.

Michael didn't trust Julia's friends. He thought that most of them were just trying to get with her. A lot of them had been with her in the past. Michael accepted that as part of her history – why shouldn't she have been with lots of men, if she'd had the chance?

Michael hadn't had those chances himself, but he would have pounced on them when he was younger. And now he could have any woman he liked, he only wanted Julia.

But sometimes all her experience made him feel weak and stupid, and sometimes he suspected her of flaunting her conquests on purpose. Sometimes he wanted to go away and sleep with fifty women, just to even up the score. He could do. He was persuasive and good looking.

Sometimes Julia's friends took liberties. They pressed their bodies too close to hers; they danced too tightly. Sometimes she encouraged them to, hoping to start a fight. They bought her more drinks than they ought to, because they knew she lost her self-control when she'd been drinking.

Michael watched all of it, and listened to everything they said, too, even when they were somewhere else.

They didn't like him.

They thought he was a nerd.

That was the word they used, time and time again, and it angered him.

What, he was a nerd because he had a degree? He was a nerd because he had interests and hobbies outside of going to the gym and preening before the mirror? Did they ever do anything else? Apart from sit in bars and talk behind each other's backs?

He wanted to – push them, sometimes. He wanted to push them against the wall and tell them to call him a nerd to his face. But they wouldn't. They would just laugh at him, even if he'd just thrown them across the room. They would say things like, 'that paranoid nerd – he's got issues, you know? You should probably leave him, Julia, before he gets mad at you'."

He couldn't fight the world. Not when the world was so unjust. Society was his enemy.

Other times he wished he could keep a record of everything they said about each other. He could have filled ring binders with their sniping and backstabbing, their insincerity and hypocrisy. He would wait until someone annoyed him, and then he would unleash! He could destroy their reputations in their small, petty circle as easily as he could their frail, weak bodies.

But what was the point? Julia would think less of him.

He had to be the Superhero.

*   *   *

In December, Michael stopped nearly one hundred crimes. He had planned on doing a *Twelve Days of Christmas* theme, stopping twelve crimes on the first day, then eleven, then ten, and so on. He liked to theme his crime fighting these days. It gave him more of a sense of purpose than standing on housing estates outside chicken shops, looking for a fight.

It didn't make him feel any better.

His work was suffering, too. His bosses had noticed that he was spending more and more time staring out of the window. He was doing the work they gave him at maximum speed. He typed so fast he broke a couple of keyboards. The computers slowed him down. He said hardly a word all day long, and then he went home.

He began to read the papers. He read about Syria. Syria bothered him. He went to the library and took out books on Syria. Then, because those books were old, he read the latest journals and articles – everything he could. He read up on the history of the country. He studied its artwork. Michael could read something like one hundred thousand words per minute. It took him a few hours to process the information, but that was how fast he could read.

He became an expert on Syria – on its history, its culture, its society.

He learned Arabic in a week.

He didn't know why Syria mattered so much to him. There were plenty of traumatised countries in the world. There were plenty of *interesting* countries in the world. But Syria mattered to him. It seemed bullied to him, by its location, by its rulers, by foreign powers, despite being so eminently worthy: ancient, mysterious, storied. It was a victim, like him.

Michael was Syria, and Michael was Syria's redemption. He could swoop in and make it all better again. He could arrest the thugs who were killing so many innocent people. He could impose democracy, bring happiness to those who had suffered – everything he had always said he couldn't do.

He would go to war, sacrifice his comfort on the altar of justice. He would be a Superhero. The Superhero. The world would see him for what he really was, and the world would admire him for it.

Syria was Michael's redemption.

In the office, he stared out of the window and imagined turning into an eagle, flying off to France, and then to Germany, and then Poland, and then through Macedonia, and into Turkey, and then into Syria. The Superman dressed as a bird.

*   *   *

In February, Julia looked at her phone. Something was wrong: it wasn't where she had put it. Or rather, it was, but it had been moved. Rotated. She wouldn't have put it on the table like that last night.

She yawned and hugged the man beside her. She was in the mood, but he wasn't, and he shrugged her off and rolled over to go to sleep.

Miffed, she scrunched up her pretty features and strolled to the window, arranging her delicate nightwear as she did so. She had the slightest limp from where Michael had broken her leg, all those months ago. Like one leg was shorter than the other now, or something. The doctors had done their best; Michael could have done better, but… no.

She looked at the snow which made Peckham seem clean and new. It had fallen overnight. She smiled. She picked up her phone again and took a photo. It didn't come out very well, because of the reflection in the glass, so she opened the window and tried again.

"Babe, close the window," said the man. Victor. She ignored him. She knew how to ignore strong men.

"Do you want some breakfast?" she said.

Victor turned his head around.

"What time is it?" he said, gruffly.

"Um…" Julia looked at her phone. "Eight-fifteen."

"It's Sunday, right?"

"That's right," she said. "No work today."

"Then come back to bed," said Victor.

"Please don't tell me what to do," she said.

Victor huffed and tried to sleep. Annoyed, Julia hobbled downstairs. She tried to stay quiet because of her housemates. In the kitchen she investigated the cereal situation. Joyce always had good cereal. She would borrow some.

There were three large boxes on the kitchen table. Surprised, Julia read the labels.

Julia.

Her pulse racing, she ripped off the Sellotape and opened a box.

"My clothes!" she said out loud.

She kept looking.

"My iPod!"

"My hair dryer!"

Then, looking around in irritation, she said,

"I can't believe he kept them all this time! He could've done this whenever he liked. Nine months. Nine months it took him!"

She shook her head.

"I can't believe it took him nine months. And even then, he doesn't knock on the door like any normal person. Just leaves it on the kitchen table. What a jerk."

She sighed. Leaving Michael had been expensive. She had had to buy everything all over again. She didn't want to go to his place. He would only keep her there. She was scared of him. She rubbed her shoulder where he had hit her nine months before.

Michael could control people's minds. He'd told her that once, when he'd listed all his powers. Super strength. Teleportation. Transmutation. Metamorphosis. X-ray vision.

Mind-control.

How many years had he used that very power on her? How long had he made her see things that weren't really there – an illusory commitment, a false promise of children? Michael's mental powers – they were his strongest, and he didn't seem to realise it. Nor had she – until she'd broken free of it, when he'd hit her, and she'd vowed never to see him again. The alcohol – that had loosened his control for a while. She did not know why. She had not even realised it, until she started doing it more and more often to be free of him.

Still, he'd brought her things back, at last. Maybe he'd gained the superpower of decency.

Absent-mindedly, she opened up her phone contacts and flipped through them. She watched the names scroll across the screen. Hundreds of friends, relatives, and acquaintances. Work and social. Taxi companies. Everything. Men. Women.

Michael.

She stopped in surprise.

His name was gone.

She mulled over this while she ate Joyce's Coco Pops. Then she went upstairs again.

"Babe?" she said.

"What?"

"Did you use my phone last night?" she said.

Victor picked himself up to look at her.

"What?"

"Did you use my phone last night?"

"No. Why would I do that?"

She shrugged.

"I'm just asking. I don't mind if you did. It just seemed out of place."

"No."

"Didn't knock it off the table?"

"No."

"It didn't ring and you pressed 'hang up'?"

"No!"

Julia nodded thoughtfully.

"Okay," she said.

She walked again to the window. She looked up into the grey sky. She did not see an eagle flying south. She went back to bed.

16 August, 2016

Eat, Drink, and Be Merry

Saturday: Be The Best You There Can Be

The sun shone through the open curtains, light streaming onto the bed, creeping ever closer to Lisa's face, threatening to dazzle her. Lisa stared blankly for a long time before doing anything about it, and then she turned over and looked the other way.

She saw the alarm clock: *07:38*. It didn't matter. She had nowhere to be. Today was Saturday.

Today was a day for lying in bed and going nowhere.

Because – really, what was the point?

She closed her eyes, determined to sleep through Armageddon if she had to.

(*"At the end of the world... only cockroaches and Roach Clocks will be alive, so buy Roach..."*)

It turned 07:39. Then 07:40.

And so on.

She opened her eyes to see 07:43 in all its novelty.

She felt empty.

Last night... all of yesterday had been a disaster. Wrong shoes on the way out; trains delayed and cancelled (*"rescheduled for your convenience"*); chewed out by Mr Sticks; pointless, worthless date.

Early wake-up the next day because she hadn't closed the curtains.

Lisa experimentally put her pillow over her face. She wasn't sure if she meant to blindfold or suffocate herself, and lacking motivation either way, she threw it onto the floor.

Mary was out. She knew because she'd knocked on her door last night to talk about Pointless, Worthless Date, and she hadn't been in. Nor had Mary woken her up on getting home to talk about *her* date. Hers must have gone better than Lisa's.

Her feet ached from yesterday's walking. She should have worn sensible shoes. Mr Sticks wanted her in heels in the office, but she'd forgotten that she was visiting clients all day. An overdose of NoTears (*"Make pain painless forever"*) and a strong will had barely seen her through.

And then, after all that, to get back to the office and be bawled out by her asshole boss for something that wasn't even her fault... Mike had that case: it was his screw-up. But Mike wasn't around and Lisa was – and, well, Mr Sticks *liked* Mike. Mr Sticks saw him as a future partner, while Lisa was a grafter and nothing more. Therefore he blamed Lisa.

For the hundredth time, she thought of quitting. The thought of walking up to Sticks' desk and tossing her resignation on it thrilled her. She imagined laughing and enumerating his personal and professional faults at the same time.

She also knew that she could never do it. Nearly thirty, and she couldn't stand up for herself like that. She needed a reference from him. She needed his goodwill. She was his hostage.

Sixty hour weeks – and all for the endless joy of looking at rows of numbers, accrediting company accounts, for people who wished you didn't exist.

And last night – Jesus! He'd seemed decent on LetsChat (*"LetsChat: the science of matchmaking, the art of lovemaking."*). It's only when you meet them in person that you realise the photo that sucked you in was ten years out of date, the nice, sensitive prose they'd composed online had been through a dozen drafts before reaching even a basic level of eloquence, and a computer system that links two people who "like having fun" actually can't predict chemistry between two strangers. In *direct* contradiction to the marketing.

And so?

Two hours of drawn-out conversation while being plied with tasteless, unwanted Drecks ("*Not having fun? Demand another Drecks!*"), being walked awkwardly back to the station for an early train home, and an embarrassed laugh as an intended peck-on-the-cheek had become a kiss-on-the-lips-and-a-grope-on-the-butt.

She'd backed off and said goodnight. Best not make a fuss.

Second date? No, thank you!

In dread, Lisa looked at her phone ("*7Gaia: The Future Literally in your Hands.*")

One new message.

Rip off the plaster.

I had a rally nice time last nite. Hope to do it again soon. X

Urgh. Translation: *sex next time, maybe?*

Was that all she could get? Twenty nine years old. A choice between *that* and a gaggle of fifty year old men who think that women two decades their juniors are anxiously waiting for their slobbering, self-entitled come-ons?

It made you want to cry.

The patch of sunlight was stroking its way along her body. Time to close the curtains, maybe. Or maybe time to get up.

Either way, today was a pyjama day.

It might even be an ice cream day (*"Fifth Street: The Healthy Ice Cream."*).

Lisa hauled herself out of bed and installed herself in front of the TV (*Keedex: better than being there."*). Maybe today was a box set day. She switched to the Sitcom Channel. That would see her through for a while. She wanted to laugh.

She wanted to laugh with people whose woes began and ended in a twenty minute arc. She wanted to smile – and feel part of – a group of attractive, well-groomed twenty-somethings who lived near their work and had plenty of storage space to put all their stuff.

She wanted to see people whose problems were themselves a joke.

She laughed for five scripted minutes (interspersed with the occasional promotional in-splice for cleaning products) and then the ads came on.

Lisa watched.

A woman stood in line at the Post Office. Everything was black and white. She had a cold: she kept on sniffling. With each sniff, people glared at her for bringing her germs near them, threatening their little bubbles of immunity and isolation. Then she was back at the office, reading through some documents: she sneezed, sending her papers flying. The woman groaned out loud. Everyone cursed her.

Then a co-worker brought a hot drink. Music came on in the background. The woman drank, and smiled. Colour returned to the picture. She picked up the papers, walked to the window, and flung them out into the street.

"*Be the Best You There Can Be*," commanded the TV. "*Buy Britannic For Happiness*."

In the next advert, a young couple – a man and a woman – were tying the laces on their lion-adorned trainers. They were dressed in equally-lion-spangled Lycra. They were beautiful. The pair looked at each other, looked ahead, and as if to a starter's pistol, they began to sprint. They split ways at the first turning, while thumping dance music set the pulse racing. Lisa watched closer.

As they ran, they grabbed an assortment of items they went by. The man grabbed an unattended racquet from the tennis court, a sport's towel from a pool, and a basketball (all emblazoned with the same African cat). The woman grabbed a coffee cup from someone at the bus stop and an apple from a grocer's. The camera lingered on the woman's Lycra-shiny backside while the grocer shook his fist at her.

At last the pair met again near the park gate. They shared the spoils and laughed. They kissed passionately.

Lionsport, the screen announced. *If sport be the stuff of life… want everything.*

Lisa sighed, unaware of the non-sequitur. The adverts were killing her mood. The couple seemed happy. Lisa didn't feel happy. Maybe she should exercise? Mary exercised, and she seemed happy. Or maybe she was too passive – she let people tread all over her.

She wondered what she would do if someone grabbed her coffee in the street. Probably nothing. She'd probably go back inside and ask for another. And have that stolen, too.

Maybe she should give up coffee?

She looked at the screen again. She'd missed the next ad. Something about the bank holiday. A DIY ad. No great loss.

The screen went blank.

Lisa looked at it critically.

"This was me last year," said a woman's voice, a slow, violin note warming up in the background. A photograph expanded onto the screen. A woman in her – what, early thirties? – stood beside a birthday cake. She was dressed sensibly. She looked okay, Lisa thought. She hoped to look as good in a few years' time.

"I didn't realise then how fat I was," the voice continued. "Or how miserable it was making me."

Lisa froze, suddenly feeling sick.

"But this is me last summer," she went on, more cheerfully.

A skinny woman in a bikini stood on the beach. An impossibly attractive man stood beside her. The long, drawn-out violin note turned into a merry concerto.

"And I found out last week… that I'm pregnant," said the speaker, who appeared 'live' on screen for the first time. "*We're* pregnant." She laughed, and her impossibly attractive man walked on camera and gave her a squeeze. "And it's all thanks to SlimmerThings. Thank you, SlimmerThings!"

Lisa stared dismally at the screen as it explained at double-speed the nature of the SlimmerThings programme.

"For terms and conditions, as well as a full explanation of the SlimmerThings Pledge, see our website at: www.slimmerthings.com/takethepledge."

"What bullshit," said Lisa, turning off the TV.

She stood up to go to the toilet. While she was there, she looked in the mirror. She looked okay, she thought. Not much worse than the woman on TV, and she looked fine.

Even so…

She dashed into her bedroom and grabbed her bikini. She only had one – it wasn't as if she used it that often. Then, slipping back into the bathroom and locking the door in case Mary came back, she changed into the bikini. She studied herself critically.

Losing a few pounds couldn't hurt. And who knew – maybe she would feel better? The TV woman seemed to. And people often said that they did – feel better for losing a bit of weight. And Lisa had heard that from some *really* skinny girls.

Still, maybe she was overthinking it. She would leave the bikini on, look again in half an hour, and see what she thought then.

Settling back onto the sofa with her tablet, she typed in the SlimmerThings address. A splash page asked for her sex. Embarrassed, she pressed the picture of a beautiful woman.

Welcome to SlimmerThings. Are you ready to Take the Pledge, and Lose Ten Pounds in Two Weeks?

Lisa scrolled down to read The Pledge. Eat what we tell you, when we tell you, and you'll lose weight and be happier.

Once upon a time, Lisa thought, you couldn't say that – not without a raft of asterisks and caveats and pseudo-studies to back up your claims. Those laws were gone now – abolished as an unreasonable restriction of trade. The new regime had raised a generation of youngsters on ads demanding everything now, and promising the earth if they got it. The dog-eat-dog rationale of marketing: survival of the least inhibited.

And even knowing it was all rubbish, Lisa was impressed. There had to be some truth there, after all. They wouldn't sell something that didn't work at all.

Order your no-risk 5 day starter pack, advised the website. *Feel better after 5 days, or your money back.*

"Hmm. Well, what's the risk?"

She tapped 'order' and went to find her credit card. As she passed the bathroom, she caught sight of her reflection again.

"Urgh," she said, and hurried along.

She hesitated again at the fifty pound price. But she was nearly there, and SlimmerThings pushed her over the edge.

Satisfaction or Money Back Guaranteed.

Rapid and Effective Weight Loss for Only Ten Pounds a Day.

A Shortcut to a Better You.

Introductory Price Only While Stocks Last.

Click here for Customer Reviews.

Lisa did 'click here'. She was a canny shopper. She skimmed the reviews of hundreds of happy shoppers. She didn't doubt that they removed all the negative reviews. Even so – that was a lot of happy customers. They couldn't *all* be paid-for.

Convinced, Lisa went back to the order page and entered her details. She looked at her body one last time before pressing 'Confirm.'

Thank you for your order, said the website. *Your product will be with you in 3-5 working days.*

"Three to five days?" Lisa exclaimed. "What is this, the noughties?"

Even so, she felt better about herself. She had taken the first steps to A Better Her. She wanted to keep the momentum going, to keep feeling good.

She looked at her feet, red from walking all yesterday. She inspected the undersides. Worn, bruised.

"I bet," she thought to herself, "that somewhere, there is a pair of shoes that is comfortable *and* elegant. And I'm going to find them."

*   *   *

Sunday: Win At Everything Or Go Home

Mary tapped at Lisa's bedroom door. No reply.
"Lisa?" she whispered.
She checked her phone. It was eleven o' clock.
"Lisa, come on! We said we'd go out this morning."
Giving up, Mary entered the catastrophe of the living room. Takeout food boxes and wine glasses on the coffee table. The wine bottle still on the dining table. The boxes from Lisa's shopping spree still stuffed in the corner.

Shoes, bikinis, new trousers. Lisa had been in a good mood yesterday. That was good – she'd been getting mopey recently. Something about work. Or her love life. Mary could never tell which. Lisa worked too hard at both.

Maybe Lisa was hungover. Sympathetically, Mary cleared up the mess. She washed the wine glasses. She rinsed the wine bottle and put it into the recycling. The fast food containers – Mary grimaced at the grease eating into the white boxes – went straight into the bin. The shopping stuff she folded up and stacked out of the way.

Eleven thirty.

She tried Lisa again.

Still no reply. Concerned, still opened the door a crack and whispered,

"Lisa, are you okay?"

"Uh huh."

Mary pushed her head through the gap. Lisa was lying on the duvet, still in the clothes she'd worn yesterday. The curtains were open. Lisa herself was curled up, facing the window.

"Hey, what's wrong?"

Mary sat down on the bed. Lisa ignored her.

"I'm fine," she replied.

"Are you hungry?"

"Not really."

"Do you still want to go out today?"

"Maybe later."

"Okay," Mary said uncertainly, standing up. "I'll bring you some coffee."

"Thanks."

Lisa still hadn't moved, or looked at her. She wondered whether to leave or not.

"Well, I'm here if you want to talk," she said.

"I'm fine."

Mary turned to leave.

"Mary?" said Lisa.

"Yeah?"

"What time is it?"

"Um… eleven thirty three. How come?"

"No reason."

"Okay. Well, I'll be right back."

Lisa said nothing, and listened as Mary left the room. The door closed. Twenty hours until she had to go to work.

Mary hung around the apartment for an hour or so, until at last Lucy's silence overcame her sympathy. She'd given her a chance; Mary had a life too, you know, and if Lucy didn't want to talk then there was no point in sitting around all day.

So she pulled on her Lycras and went for a run. She was doing a half-marathon soon, and she had to get her time down if she didn't want to embarrass herself.

Her route was a good one. She'd spent hours planning it on z-maps. It was mostly level ground and it began and ended with a peaceful jaunt through – well, through the local cemetery, but it was calm and shady, and on the way back you could push yourself without having to plough through queues of lazy slow-walkers.

The only really bad thing was having to take the high street from the cemetery to the river path. As she made her way along, weaving around two-legged traffic, bumping in to slow or inconsiderate shoppers, she saw a crowd outside the Hawthorns department store.

"Shit," she muttered. The selfish mass was blocking up the pavement. Couldn't they line up along the wall or something to let others get around?

Inside the crowd, she could finally see what everyone was looking at: a mother and her young daughter having a screaming match. The mother was holding a handbag; the daughter a top. They were standing underneath the famous Hawthorns motto: *Spend it better.*

"I want it!" screamed the girl.

"*I* don't *care!*" the mother screamed back.

"Well I do!"

"*I* want *this!*"

"Mummy, mummy!"

"I said no!"

"Aaaaaaah!"

Getting fed up, the mother stepped towards the girl and gave her a dink over the head. This had no effect.

"They've been at it for five minutes," a young man whispered at Mary. Mary looked at him. He waggled his eyebrows at her.

"I'm sorry; do I look like I want to be chatted up right now?" she scowled at him. The boy looked annoyed.

"Well, I wanted to, so I did. Sue me."

Mary shook her head in disgust and returned her attention to the show. Someone in the shop – another customer – had apparently grown bored of the shouting.

"Oh, for fuck's sake, just buy her the shirt!" he said.

The mother's eyes flashed in anger.

"Why should I?" said the mother. "I don't want to. I've got other things to buy."

"Yeah, well, you're giving us a headache. And people are watching. Do you want to be a laughing stock?"

"I don't care about them, and I definitely don't care about your headache. Go take a NoTears. If you want my spoiled daughter to have a new toy, *you* buy it for her."

The interloper, beaten, retreated, offering only a parting, "*Be a Better Mum at Bettercare.*"

He ran away before the mother could rip his throat clean open. The crowd began to disperse. Mary felt a hand around her shoulder: it was the man from earlier. Angry – she didn't want men groping her at will – she lashed out, launching her fist towards his face. By chance, she caught him on the nose.

He cried out in pain. He reached for his nose, which was already leaking red droplets, and tried to stifle the tears in his eyes.

"Fucking whore," he muttered. "Give me what I want!"

He said nothing else. Mary ran along, feeling very satisfied. As she jogged, she went past the billboard that read, *Want it? So grab it. Grab Greshams.*

She felt even more delighted with herself.

As she carried on, she went past another sign that said, *Liquid Turbo: Win at Everything…*

"*…Or Go Home,*" Mary said, finishing the famous slogan for the advertisers. She sped up a little.

When she got back, Lucy was still in her room. Mary's absence hadn't been noticed. She slumped onto the sofa and pulled out her phone. She pressed the button to say she'd finished. She felt good: endorphins raced through her body.

Statistics flooded the screen. Total run time and distance, max, min and mean speeds, average pace length, comparisons to previous runs, calories burned, and so on. She read the numbers greedily. She cursed: her run had been slower than usual. She shouldn't have stopped outside Hawthorns. And the river path had been busy today: the crowds had slowed her down. If anything, she'd run slightly faster than usual. It just wasn't showing up in the stats.

Her mood ruined, Mary stared blankly at the little 'synchronising' symbol, knowing that her poor form was being uploaded, and her local ranking would fall.

"Shit, shit, shit," she whimpered, desperate to stop it from happening somehow. Inspired, she dived towards a power socket and pulled out the Wi-Fi plug. Triumphant, she looked at her phone.

Network lost, the screen declared. *;-(*

Mary closed the app with a sigh of relief. Then she had a shower, but she still mulled over her z-maps ranking. It wasn't fair. They ought to have an option not to upload a bad run. Sometimes, things just happen.

She came out of the shower and dried herself off. She spotted something in the corner – it was a bikini. Lucy's.

"Ah!" she said wisely to herself. That explained Lucy's moodiness.

Then – as if she didn't know what she would find – she peered at the bikini label, and she smiled triumphantly to herself. A cheap win but still – a win.

"*Win at everything or go home*," she reflected. "And 'everything' means 'everything'. Even if I'm already home."

Back in the living room, Lucy was inspecting the Wi-Fi box. When Mary walked in she looked up and said,

"It's not working."

"Try the plug," replied Mary. Lucy did so. Not the brightest girl, she thought smugly to herself.

"Well, why's it unplugged?" said Lucy, testily.

Mary hesitated.

"It wasn't working for me," she said. "So I unplugged it for a few minutes to fix it. I didn't realise you were using it."

"Well, I was," said Lucy.

"Sorry! Do you want some coffee?"

Lucy accepted the offer and Mary went into the kitchen to make it. She had a real, top-of-the-range coffee maker. It was her main extravagance, and she liked to bring a Thermoflask (*"Hotter than a Thousand Suns!"*) of real coffee into work rather than risk the office stuff. She talked loudly about it, too, and made a virtue of how much she saved not going to expensive coffee shops. But mainly she liked to make people jealous mid-morning and –afternoon when everyone else was drinking the office stuff. Her machine made the *"Coffee of Kings"*, as everyone knew. She liked to put her feet up and smack her lips when she drank it, like the models on TV did. The coffee beans themselves had been used, she was assured, by Incan high priests at the end of a working day.

She passed a cup to Lucy, who drank it mechanically, hardly even tasting it. That annoyed Mary.

"Still hungover, huh?" she asked, jokingly.

"Hmm? Oh, yeah, I suppose so."

"I thought we were going out today."

"Sorry. I'm not really up to it."

"Well, that's fine," said Mary. Then, thinking of Lucy's bikini still lying on the bathroom floor, she added, "You should come running some time."

Lucy thought about that.

"Maybe," she said. "I don't have anything to wear, though."

"Oh, that's easy. We can pick up some lycras this week. I'll get them – my present." Mary was being cruel now. Lucy looked a little panicked.

Then Mary told Lucy about the fight in Hawthorns. *Both* fights. Lucy laughed. They talked until the coffee was finished, and then Mary had to work.

"On Sunday?" said Lucy.

Mary nodded.

"Of course," she said. "How else do you think I wow the boss with my amazing productivity?"

The work went slowly. Half the time, she was bothered by an email she'd received from z-maps.

We're sorry, but there was a problem with your latest upload. But don't worry, our cracking engineers (cue cute cartoon squirrels wearing hard hats) *will fix it next time you log in!*

She worked for another half hour, but the work was desultory, uninspired. She could tell that it was shoddy, hardly even worth saving.

She stopped, wondering what to do. The z-maps thing was still getting to her. The thought that all her hard work would be lost, ruined by some *stupid* mother and her kid...

Impulsively, she reached for her phone.

A few clicks and... she had deleted the app.

Horror caught in her throat.

What have I done?

She threw the phone away from her, as if she didn't trust herself to hold it anymore. Then, after staring at it blankly for a few minutes, she had an idea. She picked it up, went onto the apps store, and downloaded z-maps again.

Downloading, downloading, downloading...

Installing, installing, installing...

She logged back in after a few attempts at remembering her password.

And – joy!

All her old records were there, and, crucially, *today's run was not.*

Thank you, thank you!

She looked happily at the local leaderboard. There she was, in third place. Still gaining on the others.

And she'd discovered a new technique. Nothing she would abuse, of course. But if she ever got injured, or ran while under the weather, she could stop the app from saving her times now. That was much more fair – that way, it would only upload the right times. The ones that reflected her ability. Besides, she would bet that all the other leaders were already doing it. She would only be evening up the score.

Feeling better now, she reopened her file and glanced over her work. On balance, she decided, not so bad after all. A couple of tweaks and it would be pretty good. People would be impressed.

*   *   *

Monday: A Thousand Times Hotter Than The Sun

Lucy led Lucas up the stairwell, wondering again whether she was doing the right thing. She'd only just met the guy that evening – a last-minute message on LetsChat which she'd, almost desperately, agreed to. She didn't even like the guy that much. He was boring and oafish, and the only time all evening when he'd done anything at all to impress her was when he'd bullied another couple off the table in the pub. Lucas wanted something, so he grabbed it. She'd enjoyed having a seat while everyone else was standing. It had made her feel strong by association with Lucas.

Even so, she had misgivings. But wasn't that the point? The magazine questionnaire had told her that she was too prudish. She had 'unrealistic expectations'. And then the commentary by the magazine's Resident Psychologist had explained why that was a problem. She would be left behind, seen as 'mutton in lamb's clothing'. No one would want her – at least, no one worth having.

She had to loosen up, and that was why she'd let Lucas' come back to her place.

"Your place for coffee?" he'd said.

They'd had precious little to say on the way back – a huge, awe-inspiring silence that made Lucy want to change her mind, send Lucas home. But how could she? They were already on the train together.

She showed Lucas into the living room and bade him sit. Then she went into the kitchen and – a little cheekily – started up a brew on Mary's coffee machine. If she was going to serve coffee, it might as well be good coffee.

"Oh, wow," said Lucas, happily. "I'm actually getting coffee!"

Lucy gave him a strange look at that, but sat down with him, close to him, trying to feel comfortable next to him. Still, the talk was awkward.

Mary walked in after a while. Lucy glared at her to go away, but she stayed.

"Hi!" she said breezily. "I'm Mary!"

She reached her hand over to Lucas'.

"You two move fast, don't you?"

Lucy continued to transmit evils of varying intensity while Mary engaged in light, easy conversation with Lucas. She tried to understand what her flatmate was doing.

"I'd kill for a coffee," said Mary. "I didn't have any today. Didn't have time. I've still got a full flask for tomorrow. How is it? It's good stuff, isn't it?"

Lucas peered at his cup.

"It's okay, I guess." He shrugged. "Why? Is it something special?"

Mary smiled coldly at him, eyes deeply aggrieved.

"Oh, not really," she laughed. "It's only the Coffee of Kings. You know, ancient Incan ritual stuff. It's fine if you don't get it."

"Huh," said Lucas. "Regency, hey? Never had it before."

"Well, it's not for everyone," said Mary, condescendingly.

"No, I guess not. We use a Trismegistos at my place. That's real coffee."

"Oh, I've heard of that," said Mary, airily. "I think they came runner up in…"

"In last year's models, sure," Lucas nodded. "This year they wiped the floor with everything else. Mine's the latest model. It's pretty good."

Mary forced out an 'interested' vocal, before turning to Lucy.

"How's it going, Luce?" she said. Lucy didn't like that name: it sounded like 'loose'.

Lucas reached for his phone and began playing with it.

"Fine, Mary," she replied, stiffly. "Is there anything we can help you with?"

The rest of their conversation was inaudible, conducted in mime and gesture. Lucas had the discretion to stay out of it. In a general, silent kind of way, Mary suggested that Lucy was acting rashly, and that she shouldn't have brought a stranger home. Lucy suggested in return, in a general, silent kind of way, that Mary could mind her own business, and that she, Lucy, didn't want to die a spinster with a thousand cats

"Hey," said Lucas suddenly. "Where are we, exactly?"

"Oh, for transport tomorrow?" said Lucy. "Um, the nearest station is…"

"No, no," Lucas shook his head. "I mean, what borough?"

"What borough?" Lucy repeated in surprise. Mary's eyes lit up in excitement. Lucy didn't notice. "Um… it's Lewisham. How come?"

"Oh, it's nothing," said Lucas. Then he reached across Lucy's back and embraced her. "Now, we were saying about coffee…"

Lucy accepted Lucas' advance, leaving Mary to decide whether to watch or to leave the room. Mary stood up, looking a little disappointed – not in Lucy, but about something else, as if she'd detected the faintest sniff of scandal, but it had been snatched away before she could savour it to the full.

After a few minutes of making out, Lucas came up for air.

"Lewisham?" he said. "Definitely."

"Yeah?"

"Because we're right on the border here."

Lucas grabbed his phone and looked at it in concern. Lucy peered over and looked at the screen. Some kind of GPS map.

"We're in Lewisham," she repeated. "What's LondonLover?"

In the hallway outside, Mary became gleefully excited.

"It's just a stupid app," he said. "With crappy map data. It thinks we're in Bromley."

"No," said Lucy. "Bromley's on the other side of the road. Why does it matter?"

"Never mind; forget it."

Through a gap in the door, Mary whispered, "Ask him again about LondonLover!"

"Mary?" shouted Lucy. "What are you doing?"

Mary sauntered in.

"Go on – ask him!" she said, excitedly.

Lucy looked at Lucas. Lucas looked away and shrugged.

"Love a Lady in All the Boroughs and then you'll be a LondonLover too…" Mary sang. "It's what all the cool kids are doing these days, right, Lucas?"

Lucy stared at Lucas in disbelief.

"Sponsored by the Office of Mayor for London, no less!" Mary grinned.

Still, Lucy looked at Lucas in despair.

"Is that the reason you came over?"

"I told you, babe," he said, nervously. "I told you – I'm a LondonLover. I said it over and over again."

"I thought you meant you liked the city…"

Lucas shrugged.

"Not my fault. I gave fair warning. If you don't know the ads, you don't know what people are doing. You've got to keep in touch."

Lucy felt hollow. She didn't know what to say.

"Now," said Lucas, with some satisfaction in his voice. "What's the other thing they say? *"Want it? Grab it!"*"

He grasped Lucy's arm; she tried to shake him off; he held on.

Mary dashed out of the room and into her bedroom. She reached into her workbag and fished something out. She ran back in to the living room, where once again Lucas was pulling towards him.

"Hey!" she shouted, unscrewing the lid on the Thermoflask. Lucas looked at her in anger. " *'Hotter than a Thousand Suns'*, bitch!"

She threw the contents of the flask – completely full, and scalding – onto Lucas' face. She grimaced at the stain on the couch, and the deposit her heroism had just cost her. Lucas screamed and rose in panic to his feet. Mary half-led, half-pushed him to the door, and then to the stairs, which she pushed him roughly down. He didn't fall all the way, but he stumbled a few times. She gave chase, kicking him and hitting him until he fled out into the night.

Mary went back upstairs and knocked on the door.

"Lucy? It's me! He's gone! I got locked out…"

Lucy came and let her in, and hugged her.

"No biggie," she said. Then she stepped in to Lucy's room to check the time on her Roach clock. "Wow, it's late, and it's work tomorrow."

"I'm not going to sleep after that!" said Lucy. Mary hummed.

"Here," she said. "Take one of these."

She dashed into her own room and found Lucy a HypnoSeed.

" *'Pop the poppy and put your problems to sleep'*," she said.

Lucy took the pill gratefully.

"Just make sure to set your alarm," she said, as she put Lucy to bed. "Those things pack a punch."

Lucy was already semi-comatose. Mary shrugged. She would wake her up. Then, as a final thought before leaving her alone, Mary went to the window and closed the curtains. Then she set her alarm and took a pill herself.

28 August-30 September, 2016

Care and Share

Macmillan offer a range of support scheme for patients and their relatives, including organising volunteers, support groups, advice lines, and other information services, helping hundreds of thousands of people a year.

17447972R00143

Printed in Poland
by Amazon Fulfillment
Poland Sp. z o.o., Wrocław